The WRONG Move

LEESA BOW

Editing and Proofing by Swish Design & Editing
Proofing by Virginia Tesi Carey
Cover design by Letitia at RBA Designs

Please join my mailing list to be notified of Leesa's latest releases.

You can sign up and learn more about me on my website.

If you're on Facebook, I have a reader group where I chat about books, offer giveaways, and sneak peeks of upcoming books.

To Ashleigh,
Your passion to travel and calm demeanour when challenged
inspired me to write this story.
Thank you for staying true and being uniquely you.
The world needs more Ashleigh's to be a happier place.

PROLOGUE

GIANA

I can't tear my gaze away from him.

Caught up in the excitement, I shiver as tingles shoot along my spine. The screams surround me, reminding me I'm not his sole admirer.

He bunches his jersey in his hand mid-torso.

Byron is nervous.

His broad smile hides it, and he laughs in his defender's face. Not quite his face, as he is almost a foot shorter than his opponent. The same opponent he just dropped a three-pointer on to give us a two-point lead.

Us.

Euphoria fills me every second I'm with him. Over the last year, we have become closer, confiding in each other, our dreams and our fears, and our parents' expectations. But none of it matters right now, as the clock is counting down to the last seconds of the game. Our high school basketball team has never been invited to the championships. Who knew a tenth grader could lead us to our first?

We steal the ball from the visiting team, and Byron sprints down the court, one arm raised high, wanting the pass. The ball is thrown in the air. Byron leaps higher than his opponent and grabs the ball. He shoots while still in the air, and the crowd gasps in unison as the clock ticks down.

The ball swishes through the net.

Standing beside our friends, I jump up and down, screaming like we won the lottery. In high school basketball terms, we have.

"We're going to the championships!" Paige yells, holding my shoulders and jumping up and down like she's on an invisible pogo stick.

Mason leans in and hugs us. "I knew he could do it." We all lean our foreheads together, proud of our friend.

We break apart, still smiling, and I find Byron dwarfed by his teammates. The smallest and skinniest player on the court has more determination than the rest of his team combined.

Byron has had to work harder than all the other players. Focused and ready to give up everything just to play ball, he started the season only getting a few minutes a game, and now he's a starting-five player. With two more years of high school, he has time to improve and be offered a college basketball scholarship.

The crowd sings the school anthem as the players jump about in a circle, arms linked over each other's shoulders as they chant their team motto and the referees shake the coaches' hands. Then the players disperse, some going to their girlfriends for a hug on the sideline and others waving to their parents, who have been shouting and cheering them on. Byron has neither—no girlfriend and his parents rarely attend games. A high school final is not a priority for them. He only has us *and* the entire school backing him.

He rips off his jersey and swings it around his head revealing his scrawny midsection and protruding ribs. I don't care that he doesn't have the muscled body of the senior players. He's my friend, and I'm proud of him.

Please look up. Look at me. I'm here for you.

Grabbing a towel from the bench, Byron wipes his face before wrapping it over his shoulders. He glances up into the crowd toward our seats and waves to Mason.

Mason points his finger at him and holds it up as if to say number-one player. Byron grins, and I let out a sigh. My heart swells with something else, something I feel in my bones.

I am here for you, Byron. Look at me.

Byron scans the crowd, smiling as fans shout his name, my hands still clapping in beat to the team's chant. Then his gaze finds mine. It's as though he heard me calling his name in my head.

Byron stills. The intensity of his gaze steals my breath, and I stop midclap. A slight approving smile parts his lips as he nods subtly. Our interaction lasted mere seconds, yet it was enough to send heat to my core, to excite me more than the win. The team gathers around Byron, and our moment is lost.

Paige side-bumps me. "Someone is getting laid tonight," she sings in my ear.

"Stop it," I snap. "He doesn't think of me like that."

Paige's pinched eyebrows portray confusion. "You're the one girl he trusts and wants to be with…"

I turn my attention back to the court. My body tingles, her words not lost.

Sex.

3

We have hugged, trusted each other with our secrets, talked about our future dreams, and reminded each other dreams are that of the brave.

Taking the next step with Byron is not about being brave. It's what I fear most.

While I can see it happening and wish for it, I could also lose my friend.

Even worse, it could mean nothing to him.

THREE YEARS LATER...

I need to see you.

I stare for too long at Byron's message on my cell. Since returning from college, Byron and I have hooked up a couple of times, but I noticed something different about him.

He is handsome, wealthy, and has all the fame of an elite athlete. He is a somebody at college, and arrogance comes with the territory. Only, it's new for him.

I have to finish my art piece. You're welcome to come here.

I wait for a response, but it doesn't come. *What is his problem?*

My freshman year differed from his. While he worked his ass off in the gym, I required a more calming environment to paint. Byron thrives on adrenaline, whereas I prefer the stillness of serenity. And now he is messing with my creativity. I let out a long breath, pick up my brush, and stare at the postcard my mother gave me with an image of an Italian coastline. Her great-grandmother was from

Southern Italy, and while she hasn't had the chance to travel there, she has hope that my art will lead me there.

Adding dashes of pink to the bougainvillea flowers dotted on the canvas, I allow my mind to drift, and a sense of freedom sinks in. Time passes effortlessly, and each stroke conveys my joy. I'm transported to a time and place of comfort. With every brush stroke, I hear the village and Italian voices carried along the streets.

The door of my loft is slightly open, the chatter distracting. Byron's voice breaks through the calm as it echoes up the stairs, then the door clicks shut behind me. Before I have a chance to drop my brush in the water and turn, my hair is swept away from my neck, and his mouth is on my skin.

"I've missed you, Gigi."

I laugh. "You only saw me a few days ago." When we spent half the day having sex.

"I need you," he murmurs, trailing his lips along my shoulder and pushing the straps of my dress aside. "I want you, Gi."

Dropping my brush, I let out a long breath while staring at my almost-finished art.

I want you.

For years, all I wanted was for Byron Hendricks to pick me out of all the girls who would line up just to spend a few seconds with him. And when we graduated from high school, he did. We spent the day together, telling each other our hopes and dreams for college. Then we ended up at his parents' house, made out in the pool, and finished the day in the pool guesthouse.

Byron was my first. I know I wasn't his and won't be his last.

We hooked up almost every day before we went our separate ways to college. When I returned each break,

Byron would reach out to me. And like today, whenever I am home, he can't get enough of my body. We are not together, and I'm not fool enough to think he is celibate between semester breaks, even though I choose to be. All that matters is that when I'm home, he chooses me.

His large palms slip inside my bra to squeeze my breasts. I groan and tilt my head to rest on his shoulder. Reaching up, I rake my fingers through his silky hair, imagining how he looks since I haven't laid a single eye on him yet. Byron's other hand slides along my hip, grasping to slide the material of my dress up to my waist. Sliding his hand inside my panties, he finds my clit and works it until I'm moaning his name.

Oh God.

Spreading my legs, I roll my hips with his fingers inside me, and warm pleasure spreads through every inch of my body. His vivid heat surrounds me, reminding me it's summer despite the air conditioning being on in the loft. His scent is woody, with a hint of orange, and I breathe him in until Byron fills my senses with his whisper, touch, and smell. Hot air caresses my ear.

"Come for me, Gigi."

He sucks at my neck near my shoulder like he hungers for me.

My lids flutter, and my knees buckle as I come for him. "Byron..." I moan when he doesn't let up. "I want you, too," I whisper.

He removes his fingers. My clit pulses. My upper thighs are wet from his fingers powering in and out of my pussy. Byron spins me so his face is inches from mine. His beautiful blue eyes darken as though he is absorbing my words in a deeper way than what is happening in the moment.

Something about his eyes rings a warning bell in my

mind. His breath is minty—no hint of whiskey or beer. I don't have time to dwell before my bra is wrenched down and my ample breasts bounce free.

A growl sounds from his throat. "These are mine."

"What?"

His nostrils flare. "I love your breasts." He squeezes each in his large hands, pushing them together and up like an offering he's about to take. He kisses each breast, his gaze then lifting. "Along with your plump lips. God, I want to fuck them."

Oh.

Byron drops to his knees. My panties are tugged down, and my dress is next, pooling on the hardwood. Running his hands up and down my skin, he kisses my pussy, then licks and sucks my clit. He spreads my thighs and stares. Byron doesn't move. I lean my hands on his shoulders for balance and realize he's staring at the glistening skin between my legs.

I am so wet.

My pussy throbs, aching with the need to have Byron inside me. With both of his hands cupping my rear, he yanks my hips forward and tastes me, smearing my wetness over his lips. His tongue trails over my pussy and down my inner thigh, tasting every part of my orgasm.

"You send me wild, Gi."

"I do?"

Byron springs to his feet. Only now, I notice his blue T-shirt that matches his eyes. He rests one hand on my hip as his gaze flicks over my face. Confusion mars his expression—a look I match as I realize his pupils are more dilated than usual.

"Yes, Giana. So fucking wild. Tell me again why you decided on a different college than me?"

What?

I flinch at the harshness in his tone.

Originally, we were both intending to study at UCLA so that we could be close to home. It offered great sports and arts programs. When Byron switched to St. Mary's to accept a full basketball scholarship, I decided on the college best for me. St. Mary's is less than four hundred miles from home, and I could have seen Byron frequently during the year if we were a couple.

However, the notion of being surrounded by strangers on the other side of the country calmed me. It was the adventure I craved. So I accepted an offer from Yale. The thought of living close to New York excited me, though I had underestimated the weather. Freezing my ass off in winter was not my idea of an adventure, even with regular trips to the Big Apple with my friends.

I cup his cheek in my hand. "You know why."

My words fail to have the effect I'd hoped. His brows tighten, he grabs my hand, and guides it away from his face.

"I needed you here in LA," he growls out.

He did not just say that.

"You told me to do what was best for my career, as you did by choosing St. Mary's," I say, louder than I intended.

"What was best for your art was studying at UCLA," he says between clenched teeth.

"Says you," I snap.

His mouth collides with mine as he kisses me hard, his tongue circling and tasting, stealing my air until I'm out of breath. He sweeps his hands over my torso, then my shoulders, in erratic movements as though he is lost, unsure what do to next. I break his kiss, panting.

This is not the Byron I know.

"Why are you upset with me?" I ask.

He grabs my shoulders and stares at me as though I'm clueless. "Because I need you close to me."

"Then you should have accepted UCLA, and I would have stayed with you."

"Giana," he says, as though reprimanding me. He whips me around, and I reach for the back of the chair to balance myself. A guttural sound comes from deep in his throat. "Fucking perfect." His hands slide over my ass before spreading my legs wider. I hear foil tearing. Looking over my shoulder, I watch Byron slide the condom over his thick cock. I have half a mind to say no so I can find out what is eating at him and why he is like this. Only, the sight of his erection has me wet and ready, and I can never say no to Byron. He does something to my body no other man can.

One finger strokes my pussy, a single teasing circle. Byron lifts his finger to his mouth and sucks it slowly. His gaze is locked on mine as I watch him from over my shoulder. His eyes darken. "Hold on," he growls, his breath raspy and raw with need.

I arch my back, gasping when he pushes inside me. He holds for a moment and waits another second before withdrawing and thrusting inside me again. My breath hitches as I'm torn between pleasure, pain, and anticipation. I reach around to touch his thigh, his arm, any part of him.

"I said hold on, Gi."

Gripping my shoulders, Byron plows into me at a frantic pace. Our ragged breaths and the slapping of skin on skin fill the room. I lift onto my toes, offering him more. My breasts bounce with the force of his thrusts. Turning my face to the side, our eyes meet in the wall mirror. He leans over my back and seizes both my breasts, using them to maintain a steady rhythm as he tweaks and rubs each nipple. My breath is strangled as I try to contain the bliss of an impending orgasm. Uncontrolled pleasure rips through my body, bringing me close to a scream, the pressure of standing almost too much for my knees.

Circling my hips, I meet his thrusts. He releases my breasts, rips off his tee, then takes hold of my hips and hammers into me at an impossible pace. His stamina is astounding.

Right now, I'm commending my pussy.

Despite swinging between pleasure and pain, Byron's dick inside me is gratifying on a sensual level words cannot explain.

The first wave of my orgasm hits hard.

"Byron," I moan, my head hanging between my shoulders.

I can't go on.

But Byron shows no sign of slowing.

When the next wave of orgasm comes, I clamp around his dick, and lightheaded from panting, I see stars. I stop thinking, turn my head, and watch as Byron shudders into a deep thrust, my name rolling off his lips. He collapses over me, his arms wrapping around my middle as he lightly dots kisses along my back.

My now jelly-like legs threaten to cave. "Byron, I can't take your weight." Holding me tight, he lowers me to the floor. We curl in a ball with my back to his front. His arms are tight around me, as though he is afraid to let me go. We remain motionless for a few minutes, our breathing slowing until I can no longer hear him.

"Did I hurt you?" he murmurs.

My answer is not immediate. "No." Could I go another round? The way my pussy throbs, definitely not.

"I'm sorry, Gi." His forehead rests on the back of my head.

What is with him?

"Is something wrong?"

"Not now. I've just had a bad year. The coach hates me."

Is he serious? I push away from him, and his semihard

dick falls out of me. I sit up. "You came here to feel better about yourself?"

"What? No." He adjusts himself before pushing up onto an elbow. "I thought you'd understand."

"Understand what, your selfishness? The delusion that basketball is your entire world and your only hope to success?"

His expression slides into a frown. "Basketball *is* everything to me."

Ugh. "Stop being such a child. You're one of the most intelligent people I know. You can do more with your life than play ball."

Byron springs to his feet, knots the condom, and throws it in the trash can near my canvas. He steps into his boxers and linen shorts. "I thought you'd understand."

"Understand? What happened here wasn't you."

"Right now, you don't sound like the Gigi I know either."

"Because I'm not tolerating bad behavior?" My clothes are beside me. In one quick sweep, I collect them and dress quicker than I ever have. "You just fucked my brains out, and I allowed you to do it." He looks to the side, and I step into his line of vision. He looks away, and again, I step forward, forcing him to look at me. I'm suspicious as fuck. "Did you take coke before coming here?"

His eyes flick over my face as he clasps my shoulders. "Please understand—"

I slap his arms away from me. Sucking in a deep breath, I stop myself from yelling at him. His eyes glaze as though he wants to cry.

"I never meant to hurt you, Gi."

"You didn't. But using people *is* hurtful. Stop acting entitled. You told me we all have to earn respect, and as a freshman, you have to earn the coach's respect."

He tilts his head at me. "I'm sorry."

"Sorry?" I shake my head. "What if you were caught?" Suddenly, it dawns on me. "Did you snort it in the car before coming inside?" He stares at me, his lips pressed into a thin line. "Fucking unbelievable." I straighten my dress. "While your reputation is safe with me, I hope no one saw you from the street. What if my parents saw? Or worse, what if you were tested? What would happen to your precious basketball career then?"

"We all deal with things differently, Gi." His eyes soften, my harsh words failing to spook him.

My throat burns. I swallow down the emotion of knowing Byron came for sex and had to be high to do it.

"I thought I knew you," I murmur. "Clearly, I don't."

His blue eyes narrow, and a cynical laugh escapes him. "You are the one person who truly knows me. Guess I was wrong for coming here for advice."

"Advice?" I shake my head. "Just what did my pussy tell you?"

By the look on his face, I definitely hit a nerve. He steps closer. "I'm not delusional. You want me as much as I want you."

"Not like this, Byron," I say, my words gentler this time. "You came for sex, not to talk."

"That's where you're wrong." He smirks, and I want to smack it from his face. "I can get sex anywhere."

"Leave," I say between clenched teeth. "Think about what happened here before you talk to me again. Oh, and here's some advice... don't come back until you've grown the fuck up."

He pulls his T-shirt over his head and tugs it over his ripped abdomen. His throat bobs. I hope I made sense, and he'll think about his recklessness. I try to put it into words he'll understand. "Your entire life is about plays and making the right call. Well, this was your worst. The ultimate wrong move."

With a nod, Byron turns and quietly closes the door behind him.

I pull at my hair and spin on my heel. "Damn his stupid game."

1

BYRON

Six years later...

"The email for this lame high school reunion clearly states a reply was required three weeks ago." I feign disappointment to hide my relief. It's not how I want to spend my Saturday night. It's the last place I want to be.

"Come on, Byron. I could use the support. Paige will speak to me if you're there."

"Mase, you've got this. Paige already likes you. Talk to her whether I'm there or not."

"You know I always freeze and then sound like an idiot."

Mason doesn't need me for this. "We're no longer at school. Just talk as though you're in a meeting. Wait, no. Engineers bore the fuck out of me."

Mason laughs hard. "You're one to talk. I still don't understand the rules of basketball, and with all that shit-talking you do on the court, *you* sound like you're still in high school."

I grin even though he can't see my face. "King of the court." He laughs again. "Act like it's me you're talking to. It'll bring out the best in you."

He moans, and I hear it through my AirPods. "You know they'll make an exception because you're *the* Byron Hendricks."

"What's the dress code?"

"Smart casual."

"Just so you know, I won't be staying long enough to eat, so my being there won't mess with their precious numbers."

"They won't care. Just pose for some photos to keep the prefects happy."

Before I curse, an alarm goes off on my phone. "Hang tight. Someone's at the door." I check the security camera on my app. "My sister's here."

"You have an hour to get ready. I'll wait for you at the bar."

"No promises."

I end the call and jog down the staircase to answer the door. "You have the new code?"

Charlotte pushes past me. "You keep changing it. That tells me too many girls stay over," she says aggressively. She has a point. "Get yourself a security guard."

"I have one when I go out. What's up? You're not here to discuss who I sleep with or my protection."

She digs her fists into her hips. "No, because everyone knows you're not *sleeping*." She rolls her eyes. "And God, I hope you're using protection."

Charlotte is the female version of myself—blue eyes and light brown hair. We are closer in age than our other siblings, and for the most part, we understand each other. Though she is hard to read of late, and tonight, with the shadows under her eyes and the agitation in her expression, she looks ten years older than me.

"Wait, who is *everyone*?" I ask.

"Everyone in the office. Every player is watched. We prepare for collateral damage."

"Jesus." I tilt my head to the ceiling. "Does admin need to know every detail of what happens off the court?"

"Yes. I'm not about to let anyone fuck up and ruin our team, and that includes my brother." She walks into the living room and pours herself a whiskey.

"Help yourself."

She glares at me.

I shove my hands into my track pants pockets. Charlotte doesn't intimidate me. Ever since she left college and began working at the LA Sharks' administration department, she has taken on personal responsibility for keeping the players in shape and in line. It might be my father's team, yet her personal investment in the team is too much for my comfort. She knows *almost* everything about me.

She raises an eyebrow. "How many times have you changed the code on your door?" She walks to the balcony and takes in the sprawling city at dusk as the sun sets over the ocean. The view is one of the best, and I'm lucky to have a brother who works in real estate who discovered this beauty in Hollywood Hills for me.

Charlotte tilts her back and neck before taking another sip. She's doing this more often lately, as though it somehow relieves her tension.

"Are you okay, Lottie?" I despise her treating me like I'm a teenager, but I hate seeing her stressed out like this.

"Of course I am. I just need you two douchebags to pull your heads in."

Why does she always bring Brandon into this?

"As my sister, you get away with snarky remarks about me, but you don't have the right to do it to BJ." I shake my head. "And as much as I want to stand here and chat about

17

trivial things, I'm about to head out." I press a button, and the twenty-foot glass doors slide closed.

Charlotte walks inside and eyes what I'm wearing. "You're not going anywhere important dressed like that."

I grin. "Observant. I was upstairs about to get dressed. I'm attending our high school reunion with Mason."

Her eyes go round. She looks like our mother when she is surprised. "It's not on your calendar."

"Do I have to report to you every time I want to piss?"

"No, and don't talk to me like that." She downs the last of her drink.

"I'm not a fan of being managed like I'm still at school."

"If you and Brandon didn't mess up so spectacularly on your last away game, we wouldn't be in this position." Her edgy tone sharpens as she mentions Brandon's name.

"We apologized, and all parties were consenting adults."

"If photos are leaked—"

"There were no photos. How many times do I have to say it?"

She stares at me. "Fine. But it's the last week of August. You need to be at your best for training in the morning."

"Lottie, this is not my first rodeo."

She places her glass on the tray. "Don't be a dick when you're out tonight. Call if you need me."

"Thanks, Mom. I'm going as a favor to Mason. I'll be bored as fuck."

She smiles, and it reminds me of the Charlotte I knew before she started working for the team.

I follow her to the door. "Did you visit for a reason?"

She turns, and for a moment, I see her vulnerable side. "Have you heard from BJ? He's not answering my calls."

"He doesn't need to be lectured by you."

Charlotte's expression changes, leaving me confused.

"All right. Enjoy your night."

An hour later, I'm walking into the ballroom decorated with red and black balloons—our old school colors. Flags with our school emblem are displayed on the stage. I look around at the same people gathering in the same groups and find Mason talking with Paige not far from the bar. I should walk out and text him *I told you so*, but he turns and waves before I do.

"Hey."

"You made it." He pats my back. Mason is dressed in a suit with a paisley pocket square, and Paige is in a long red evening gown, her blonde hair swept up off her bare shoulders.

"Smart casual, hey?"

He grins at me. "If I said it was formal, you wouldn't have come."

I huff out a laugh. "My fault for not reading the email thoroughly. It did make my job convincing security tougher than usual. He said you added my name to the list."

"Looking out for you, bro." He pats my back harder than before. "You remember Paige, right?"

I lean in and hug Paige. "Of course. How are you, Paige?"

"Great. It's really good to see you both again." I smile and turn to Mason. His beer glass is half full. "I'll grab you both some more drinks?"

Making a mental note that Paige is holding a crystal champagne glass, I make my way to the bar and stop when a woman steps in front of me. She is my height in heels and looks directly into my eyes.

"Byron Hendricks. I missed your email response." Jessica James's expression is not joyful. She was prom queen and queen everything in high school—her best years. I haven't heard anything about her since, which I'm happy about because she spent every day at school giving me hell.

"Sorry, Jess. It was in my spam. Mason convinced me it was okay to come." She doesn't smile. "I promise I won't eat a thing, and I'm on the water, so..." I shrug. "I'm getting drinks for my friends."

She presses a hand to my shoulder. "I guess it's okay, then." She straightens her back, full of authority. "I made sure there is plenty for everyone, so please enjoy yourself." Her eyes lower and track over me before meeting my gaze again. "I heard you're in the big time now. The first student from our school to make the NBA. You look fit," she drawls.

"I was always fit, Jess." I wink at her, then sidestep her and head toward the bar. I order drinks and a bottle of water, then gather the drinks with the bottle tucked under my arm. Before leaving, I catch the sound of a familiar laugh, and it stops me in my tracks. My chest constricts as my body remembers her.

At the other end of the bar, Giana Monroe talks with some friends. For a moment, I allow myself to watch her. She smiles, her brown eyes full of life. There was a time she smiled like that for me.

Long dark hair falls over her tanned bare shoulders. From here, I can see the way her full breasts fill out her dress and spill over somewhat.

My throat tightens. I thump my chest, not getting enough air to my lungs because I'm thrown back to a time when we were at school, and I'm remembering things I had pushed out of my mind.

The last time I saw her...

"Are you finished, Byron?"

A voice snaps me out of my daze. "Yeah, sure. How are you, Carter?"

"I'm good. And you?"

"Good, man. I'll come and see you later."

He nods. "It's been a while."

I move so he can squeeze past to get to the bar.

Most of the people here I haven't seen since school. It's not that we didn't get on, but our lives took us in different directions. I quickly learned who was fake and who I could trust. It's why my teammate, Brandon, and I got on so well. We met at college, and his laid-back Aussie attitude resonated with me. Apart from my basketball friends from college and the LA Sharks, I only stay in contact with a few friends from high school.

When I find a space, I turn and look back to the bar, where Giana is still smiling. There was always something about her. She was *almost* the one.

Mason and Paige take their drinks and thank me.

"I see you ran into Jessica." Mason smirks, understanding what would have gone down.

"Yeah, but I sweet-talked my way into staying. She told me to enjoy the night."

Paige laughs. "It's because she had a crush on you."

I choke on the water. "She hated me."

Paige rolls her eyes. "Secretly, she was in lust with you. She wouldn't chase you because she thought she was too good for that, so she got you to notice her in other ways."

I shake my head. "I think you're delusional. She treated me like I was scum."

"Yeah, I agree with Byron," Mason adds. "She said some pretty awful stuff to him."

I stare at Mason. "Don't bring it up. I don't want to remember the bullshit." I was the skinny, geeky kid back then, and she squished my confidence like I was nothing but an insect. I look at Paige. "She tried to get me kicked off the basketball team. She wanted to ruin me."

Paige shrugs. "I'm not saying what she did was right... only what I heard from others."

"News flash. If you want someone to like you, don't set out to destroy their future."

Mason clicks his glass with my bottle. "That's a warning label if ever I heard one."

"Damn straight."

"Hello, Byron."

Giana's gentle voice wraps around me, and Mason has that knowing look in his eye. I turn.

"Giana." I lean in and kiss her. "You look beautiful."

Her dark waves fall over her shoulders as her large brown eyes meet mine, her smile shy. She lowers her gaze. "You didn't get the memo?"

"No. My fault for skimming the email." I grab Mason's shoulder. "My friend here mentioned the dress code was smart casual. If you can't trust your friends, who can you trust?" Everyone laughs.

"He wouldn't have come if I said he had to wear a suit."

Giana smiles at Mason. "He never did like suits, not even for prom."

"How are you, Gigi?"

"I'm wonderful, thank you."

"The Mediterranean sunshine agrees with you," Paige says to Giana, then glances at me.

"Absolutely." Though her glowing skin is not the reason I can't take my eyes off her.

"How long has it been since you two have seen each other?" Mason asks.

"Too long." I smile at Giana and allow myself to admire her for a few seconds before it gets weird. She is even more beautiful now, and my body hums with the attraction. After high school, we caught up after our first year at college. My memory of the last time is blurry, but I left her on not so good terms. I can't recall the exact reason why we stopped texting, except that we were both busy. All those feelings I had for her then rush back to me now, and I'm kicking myself for not trying to stay in her life. I tried to reach out again years ago, but she had disappeared. It was as though she didn't want to be found.

"Gigi is now famous," Paige says excitedly. "Her art features on Isabella Leto's new fashion line. She is a fabric designer and works with the chief textile designer for Leto Designs."

Designs? My brain catches up.

"After graduation, Byron and I spent an afternoon talking," Giana explains. "He knows I've always wanted to be a working artist."

We did more than talk. It was a fun, intimate day. Giana told me her concerns about being an impostor in the art world. She didn't think she was good enough, even though she was accepted into one of the best creative colleges in the country. I emphasized her talent, and she had a way of extracting all my doubts about making it to the NBA. Every insecurity I had about not being big enough or good enough, she squashed with her wise words.

"Yet here we are," I whisper. We had a connection, one I cherished. We were young and reckless, and on different career paths. It wasn't the moment our story began. The last time I saw her hits me, and my gut tightens. I had almost managed to push it out of my mind.

"And yes, he has seen my work," Giana says to Paige gently. "At the end of our freshmen year, I came back to LA and we caught up." Her brow flinches. I swallow, hard. It was my mistake. "You might not remember," she says to me. "You came to see me, and I showed you my work."

Mason lands a hand on my shoulder. "I remember

Byron mentioning it." His fingers dig into my muscles. He gives me a look, and I fake recognition.

"I remember. I can't for the love of God remember your piece, but I do remember loving it."

Giana looks down, and her smile fades. "I really should get back to my friends. It was lovely to see you again. See you soon, Paige." She almost floats across the floor, and I can't tear my eyes away from her. I check out who she is with.

Ugh. Jessica freaking James is in her circle of friends.

"Byron," Paige snaps. "You looked clueless."

"It's because he was as high as the Empire State Building," Mason quips.

Fuck. "Why didn't you remind me of this?"

"It was your worst year at college. Between fighting with your parents and being dropped from the team for finals, you were struggling." He shakes his head. "Man, that was some bender you rode over summer break. I do recall you talking about her parents' house, but you didn't say much else."

Paige coughs. "No need to elaborate, Mason."

Every time I sneak a glance at Giana, she is laughing with her friends.

"Paige, do you happen to have her number?"

Paige's smile is understanding. "If I give it to you, don't mess up this time."

A deep frown creases Mason's brow. "You never told me about the last time you saw Gigi."

"I never told anyone," I murmur.

"If you want to make amends, you're in luck," Paige adds. "She's home for a few months until she decides where to travel next, and tomorrow, she'll be at a fashion show, but it's booked out."

My smile grows. There is always one more seat when you know the right people.

2

BYRON

MY SISTER CAME up with the goods.

Charlotte questioned why I needed tickets to LA's fashion night of nights until I mentioned Giana. After a few phone calls, she managed to get me inside, but standing room only—at the back of the room. Fine by me. I only need a moment to catch Giana's eye.

I hold out my cell, and the security guard scans my ticket. He squints as though he has a moment of recognition. I offer a nod before proceeding and fall into line with the crowd. While I love trending in style, I'm out of my league here. I should have taken a moment to consider my choice of shirt because tonight, I am bland. If it were another occasion, I'd be happy to fade into the background and dodge strangers telling me how I could play on a certain opponent or asking to grab a quick selfie. How is Giana going to see me behind this ocean of color?

The catchy beat blasting through the sound system

distracts me momentarily. Leaning against the wall, I scroll through social media looking for updates on the fashion show and searching for Giana's name.

The fashion world loves Giana's bright floral designs and how her art infuses the elements of nature onto the fabric in bold, beautiful color. I can't help but smile at the praise for her.

Giana, you did it.

The goals and dreams she shared with me in high school came to life, and I'm about to witness her brilliance. I'll likely appreciate it more than the others, too, because we shared secret daydreams about our futures before college.

Scanning the crowd, I wonder about the influential guests and if her designs please them. If they don't, well... An odd sensation builds inside my chest at the thought. My fists clench, and I'm thinking about ways to help and protect her if the media decides to focus on that. I have been in the spotlight for unfavorable reasons, and I don't want Giana to experience the pain of being publicly humiliated.

She will kill it.

Then I lock eyes with Holden Hayes, the best point guard for the LA Stars and my main competitor. I never took him for a fashion lover. Front row seats? What the fuck.

Jesus, Charlotte, was standing space really the best you could do?

How did I overlook this event and not know Giana would be here? I need to get my head out of my ass and look at the world beyond basketball.

Hayes is sitting beside some teammates, and near them are some NFL players. Why were the LA Sharks overlooked to be represented here? It's no secret I have a healthy passion to win on the court, and that's now spilled over to a fashion show. If any of them even look sideways at Giana...

The music switches a beat as the room darkens and

silence falls over the crowd. Spotlights brighten the stage, and pink and green stage lights flick over the runway.

Applause.

The presenters walk out and address the crowd, then announce the first fashion label. I'm zoning out between checking out the guests and thinking about training tomorrow.

The first group of models walks onto the runway with exaggerated steps, looking straight ahead. The presenters describe the fall and winter line with soft oranges and pinks, dominant colors among the beige.

My interest piques when the male models walk out. Is this what I should wear to get Giana's attention? Not a chance. My brother, Jobe, is known for his outlandish outfits, and even he wouldn't wear anything that colorful.

I sit through three more designer parades before someone announces, "Our next label debuted in Italy, and we are honored to have them joining us tonight. May we present *Leto Designs*."

I push off the wall. The presenters have my full attention.

"What you're seeing tonight is more than clothing on a runway. It is an innovative creation to take art to the fabric. Isabella Leto and Giana Monroe have worked tirelessly to create forms that function as both fashion and art."

Each model appears wearing a flowy, sexy yet classy gown. Giana's art is splashed over the entire dress. After stalking her work, I immediately recognize her style. As more models grace the runway, the presenters continue.

"Giana has been on the cover of *Vogue* in Italy, France, Turkey, and multiple times here in America." The applause has me smiling, and I tap out a quick text to Charlotte.

Can you get hold of the issues of Vogue that feature Giana?

"And Isabella Leto has thirty years of fashion under her stunning designer belt. She knows what the people want and changes her designs every season to give us something fresh and awe-inspiring. Her designs have been worn on television and the big screen, and even by the First Lady, who was photographed in a Leto Designs hydrangea flare dress while in France."

An image flashes onto the screen of the First Lady, and goose bumps trail along my arms. But with every piece paraded by the models, I only see my *Giana*. Each model fades into the distance as I envision her in the dress, laughing, twirling so the material fans out. Off to the side, the real Giana gazes at her creations with pride.

Damn. My chest swells with emotion.

"The beautiful artwork of Giana Monroe highlights her love of nature, and thanks to this collaboration, we get to wear these beautiful designs. Let's hear it one more time for Leto Designs."

The crowd cheers, and I'm there cheering along with them as the last model takes the runway. Isabella and Giana walk out holding hands. They take a bow, and the crowd stands, the applause louder. Giana's gaze roams over the crowd. She waves and smiles with joy. Just when I think our eyes will meet, hers dart in the opposite direction.

Giana's smile is broad, and I want to bottle it and memorize her happiness. We have both found our paths in life. Her success will take her around the world and farther away from me.

I have not even got her back yet, and the idea of her leaving cuts deeper than a blade through the heart.

I cough and straighten my spine.

That's when she sees me. First, her head tilts to the side as if she is figuring out if it's really me. Her brow pinches ever so slightly.

Good.

She is thinking about me, even if she's thinking, *Why?*

I offer a subtle nod, then mouth, *Congratulations.*

She bites her lower lip, her brow remains tight. Isabella sweeps up her hand, and they take another bow. My cue to leave. I achieved what I wanted. It's time for Giana to celebrate her success with her fashion family, and I need an early night before my red-eye practice session tomorrow morning.

3

GIANA

WHAT WAS with him showing up yesterday? I can't explain it, nor can I explain the text Byron sent this morning. It's messed with my head since. I remind myself it's a friendly chat over coffee, nothing else. Definitely not a date.

Yet my heart beats nervously, and I checked my hair and lipstick three times before walking out the door to drive to Santa Monica. I know what he's doing. The last time we met out, we were in Santa Monica, and I told him how much I loved the beach. He booked the same café where we used to meet before I went to college. One particular time is ingrained in my memory—the day after we drank too many cocktails by his pool and ended up in bed together. The last time I saw him, he was not the Byron I thought I knew.

I was one of *many* who fell under the charm of Byron Hendricks, and today, I won't be added to the count again. I need to maintain us being strictly friends so my thoughts aren't confused by what my heart feels if I'm going to take the next step in my career.

A giant step out of LA.

Don't be a prude.

It's not like I haven't had men in my life. They helped with the lonely nights spent in foreign countries. Italian men are fluent in the language of love, but Byron does something to me no other man can. I keep telling myself we were kids, and my first was special. Maybe it was the cocktails or the guesthouse overlooking the pool. Byron made me feel beautiful and caressed every part of me as though he loved every inch of my body. With him, sex came as a natural step in sealing the bond between us.

Until I went to college, and then I knew I wasn't a love interest he wanted to pursue.

Before college, we told each other about our hopes for the future, and I don't blame him for being focused on making his basketball dreams come true. We both did what it took to pursue those goals. After the last time we had sex, I tried to forget him. Within two days, an offer came through for a mentorship in Italy—an opportunity I ran to, leaving my heart back in LA.

So here I am, back where our story began. We are going to visit the place where we shared our fears. What Byron didn't realize was that not keeping in contact after everything we shared was one of my fears on steroids. When he stopped texting, it meant I wasn't someone he respected, not even as a friend.

After I park, I take my purse, which matches the tulip print of my Leto Designs dress, and walk the block to Coral's café.

Byron waits out front. His foot is perched against the shop's discolored white, rendered brick wall, his head lowered as he scrolls on his phone.

"Too vain to wait inside alone?"

He looks up at me, and a smile grows on those lips that have me swooning on the inside. "Giana. You're late."

I check my phone and roll my eyes. "By one minute."

"Still late." He leans in and hugs me. "It's good to see you."

I'm hugging him tighter than intended because being in his strong arms feels good. He releases me, takes my free hand while holding the door open, and leads me into the café. Is it so wrong I like that he has shifted into protector mode? My brain is telling me to set boundaries, and hand-holding is a no because Byron accelerates to familiarity faster than Maverick testing the limits of the Darkstar.

He pulls out a chair for me to sit, and I'm already liking this gentlemanly side of him. For a moment, I'm curious. I want to know more about the man Byron has become, but I squash that idea flat.

Rule #1: Do not get your heart broken in LA.

"Soy latte?" He eyes me, and I notice the slightest grin. No points to him, even though I'm impressed he remembered my choice of coffee.

"No. I take almond milk occasionally, though I prefer a short black these days."

"Noted." He orders my coffee and adds a green energy juice for himself. While he reads the menu, pondering food, I take the opportunity to make some mental notes.

His face has changed from a boyish look to that of a man, with an angular jaw and high cheekbones. His blue eyes remain deeply set with dark, thick lashes most girls would give a kidney for. Eyes that cause me to inhale ever so slightly, even though I worked hard to erase that face from my memory.

It's not that he hurt me. More what we could have had, and he didn't try. My stupid pride made sure he never got another chance.

"So, Italy..." He places the menu on the table. "How long were you there?"

"From the last time we saw each other, up to a week ago."

His eyes flick over my face, his grin lost to an expression of deep thought.

"What?" I ask.

"You didn't mention it last time—"

"You were high, Byron. I doubt you even remember."

"I remember everything," he says, his voice low and deep. His eyes narrow. "Did you know you were going to head to the other side of the world when you were with me?"

"Does it matter?" I ask gently.

"Yeah, it does."

How is he turning this around on me?

Fiddling with the fork, I meet his gaze. "No. Watching you achieve your dreams kickstarted my brain into chasing mine harder."

"So it had nothing to do with what happened between us that night?"

I twirl the fork a little faster. "I thought this was a coffee date between friends? It's feeling more like an interrogation."

"You changed your cell and made a new private Insta account. As one of your friends, not being privy to your life hurt some."

I let go of the fork and place my hands in my lap. We were young, and it was all so inconsequential. We were friends.

"There are some things a girl doesn't want to see on

34

social media. You had your new life and were soon to be in the NBA. Your new friends were strangers to me. As to how you spend your time off the court, you and the team had access to a fast-flowing river of fish."

He pulls a face at the analogy. "We agreed not to wait for each other," he murmurs. "We supported each other's aspirations, and I wanted to watch you achieve everything you hoped for too. Instead, you cut me off like I was nothing to you."

"No." I shake my head. "I didn't think you cared for art, and believe me, my account was all paintings. That was until some big collabs, then I needed another Insta account for the business."

"Yeah, I found it." He smiles at me, and this time, it reaches his eyes. "You're a big deal, Gi. I'm proud of you."

More than anything, I want to hug him, fall into his arms, and absorb every word he is saying. It's the one thing I remember from when we sat here after graduation. He sang my praises, made me believe I could accomplish anything, and told me to chase my dreams without limits. He made me believe, but I struggled to let go of him.

I needed him in my life.

"If I didn't cut you off then, I wouldn't have achieved anything you convinced me I could." I watch his face change as he absorbs my confession.

"You would have stayed for me?"

"I knew there were no promises, but I couldn't handle seeing you with other girls." I make a face. "Selfish, I know."

His lips twitch. "Do you have a possessive trait I'm unaware of?"

"I have been known to be jealous maybe once or twice."

"And was that directed my way, or did you experience these feelings with an Italian lover?"

"Ah, my Italian lovers. A girl never kisses and tells."

He leans forward and holds my gaze. "I'm glad I didn't see."

My stomach flutters, but we are interrupted by the waiter. "Coffee," I enthusiastically say as it is placed in front of me. "If we're here to fill in the void, let's backtrack a few years. Tell me what I've missed and about your new goals in life."

Byron takes a sip of his green drink. He fills in the gaps about his family—his brother's new wife and how his father bought the basketball team. "There were whispers he did it so I could play in the NBA. It's such bullshit," he says in a way that reminds me of a younger Byron. He was skinny and smaller than the average basketball player but had the tenacity of a tiger. If Byron set his mind to something, he always achieved his goal. It's why I listened to him about my career. His advice was influential and motivating, though he struggled to cope with his own doubters. Still, Byron was filled with determination.

"I'm not sure if you remember..." he continues, "... but in high school, my father rarely attended a game. He was always busy with work or traveling. Basketball was insignificant to him. I remember his embarrassment at my choice to play in college. He believed it was taking valuable time away from study. Frank spent most of his years at college working his ass off for my father's approval, then Jobe partied his way through. I have nothing in common with either of them."

I tilt my head at him and pull a face. "I remember when you—"

"Okay, I maybe have *something* in common with Jobe, but I knew I didn't want to work for my father, pumping out numbers all day in an office."

"And yet here you are, employed by the team your father owns."

He rubs at his temple for a few seconds before taking another sip of his energy drink. "Yeah, but it's the *family's* team. When I announced I wanted to go pro, my father couldn't see how it would assist the family name. The Hendricks work so millions accumulate in the name of family. Going pro would help me as an individual. If anything, it was an insult because my father didn't hold elite athletes in high esteem. Then Lottie suggested he buy the team." Byron chuckles. "Back then, she told me if I weren't up to the level, I wouldn't be selected. She made it clear there were no favors, even for family, because business is business."

"Lottie said that?"

"Hell, you wouldn't recognize her now. The team is her life. She's working her way up the corporate ladder."

"Our little Lottie?"

Byron's lips curl. "She watches me like a hawk so I don't mess up."

I can't help but giggle. "She was so cute and fun."

"Emphasis on the *was*. It's why I never wanted to work for my father."

Reaching across the table, I take his hand and give it a gentle squeeze. "Look how far you've come. I'm also proud of you, Byron. It's hard to believe we sat here years ago and told each other our hopes and fears."

His eyes are gentle and caring. "I never forgot you," he whispers.

"Neither did I," I murmur. No matter how hard I tried.

His voice is gravelly and deep as he says, "The one that got away."

I shake my head. "No. We knew each other's dreams."

"Right." He holds my gaze.

Oh shit. The way he is staring at me makes me feel like I'm his new goal.

Rule #2: Only date people you're not attracted to.

As much as I want to be his new favorite toy, I'm not prepared for the disappointment until I convince my brain that we're merely having fun and can let my guard down. Right now, everything is still fresh in my mind.

His eyes twinkle. Already, I can't picture saying no to whatever he suggests. But it's too soon. I still remember the pain.

I look at the time on my cell. "Sorry, Byron, I have to go. Can we do this another time?"

4

BYRON

MY THOUGHTS whirl from this morning. I still haven't processed Giana's words and the way she rushed off. *Fuck.* I'm an idiot.

My phone pings. It's Brandon sending me a reminder about picking him up for training. His BMW is in for service, and even when it's not, we often share a ride since we usually stay back for a shooting session after practice. Throwing my training bag over my shoulder, I head to the car, tapping out a text to Brandon as I walk.

> On my way.

Twenty minutes later, I pull up at the front of his condo. He throws his bag in the trunk and jumps into the passenger seat with the energy of a kid.

"Ready to slay?"

"I will beat your ass."

He laughs as I merge into traffic, taking the route to the LA Sharks arena.

"Did Lottie call you?"

"Yeah." His fingers thrum along the edge of the door handle. "She's pissed."

I shake my head. "She has more of Dad in her than I realized. Sorry you have to suffer her outbursts."

"It's fine."

"No. She's gotten out of hand. She came at me with what everyone in the office is saying, and I couldn't give two fucks about their opinion. She wouldn't come down as hard on you if she didn't consider you family."

Keeping my eyes on the road, I sense him staring at me.

"Lottie doesn't treat me like a brother."

I laugh. "I assure you, the new *Lottie* is testing all of us. If she hadn't known you for seven years, she wouldn't be acting like such a bitch."

"She's just doing her job. I can handle her wrath."

"That's big of you. If she gets out of hand *managing* you, I can tell her to back off."

Brandon remains quiet for a moment, then says, "Hey, how did the coffee date go?"

I shrug. "Shorter than I anticipated. It's going to take a while to get to know each other again."

"She's not into you." He laughs and jabs my ribs.

"She is. She's just forgotten how charming I can be."

"Gonna bring out the big guns?"

I laugh at him. "We'll see."

After parking the car in the secure parking lot, we stride into the arena like it's our second home—familiar and excited to be here. We take the underground tunnel, avoiding the office suites, to the changing room. LA Sharks memorabilia lines the walls. Famous names on jerseys hang high on parade, reminding everyone of the pride we have to play for the team.

My cubicle displays the number nineteen. It was also my number in college, and everything about it is lucky for me.

Brandon sits in his cubicle and pulls on his training top. Minutes later, we are on the court, just the two of us, surrounded by stands of empty seats.

We warm up in silence.

Heavy breathing fills the quiet arena, yet I can visualize the fans standing and screaming our names. The memory of winning spurs me on. We shoot, play one-on-one, and shoot some more. Before we call it a day, we hit the line for some foul shots. Brandon rebounds for me.

I make fifty shots, then we switch. He makes the first shot.

"What did you do last night?" I ask, throwing the ball back to him.

He shrugs, bounces the ball three times, then takes his shot.

Swish.

I throw it back.

"Stayed in and watched some footy." He pauses. "AFL. Aussie footy."

"It's not football, man." I grin at him. "How's your team doing?"

"In the top four. Grand final is some weeks away."

"I should go to a game with you sometime."

"Mate, you'd love it. When I went home for a month, I got to some games. Next time, during our offseason, come with me. This time of year gets intense, and I love being here, but... I'm also pissed to be missing Mum's sixtieth birthday."

"You're not going?"

"It's in a week." Dead in the heart of preseason games.

"Have you talked to Coach?"

"Nope."

Swish. He claps his hands, demanding the ball. I get that it's a hard conversation for him, and I know he misses home. I keep passing. Brandon doesn't miss a shot.

ON WEDNESDAY MORNING, I PICK UP BRANDON, AND WE head to a peak performance center in Santa Barbara to train. This place is like being on a movie set. Tiny silver balls that hook up to a bunch of cameras get attached to our joints. The staff studies how we jump, run, dart, and leap. The data is analyzed, and the results offer ways to improve our bodies and modify our training to gain strength while minimizing the risk of injury. The intensity of pro-level basketball leaves us at risk for major knee trauma, and I'm doing everything I can to reduce my chance of injury and missing games. Preseason after the offseason is when I build strength and not only on the court. This preseason, I improved by shifting my mechanical baseline.

We switch into training mode. Quick feet are essential in this game, and the performance center equipment and drills enhance that skill. I need to catch my breath. I stop to grab a towel and wipe the sweat from my face. Brandon grunts on the opposite side of the room. He has a three-foot iron triangle with a bar of one-hundred-pound weights on top. With a thick leather belt around his torso and a rope connecting him to the weight, he drags the weight behind him. Like a runner springing from the start blocks, he remains low to power forward.

I continue with my footwork drills before heading to the strength corner.

I groan as I finish the one-hundredth pull-up, drop down from the bar, and clap my hands together.

"Looking fine, Byron, looking fine," Nate says. I laugh at his enthusiasm.

He holds up his tablet. "The data is showing a slight twist in your left knee as you leap up. We want to rectify your technique, so I'm emailing you some exercises for when you're in the gym and for drills on the court."

"My knee?" My knee feels freaking great.

"We think it's stemming from your ankle."

The fuck?

I glance down at my feet.

Nate rests a hand on my shoulder. "Nothing to worry about. It's why we're here to prevent any potential injuries by improving your training. There are a couple of minor adjustments. You're otherwise in perfect shape."

I wipe my face with the towel. "Thanks, man."

Nate stressed that it's injury prevention data, but my gut is in knots. Ankle sprains are common, and a career-ending injury is my worst nightmare.

As we walk back to my Porsche, Brandon taps my back. "You okay?"

"Yeah, of course." I'm doing my best to push out any negative thoughts.

On the drive back to LA, I barely speak to Brandon. He closes his eyes, takes a nap in the car, and wakes when we're close to home. He opens his cell.

"It's my mum's birthday," he says quietly. "She's sent photos of the family dinner." Brandon swipes across the screen.

"Today?"

"Well, today for us. These were taken last night." He looks up and grins. "You know us Aussies are from the future."

"You idiot." I laugh once, but he's back to swiping his phone. "The party is this weekend, right?" He nods without taking his focus from the screen. "Why don't you go back and surprise her?"

He stares at me as though I've lost my mind.

"Seriously, Brandon. My dad can talk to the coach. It's one weekend—one preseason game. Being with your family is more important. We can chat to Dad tonight over dinner."

MOM HAS ASKED THE ENTIRE FAMILY OVER. BRANDON AND I arrive before Jobe and Charlotte. Laughter comes from the family room. Franklin and Penny are on the couch with Mom while Dad pours his standard predinner whiskey and hands Franklin a glass. My father and brother wear their standard trouser-and-shirt dinner attire despite the weather being above ninety. Brandon and I are dressed in chinos and a T-shirt, standard smart casual.

Mom springs from the white suede sofa to greet us. "Byron. Brandon." She hugs me and kisses my cheek, then moves to Brandon. She treats him like he's one of the family.

"We could hear your laughter a block away," I jest. I shake hands with Dad and Franklin, then lean down to kiss Penny on the cheek. Penny smiles up at me and rubs her rounded belly.

"Byron, it's good to see you." Her bright eyes sparkle. "We were laughing at how this little one will soon be putting her dirty hands all over Grandma's couch."

"*His* dirty hands," Franklin corrects.

Mom places a hand on Penny's knee. "And I'll be delighted to see the dirt if it means our grandchild is here with us."

I look at Penny, then at Franklin. "Do you know?"

Franklin stares at Penny, and she giggles at her husband.

"I went alone to my last appointment, and I tease Frank that I know the gender. I keep changing from saying he to she." Their cheesy love is sometimes sickening, but if I were to find love, I hope we are as happy as Franklin and Penny.

"Franklin, next time you make Penny's appointment your priority," Mom scolds.

Franklin raises his arms. "I was in New York. Penny said she was fine to go alone."

"Of course, she's going to say she's fine. You should arrange your travel around Penny. She's carrying your child."

Penny giggles. "It's fine, Sophia. I told him to go." She continues rubbing circles over her stomach. "I love seeing him get into trouble."

Franklin arches one eyebrow at his wife.

I grin at Franklin. "Not going to say something back?"

Ever since he married Penny, he never argues with her. She has calmed the ruthless negotiator, and he sees her as a life force. In a way, she is, now that she is carrying his kid.

"No, but I will to you. At least you didn't wear sweatpants to dinner."

I chuckle. "It's summer. Why are you in trousers?"

"Brandon," Mom says, interrupting us. "You're quiet this evening. Is everything okay?"

"I apologize, ma'am." He runs his fingers through his blond waves. "I'm tired from training."

"It's BJ's mom's sixtieth birthday today. The celebrations are this weekend." The room turns quiet. Everyone stares at Brandon.

"Oh, darling. You should go back."

Brandon's gaze lowers to hide his disappointment.

"He has a game, Mom."

Mom stares at Dad. "Carson, you can talk to the coach about Brandon having one game off. This is important."

I hide my grin. That was all I had to say for my mom to get this moving ahead.

"Possibly, but the coach's decision is final." Dad rolls the ice in his whiskey glass. "I don't interfere with team matters."

"Rubbish. You'll call him tonight." She turns to Brandon. "You *will* be there for your mother, Brandon. I promise."

Franklin coughs. "Maybe I can help?" He glances at Penny. "I have a quick trip to Australia and Singapore this weekend. It's the last time I travel before Penny has the baby."

"Franklin, you shouldn't be going away. Penny is due in three weeks."

I can't hide the smirk on my face. My perfect brother has been chastised more times tonight than in his lifetime.

Mom stands. "We need to move to the dining room. Lola will be waiting for us."

Dad stays back to make the call, so I keep in step alongside my mother. "Is Lottie coming tonight?"

"She is. I have no idea why she's late."

I drop back to walk alongside Brandon. *Thanks,* he mouths.

We take our seats at the table. Lola serves our appetizers of smoked salmon, prawns, capers, and a tangy side salad. As Lola clears our plates, Charlotte arrives.

"Lottie," I pipe up. "Your punctuality is of concern." It's the same words she has used toward me many times.

She rolls her eyes. "I was working, you idiot." She greets the table, stops at Penny, and wraps her arms around her shoulders. "When do we get to meet the little one?"

"Three more weeks," Penny says with a grin. "I'm tired and uncomfortable but excited as well."

"Well, I can't wait. Talking of waiting, where is Jobe?"

"He's tied up with the London contract," Dad replies.

"London? What's happening in London?" Charlotte takes a seat next to me and gives me a slight elbow.

"Commercial property investment opportunities," Dad enthusiastically says as though he could talk more about it, but my mother gives him a look.

"Cool." Charlotte is as disinterested as me. "How was training today?"

"Good. Nothing to report." I'm not ready to share the data on my ankle with anyone. It's a precaution, and we're rectifying any potential problems.

She glances at Brandon, who is staring at his dinner plate. "BJ." She waits for him to look at her. "Did you work on your leap?"

"Jesus, Lottie." I shake my head. "You're not our coach."

Her brow pinches. "Why are you in such a bad mood?"

Dad grunts. "Please stop acting like teenagers. Excuse me while I take this."

"Carson, no cell phones at dinner," Mom says exasperatedly.

"That's great news. I'll pass it on." Dad gestures to Brandon. "You're not required to attend the game. Neither is Byron. Coach is playing the two rookie guards."

"What?" Charlotte's eyes round. "What did I miss?"

"It's my mum's birthday," Brandon says, all white teeth showing. He looks at my father. "Thank you, sir."

Dad pats Mom's hand. "It was an important call."

Lola brings out the lamb with multiple side dishes. "Thank you, Lola," Mom says gratefully.

Brandon is still grinning. "Now to book flights home."

"BJ," Franklin says from the other end of the table. "I'm taking the private jet to Australia. You're welcome to join me." He glances at Mom. "I'm sorry, but this trip is a

47

necessity... four days at most. Penny knows to call you if she needs anyone."

"Thanks a million," Brandon says. "I don't know what to say except thank you. My mum will be surprised to see me. And your private jet..." He's smiling like he's won the freaking championship.

"It's okay," Penny says to Mom. "Zara is staying over, and my mom will come if I need her."

Mom reaches for Penny's hand. "You can call me anytime. I'm more than happy to come to you."

"Same," Charlotte pipes up. "But *Australia*? If Frank's going for business and BJ is hitching a ride, maybe I could tag along? This could be great PR for the team. *Australian LA Sharks star heads home for his mother's birthday, team supports family.*"

"This is not about the team, darling. It really is about family," Mom says gently.

"After the scandal these two idiots created, we could do with some good publicity to rebuild the team's wholesome image."

"Do you have to keep bringing up the past?" Brandon murmurs, lowering his gaze. "You're welcome to come, Charlotte, if you think it's best."

They'll kill each other by the end of the trip.

"Are you coming, Byron?" Franklin asks.

"And start a war? No, thank you."

Usually, I would be disappointed in not being named on the team. Not this time.

Giana is home, and I have something to prove that's not on a basketball court.

5

GIANA

Mom rests a hand on my shoulder as she places a glass of iced tea on the wooden table in front of me, then sits beside me. "What are your plans for today?"

"Painting. I'm creating more pieces to send to Isabella for their spring designs."

"I'm so proud of you, Gigi." Mom squeezes my hand. Her smile reaches her eyes, and the lines deepen at the corners. "I'm proud you chased your dream and didn't give up."

"I almost did, many times." I sigh. "I wanted to come home. Not speaking the language and the loneliness got to me. But I'm glad I stayed." I squeeze her hand. "And I'm also glad to be home. While I told myself it's for a few months to see you both, it's going to be a struggle to leave."

My father's dementia is progressing. While Mom manages Dad at home, we are discussing their options for the future. It breaks my heart to see him not himself some days.

It's one of the reasons I came back.

I missed my family.

I missed my home.

While I enjoyed my adventure and advancing my career in Italy, I needed to come home. It's where my heart is.

Mom glances at the glass doors. On the other side, my father putters in the garden. He loves being outside. Always did. When the gardener came on the weekends, Dad would follow him around, observing and learning. He nurtures every plant.

"While I understand you wanting to see your father..." her eyes glisten with emotion. "... you can't put your career on hold."

My mother is so brave. "I appreciate you saying that. Lucky for me, I can work anywhere in the world. If I continue with Isabella, I'll travel back and forth if that's what it takes to keep my contract. I might be gone for a couple of months at a time, but at least home can be my base."

"Gigi..."

"And with the studio upstairs, I have everything I need." I smile at her. "Today, I'm going to work outside while Dad is in the garden. Watching him warms my heart, and your flowers inspired my lines for the last designs."

Mom swipes a tear. "When I saw the poppies on the model's dress, I wondered if they were from our garden."

"Oh, Mom. I draw so much inspiration from home. It's why I wanted to come back."

Her gaze meets mine. "And having your heart broken doesn't help."

"No." I let out a long sigh. "But I didn't love Dante. He was a source of affection, security, and comfort. For a while, I thought I loved him, but looking back, I was never *in love* with him."

"Have you ever been in love with someone? Do you have something to compare your emotions to?"

I take a sip of my iced tea while gathering my thoughts. "No. Although it wasn't how I imagined it to be." There was a time I thought I was in love with Byron, as I had all those feelings of love, even at seventeen. I'm never this way with anyone else. But Byron didn't give me the security and passion Dante did. Byron and I didn't last long enough to discover if our love would thrive.

My cell vibrates with a message. *Byron.* My heart thuds hard. Is it a coincidence he is also thinking of me?

Do you have any plans today? I would love to see you.

I quickly tap out a reply.

Staying home to paint. Maybe another time.

While I wanted to say yes, I would love to see you, I'm not ready. My heart is still healing from someone tossing me aside for someone else with no explanation.

It hurts, even if Dante wasn't the right person for me. Another lesson in love, and when the time is right, I've considered what I want in a lover. When it comes to love, I have also made a mental list of what I need and what I don't. A gorgeous man with an equally gorgeous body is not a combination to say yes to, even if my hormones argue otherwise. He has to respect me. We have to be able to have long chats and connect on a level other than physical. I want to laugh and cry with him, and he has to be there when I need him most.

"Byron Hendricks," Mom says. "Sorry, I saw the name, not the message."

"We met for coffee the other day."

Mom listens but doesn't say anything. She doesn't have to. She knows how he hurt me the last time. She also knows he's basketball famous and what fame can do to young men. While I have found fame in my own way, it doesn't come with the stardom or fan base of a music, film, or sports star, and I'm thankful for that.

"I'd better get started before the morning is over." I kiss Mom on the cheek, then head to the studio to grab what I need to sit outside and paint.

THE PURPLE OF THE BOUGAINVILLEA IS MY FAVORITE COLOR.

I'm creating a piece of art where, on a larger block canvas, the design can be transferred to fabric. I'm imagining a flowing white dress with all the colors of the bougainvillea. Dad comes to stand behind me and peers over my shoulder. "Do you like it?" I ask gently.

He steps aside and rubs his gloves. Dirt falls to the ground. "Very much, Gigi. Are you going to add the white variety?"

I smile at my father and wipe the smudge of dirt from his cheek. "I will. It needs more shading around the flower for it to pop."

His eyes glaze as though he is remembering something. He stares at me for a few more seconds, then totters off.

The shade shifts, and before long, the hot morning sun is almost directly above me. Gathering my easel, I move closer to the house while still under the shade of the jacaranda tree. The purple flowers are beginning to bloom for the second time this year. We're lucky to have a tree that flowers twice a year, and while I love the purple rain of the flowers falling to the ground, my canvas is not where I want buds to land. Mom is fond of seeing color throughout the yard, so Dad cleans the foliage from his mass of trees every Sunday. It's his routine.

I retrieve my palette and stools and get back to painting, ignoring the sound of Mom chatting in the background. At least a half hour passes before I'm too hot to stay outside any longer, even after four years in Italy acclimatizing me to paint in the heat. I stand and wipe my brow, and all the air leaves my lungs. Byron is sitting on a chair, watching me.

"Um... hi."

"Hey." He stands and shoots his heart-winning smile, and it hits me right in the chest. "Your mom said I wasn't allowed to disturb you."

Oh my God, why?

"I don't mind being disturbed. I can do two things at once." How long was he watching me?

He closes the distance between us. Out here in the fresh air, I can smell him more than I care to. I close my eyes, remembering how good he smells up close. "Can I give you a hand?"

"I'd appreciate it." I ogle his designer shorts and T-shirt while I wipe my hands on my old shirt. "Careful with the paint... you don't want to get it on your clothes. I need to get this upstairs. Could you bring the easel?"

Byron follows me through the house. The last time he was here is something I have tried to forget. After speaking to him at the reunion, I sensed he barely remembers what happened that night, and I'm not about to remind him. I turn and watch his long muscled legs take two steps at a time. I wait for him to set up the easel inside the studio, then I position the painting on it and stand back to stare at it.

"It looks good, Gigi." Byron turns in a circle, taking in my studio décor. There are more shelves, paints, markers, and pencils in jars on the table against the wall since he was last here. Plus, extra easels for sketching and blank canvases that line the wall ready for the next project. "I remember some of these."

"You do?" There is an array of unfinished works. Many are my early pieces, but Mom refuses to throw them out.

"Yeah." He picks up a smaller canvas of the beach—the one with the Santa Monica pier. "I remember you had just finished this and hated it, yet I thought it was brilliant." He stares at me. "Why is it hidden up here?"

"It's not that good." I take it out of his hands and place it back on the floor.

"Gigi, we spoke about this. About believing in ourselves."

"I do believe in my work, but this piece is from inexperience. If you like it, then it's yours."

"It reminds me of us," he quietly says as he retrieves it from the hardwood floor.

He's studying the painting as though it is an image of us. My heart races, remembering the fun we had at the beach. He was not a boy or a man back then. He was something in between. While he looks like a man now, with his thick biceps, muscled chest, and rounded shoulders, his decisions are yet to be judged. Byron was stubborn, determined, and loved attention. He had all the qualities of an elite sports star, but I got to see his gentle side when he was with me. Before his fame, my memories were of the skinny boy who was not strong enough, not tall enough, and couldn't make foul shots under pressure to win games. He glances up at me, his face serious.

"What are you thinking about?"

I suck in a breath. "The school game when you missed the foul that would have put us in the finals for a second year running."

His face falls. "Why were you thinking about that game? It was my worst moment."

He doesn't get it. "It's when I was closest to you. When you started opening up to me, and we started to talk to each other. Really talk." We were friends first.

He stares at me for a moment too long, then shifts his focus back to the painting. "So I can keep this?"

"It's all yours."

"Good, because this reminds me of a time when I thought *we* understood each other." He walks over to me and takes my hand in his. "We had some good times, Gi."

"We did," I murmur. His beautiful blue eyes hold mine captive, and I sense he's going to kiss me.

"Why don't we head down to the beach for a swim this afternoon?"

"Sure," I say without thinking. "I can meet you there. I need to do a little more to this piece before I finish for the day."

"I can swing by around four? Does that work?"

"It works fine."

He tucks the beach painting under his arm. "See you then."

After he leaves, the realization hits that Byron hasn't seen me in a bathing suit since high school. I've changed in more ways than one. Genetics hasn't helped, but I also fell in love with Italian wine and pizza. *What the hell was I thinking?*

A minute before four o'clock, Byron pulls up out front.

I kiss Mom on the cheek. "I'll call you later."

"Will you be back for dinner?" Her eyes tell me she doesn't expect me to be.

"Maybe not. Bye, Dad," I call out. I'm out the door before Byron reaches the garden gate.

"Your garden is stunning." He opens the door of his black Porsche for me.

"It is. My dad spends countless hours pruning and nurturing." I wave to my mom, who is peering through the blinds.

"Your dad has retired? He looks so young. Mine is retired, but I have a brother twelve years older than me."

"He has the beginnings of dementia. He had to retire in my second year of college."

"I'm sorry. I didn't know."

I stare out the window at nothing in particular. "It's fine. We didn't stay in touch."

"For that, I'm also sorry. There are no excuses for my behavior other than being selfish and loving the limelight."

"I also know the real Byron."

"You're one of the few people who do."

It's why we clicked. I didn't have many friends at school, and neither did Byron. We formed our little group and kept to ourselves. Byron trained on the courts every lunchtime and sometimes before and after school. He was never a main player until the last three years, and that's when he stepped up as he wanted a college basketball scholarship. He could have gone to any college based on his grades, except he hated being the smart geek. He wanted to be recognized for his basketball talent, something I remember his father not being happy about.

Byron finds a parking space, and we grab our bags and walk the path to the sand. We find a spot on the crowded beach to spread our towels. Byron removes his T-shirt, and I can't stop ogling his abs. I force my eyes away only to notice the teenage girls surrounding us also ogling him and whispering.

Oh shit. They recognize him.

I sit on my towel, leaving on my top and sarong.

He rolls onto his stomach. "Do you have any sunscreen?"

He knows I do as I am a stickler for being skin-smart, even with my olive complexion. I ruffle through my bag and then hand it to him.

"Could you apply it to my back?" he says. "It's the one spot I missed."

I inhale deeply, knowing I need to touch him.

Being with Byron is hard. Touching Byron is breaking all the rules. I squeeze the cream from the tube, and it makes a fart sound. Byron chuckles.

"You're such a child."

I smooth the cream over his muscled back, and *oh my Lord*, he feels so good. Soft yet firm. My hand almost bounces over the mounds of each muscle. It sends my thoughts crazy. I slide my hands down to the band of his shorts, and his tight ass clenches.

My gaze lingers as I imagine him without his boardshorts.

I bite my lip.

I circle up to his rounded shoulders and allow myself the pleasure of feeling his skin for a few more seconds until a quiet moan comes from him.

Shit. I need to stop. We're in a public space.

"All done." I wipe my hands on the towel and pull out a book to read. I position my hat and place a small pillow behind my head. I read the first few lines before he interrupts.

"What else do you have in that bag?"

"Not much."

"Am I bad company?"

Is he kidding? Does he know how nervous I am? I need to distract myself.

"No. I thought you were closing your eyes for a bit. Did you train today?"

"The standard five a.m. training."

"You still get up and practice on your own, even with all your other commitments?"

"Five days a week. And I'm not closing my eyes when I'm lying beside you." He rolls onto his side. My skin heats with his gaze tracing over my every curve.

"I don't mind, Byron. If you need to rest, I understand."

His gaze fixes on me. With one finger, he lowers the book from my face. "I thought we could talk."

"About what?"

"Us."

"Us?" There is no us.

"I want to spend more time with you," he says softly.

"I'd like that very much." We hold each other's gaze for a few seconds. "But I can't get past why you're suddenly interested in me. I'm too scared to look around because I know every girl here is looking at you and judging me. I'm uncomfortable, and I *thought* I buried those feelings a long time ago."

He leans in close to my ear. "I don't care about them. I want to be with you."

"You could have anyone..." He grins, and I shake my head. "It's not attractive to know it."

"No. But *you* know me, and girls never looked at me this way in school. I was the skinny, geeky guy. While I might like the attention, it doesn't mean I'll act on it. I've never had a girlfriend, and the one-nighters aren't as regular as you might think."

"I don't want to think," I snap. And he's wrong. Girls have always flocked to him, even at school. He just didn't notice back then because his focus was basketball. He wanted to be admired on the court, not for his good looks— even if he was a little geeky—or for the name on his back that represented his family more than his basketball ability.

He chuckles. "Are you jealous, Gi?"

"No." I raise my book to my face, but he lowers it again.

"What about you? Did you have someone special in Italy?"

"Byron, I..." I place my book on the towel and roll onto my side to face him. "Yes. I don't think you want details any more than I want to know about the girls you've slept with."

"That's where you're wrong." He grins at me. "I want to know who I'm competing against. Study everything about them to plan my attack." His smirk remains.

The Byron I know would be seething inside if he perceives his opponent to be better than him, not that they were. No one came close to him. How could they, with his blue eyes and the longest lashes? The way he looks at me, *God*. One look and no words, and I would slide beneath him.

"It was Italy," I confess. "Love is a second language." His brow furrows. "While I had lovers, there was one guy. After a year or so, we called it quits. I came home not long after we separated."

His smirk is long gone. "Is he the reason you came home?"

"No." I sigh again, finding it hard to talk about this with Byron. "He was the reason I stayed longer than I intended. While I thought I might have loved him, I wasn't in love with him."

"Of course you weren't." He grins at me and takes his sunglasses from the top of his head. "You were in love with me." He's smiling as he rolls onto his back and covers his eyes with the glasses.

"You're infuriating." I raise my book again and begin to read.

We remain quiet for a few minutes.

"Why did you stay with him?" he whispers. All the cockiness in his tone has disappeared.

Stay with him?

Why is he thinking about this now?

While Byron exudes confidence, it's a cover for how he feels on the inside, and right now, he feels threatened. He admitted to never having a girlfriend. He was, and still is, focused on his goal—his basketball dreams. If he lets someone in, they might discover he's not the self-assured guy he makes out to be. He has this intense energy for anything to do with basketball. Away from the hype, he's humble, kind, and rather normal. Fans are always looking for excitement. He can't run on that energy twenty-four seven—it's exhausting. I just admitted to being intimate with the same person for a year. He hasn't done that.

I keep the book elevated. "I was lonely."

"Why didn't you call me? I didn't know you were alone?"

I lower the book and glare at him. "If you remembered what happened the last time we saw each other, then you'd have your answer to why I didn't call."

"I'm sorry, Gi. It wasn't a good time for me. If I could take it back..."

"It's always about you, Byron," I say louder than normal, and heads turn. I don't want to stay here. I rip off my sarong and top.

"Finally," he says with glee.

He is infuriating.

I storm toward the water. I dive in and enjoy the sounds of the ocean for a few seconds. The noise from the surface is muffled, and it's comforting to escape, albeit only for a moment. The waves roll in, so I concentrate on floating over the swell before it breaks over me.

Byron appears beside me. "We need to swim farther out." He flicks his long bangs, and water smacks my face. I giggle.

"Wait. Who is watching our stuff?"

"I promised some chick two tickets to the game tonight to guard it."

"There's a game tonight? Why are you here?"

"I'm being rested." His eyes darken. "Tonight, I'm all yours."

I swivel in the water to scope out my towel and bag. Paddling to keep afloat, I spy a bikini-clad girl standing near our belongings. "You picked her?"

"Yeah. She was sitting closest to us."

"I doubt she could even tackle me."

This is the Los Angeles I remember. Gorgeous women are slim. I now have curves—more than I did the last time I saw Byron.

"Twenty yards from our towels, there's a guy with a red umbrella and a black top."

I strain my eyes, barely making him out.

"That's Colton, my security guard. If anyone touched you, they would have me *and* him to answer to."

What? But we drove here together. "How is he here?"

"I gave him the details before coming to yours. And he tracks my cell."

"Is he undercover?"

Byron's lips curl into a grin. "Good security isn't seen unless they need to be."

"Your life is very different than what I remember."

He reaches for me and pulls me close. Both hands are on my back, and we are squished together. This close, it's difficult to stay afloat. Byron guides my legs around his waist. I use my hands to paddle like mad because I'm scared what it could lead to if I touch him. He takes my face in his hands and kisses me. It's light and salty. Lost in the moment, a wave dumps over the top of us, and we surface, spluttering, my hair covering my face like Cousin Itt.

"Jesus. I'm used to swimming in Mediterranean oceans."

Byron's expression drops. He takes my hand. "Let's go ashore." He holds my hand while we paddle in, not letting go as we emerge from the water.

Thank God I'm wearing a one-piece bathing suit.

With my free hand, I adjust my red bathing suit, but it's tight and has barely moved. Both girls are still safely tucked in. While I bathed in a bikini in Italy and topless at Dante's private pool, I'm not as comfortable in my skin in LA, especially not around Byron.

Byron releases my hand and chats to the girl, who eyes me up and down. I lie on my stomach, my forehead balancing on the back of my hands.

"Lorraine, our PR administrator, will email the tickets to you," he says. He then talks to someone on his cell. Byron has always been good on his word. "You should have them in your inbox any minute."

"Thank you so much," the girl says excitedly. "Will we see you there?"

"Not this week. Thanks again."

There is movement beside me.

I take a discreet peek under my arm. Byron lies on his back, perched on his elbows. He's staring at the water, deep in thought.

What am I doing? I've been home ten days. I go over my mental list about dating again.

Rule #1: Do not get your heart broken in LA.

I should have added stay away from Byron Hendricks.

Rule #2: Only date people you're not attracted to.

I wanted to date people who are good communicators. I'm done with monologues with men talking about themselves. And there's much more to life than seductive eyes and a hot body.

Rule #3: Be open to new things.

Number three is my new priority.

I barely hear his question when he asks, "Have you ever been to an NBA game?"

"No."

"Would you like to come and watch me?"

I lift my head. While I watched Byron in high school, it was more about cheering for the pride of the school and my friend, not about the game. I've never been a fan of testosterone on the court. But the way Byron said *watch me* has my heart beating faster than it should. *Be open to new things...*

"Watch you, yes. But I'm still not a fan of basketball."

He laughs. "I suppose you're into soccer now?"

"It's called football in Europe."

"But you're LA born and bred. It's soccer."

I laugh and lower my head. "I didn't get into that either. When my friends were watching the games, I painted."

"I'll get you in the corporate seats with my family."

I roll onto my side. "I don't need special treatment. I'll sit anywhere. I'll be there to watch you, not cheer on the team."

His brow furrows. His eyes lock with mine, then lower. My skin heats as his gaze trails lower, then lower still. His hand lifts to rest on my hip. "You will not be sitting just anywhere," he says in a husky voice.

"I don't mind." I roll onto my stomach, and his hand moves to my lower back. "We're friends, Byron. I don't want to ruin it before we get to know each other again. We have both... I was going to say changed, but I think matured is a better word. There are things we should talk about. I don't want to be hurt again."

"Have dinner with me."

"No. Being charmed by you at dinner is not what I need."

"What if I promise not to charm you?" he asks, his voice flat.

A laugh bursts from me. "You can't promise me something that comes naturally to you."

A slow grin spreads across his face. "Giana Monroe finds me charming." He rolls onto his back with the smirk firmly in place.

"You're back to being infuriating, which also comes naturally to you."

"Charming," he repeats, ignoring my words.

Ugh.

WE SHAKE THE SAND FROM OUR TOWELS.

"Is it too late to eat now?"

He glares at me. "You're not getting out of dinner that easily."

I tie my sarong around my hips, then shove everything in my bag.

"Walk with me," he says.

"Now?"

"Yes, now." He stands and waits for me to sling my bag over my shoulder. He takes my hand in his, and we walk down to the water and stroll along the wet sand.

I inhale a deep, cleansing breath.

"You love it here," he says.

"The beach?"

"The beach, home..."

I think for a moment before answering. "There is comfort in being home, but I also found comfort in being somewhere nobody knew me."

"I thought you were lonely?"

"At night."

A soft growl sounds from his throat.

"Most days, I painted or worked with people, and I loved it. Most nights during the first few years, I came home to an empty bed in an empty house in a strange country."

"I was going to say my bed is empty ninety-nine percent of the time, but we are discussing different situations here."

"We are. You were living in a familiar place, and if you wanted, someone would be in your bed within seconds."

"I didn't want people in my bed. But that's me."

I know it is. Byron's focus is next level. "They never stayed the night?"

"Rarely."

"You wouldn't want me either."

"Don't tell me what I want, Gi," he says in a gentle but firm voice.

I need to backtrack. "We should go. If we're having dinner, I need to shower and make myself beautiful," I joke.

"We could have dinner like we are."

I pull a face at him. "Restaurants have standards."

"Not at my house."

It's my turn to grin. "Are you going to cook dinner for me?"

"I am."

God help me. I should tear up my rule book right now.

<small>We drive directly to Byron's house.</small>

On entering his driveway, we stop on a turntable, and it

spins us around so we reverse into the garage. The huge space oozes class, with polished floors, inbuilt cupboards, a kitchenette, and two more lavish black sports cars—a Lamborghini and a Range Rover.

"Are these yours?"

"They are, although I mostly drive the Porsche." He takes my hand and leads me through a door to the hallway. A little farther along, we come to a dead end with three more doors. We enter through the middle door and take the stairs to the next level, which leads us into a vast marble kitchen.

He points to the stools at his kitchen island. "Take a seat." With every step, I have turned my head like a sideshow clown as I take in his impressive home. Black is clearly his favorite—black leather stools, black faucets, black light fittings. There is a hint of brass, but even the marble counter has streaks of black and gold.

"Who styled your home?"

"My sister-in-law and I did most of it."

"It's stylish."

"She's in the business, and I have great taste." He looks at me and smirks.

"Finally, we agree on something."

He pulls food from the refrigerator and specialty cookware from the deep drawer beside him, then turns on the induction surface plate.

"What are you cooking?"

"Seafood and a salad. I thought it would appeal to you."

For real? "A Mediterranean meal?" His smile grows wider. "A meal straight to my heart." I'm impressed by Byron's attempt to please me. "Do you have any wine?"

"In the cellar."

"Which is?"

"Downstairs. You need to walk through the movie theater."

I slide off the stool and trot down the staircase to the ground level. The staircase to the lower levels is on the other side of the foyer. I head down the stairs, walk through a movie theater, a gym room, and then behind a wall of glass...

Holy Mother of God.

This is the cellar of all cellars—a complete room of refrigerators with floor-to-ceiling glass doors. I walk past each section—champagne, white, rosé, red. I open the red wine refrigerator door and step inside to browse over the labels. I choose a Nero d'Avola, my favorite before leaving Italy.

I scan the other bottles, and all the air leaves my lungs. His collection is amazing and worth hundreds of thousands of dollars.

Who needs Italy when I have Byron Hendricks?

6

BYRON

GIANA POPS the last shrimp in her mouth and groans. Damn, I love watching her eat. She forks at the salad. "What's in the dressing?"

"Fresh herbs."

"You're in the wrong business."

I raise a brow at her. "Watch me play and then compare my cooking to my ball skills."

"I'm sure they're equally impressive." She eyes me over the rim of her glass before taking a sip of wine and staring at my untouched glass. "You don't agree with my choice of wine?"

"It's one of my favorites. The window where I allow myself to indulge has almost closed."

"Because of training?"

I take her dish and place it in the dishwasher. "Yes."

"The season doesn't start until October. You have two months."

"I do, but tonight, I'm choosing not to drink for other reasons."

Her glass is almost to her lips when she freezes. "Byron," she whispers.

I round the island and take her hand. "Come sit with me. Outside." The glass doors to the outside pool have been open all night. The lights of LA twinkle below us, and Giana has turned her head throughout the meal to sneak glances at the impressive view. It's one of the reasons I bought this house. The sun has almost set, and the sky is a burnt orange over the ocean with the entire city below us.

"It's stunning," she whispers.

"It's my favorite time of night. Nothing better than sitting out here with a wine at dusk."

"I can't look away."

Normally, I would agree, except tonight, I'm struggling to take my eyes off her. While her cover-ups conceal her beautiful body, the image of her on the beach is unforgettable. Giana is the most beautiful woman on the planet. While my attraction to her at school was undeniable, I'm now fighting it at another level.

It's considerably hotter outside, even with the breeze of day changing to night.

Giana stares at the infinity pool.

"Jump in. It will help you cool off. I'll pass your wine over, and we can watch the last of the sunset on the edge."

"I don't know..." Her gaze flicks between me and the pool, then she shrugs. "Why not? We only live once."

She slides her shirt over her arms, and it falls to the pool lounge. She unties her sarong. "Are you coming in?"

She catches my admiring gaze. "I can if it's what you want."

"I'm not swimming alone. I did enough of that in the last four years."

It's like a knife to my gut. Why the hell didn't I call her? The fact she cut me off is a fact I don't miss, and we still need to have a conversation at some stage. But not tonight. It could ruin what we're building.

Giana slides into the pool, and I'm doing all I can to tame my raging thoughts. I hand her the glass of wine, slip off my shirt, and follow her in. We push through the water to the other side of the pool, and Giana rests her wine glass carefully on the ledge.

She pushes up to look over the edge. "Woah. That is a drop."

"Fifteen feet." I place a hand on her back as she stares down to the pool water catchment.

"Has anyone walked along this ledge?" She gapes down the rugged mountain edge to the properties below.

"No, and neither will you."

She giggles at me. "I'm not that brave."

"Brave? I'm not about to let anyone risk their safety by being a daredevil."

"I like this side of you." She turns, and her gaze fixes on mine. My hand is still on her back as she slides into the water. "You were always focused, but something is different."

"Focused? As in not risking everything I've worked so hard to achieve?"

She turns to the house, taking her arms wide. "What you have achieved here is remarkable."

"Glad you approve."

"I'm sure *many* do."

The way she says it isn't a compliment. "It's not a party house."

"No girls?" She pulls a face as though she doesn't believe me.

"I never said I was a priest."

"I bet they prayed to you."

This isn't the conversation I'd hoped for. I move directly into her line of vision. "There was only one girl I wanted to want me in that way, but she cut me off like I was nothing. A man does things to forget."

"You didn't want me," she whispers. "You were high the last time we were together. I was nobody, just a warm body to you." She shoves her wine glass toward me in emphasis, one finger pointed my way. "You came for one thing. Fucked me in my studio like I was nothing, then got up and left when I called you out on it."

Jesus. I was a mess, I admit, and I didn't expect to have this conversation now.

"I waited for a week," she continues. "But I never heard from you. Lesson learned. I don't want to feel like that again." She looks at her wine glass and takes a sip. "It was a douchebag move, and it meant nothing to someone I deeply cared for."

My chest is so tight I'm struggling for air. "Gigi, I'm sorry. While I can't fix my past, I can promise you I'm no longer that guy. It was a shitty six months of my life, and I'm sorry you had to see me like that."

She stares into my eyes as though she is looking for who I am and if it's the truth. I place my hands on her hips. "I'll never hurt you again."

She shakes her head. "Another promise you can't keep. Or maybe it's me that won't make any promises."

"I don't follow."

With her free hand, Giana cups my face. "We have tonight. That's all for now."

While I'm not happy about being with Giana for one night, I'll take what she offers. I lean in and kiss her mouth, tasting the red wine, tasting her. Our tongues clash, and the heat between us escalates. I pull back, and she pants, her chest rising and falling. I take one of her straps and slide it over her shoulder, kissing her shoulder and neck, then the other. Her eyes lock with mine as we watch each other's expressions. I tug her bathing suit over her curves, and those full breasts bounce free. The water hides most of her body. "Fuck, I need to see you." I go underwater and suck each nipple until I need more air.

"Get this off," she demands.

Happily.

Dropping below the surface, I tug the material over her hips, and she lifts each leg to accommodate me. Turning back to Giana, I rub my hands up and down her arms. "Are you sure this is what you want?"

Her lashes flutter. "I want you to touch me."

She doesn't need to ask again. Tonight, Giana has my entire focus.

7

GIANA

THERE IS NOT enough oxygen in LA. Not when Byron's mouth is all over me, his fingers bringing me to climax. I feel his every touch and caress when I had hoped the alcohol would numb his charm.

Nothing can dull Byron Hendricks.

He has a power over me no one has come near to, and it started the first time I was introduced to him in high school.

"Oh God," I moan.

There's a faint chuckle.

He remembers where I like to be touched.

I tilt my head, hanging onto his shoulders with my legs wrapped around his strong hips. Three fingers pump into me, circle inside me, and rub over my G-spot in the most delicious way.

"Byron..." I cry out in a moan as I come, color lighting up my thoughts. An orgasm so fantastic whips through me that I can't help but smile through heavy breaths as my body becomes limp. A strong hand glides from my stomach up to my chest bone. I tilt my head back until the bliss scatters.

Byron takes me in his arms. "You have the best orgasm face," he whispers.

"How so?" Who even knows what their orgasm face looks like?

He nuzzles my neck. "You're even more beautiful when you climax."

"Are you implying it should be part of my beauty routine?"

I open my eyes as my body floats back to reality. Byron's gaze is locked on me. His expression darkens as though it has aligned with his thoughts.

"You don't need a beauty routine, Gi."

That's not what he was thinking.

My breath stills, knowing what he wants.

"I want you, Gi, but I can wait."

He's giving me a choice, and it orients me quicker than any smelling salts. I only asked him to touch me.

I want to...

The time-lapse in my reply is answer enough. Byron kisses my cheek, grabs the glass from my hand that I miraculously didn't spill, and wades through the water to the other side.

"Where are you going?"

"To get you a towel," he says gently.

He steps out of the water, his huge erection pushing against his shorts. I can't help but stare and remember what he used to look like naked. Now he has more muscle, more strength, and more stamina—the perfect combination in bed.

What am I doing?

Without a doubt, I want to have sex with Byron, but this is happening faster than I intended. I needed to be touched while also protecting my heart. Why not Byron? He is as good as any lover.

Because Byron is the one who can hurt me more than any other man.

He returns with a towel wrapped around his waist, his erection still evident. He holds another towel open for me to step into.

Swimming naked is not new for me, yet I feel nervous as I take the first step from the water. Byron watches my every move. His eyes are all over me, and when I press against the towel, he holds my gaze, the lust swirling between us. He wraps the towel around my body and takes a step back to give me space, his erection pushing his towel even higher.

He rubs at the material caging his dick. "Seeing you like this, with water running over your beautiful body, doesn't help."

My beautiful body. His words are like a song in my mind.

"What will help?" I whisper.

"Not imagining you in my bed, for a start." He turns aways and rakes his fingers through his wet hair.

"I'm assuming you have regular checks."

His head whips around, understanding what I'm asking him.

"Just last week. I'm clear. I also always used protection."

"Same. I have contraception."

His eyes widen, his chest rising and falling rapidly.

I turn away and look out over the million-dollar view. "No one can see us here, right?"

"No."

I drop my towel, and in an instant, his hands are all over me, his mouth on my breast, my stomach, my inner thigh.

This has to be sex, not love.

Do not fall for him.

His kisses trace over my stomach, up to my other breast,

to my shoulders, and then to my face. His lips take mine, and my body screams for him. Our kisses are passionate, his tongue wrapping around mine like a snake dance. We breathe the same air through loud, desperate breaths, our needy hands all over each other.

"This is just sex, right?" I say.

His face drops, then understanding crosses his expression. He spins me so I'm facing toward the pool, his cock pressing into my lower back. Both hands wrap around to massage my breasts while he kisses the nape of my neck. I tilt my head to rest on his shoulder and circle my hips against him.

This is perfect. No gazing into his eyes when I come, no kissing intimately. A hand reaches, and I spread my legs for him while the other squeezes my boob and rubs my nipple. His fingers own me. This time, I'm bucking and circling in rhythm as desire builds again. "Now," I demand.

I step away and place both hands on the chair, bending my ass to him.

He hesitates, then steps closer.

I focus on the city lights twinkling as the night begins to set in. His hands grab my hips. Looking over my shoulder, I catch him staring at my pussy. "You are fucking gorgeous, Gi."

He's making me nervous.

It's just sex.

Only one night.

Byron slides inside me and stills, giving me a chance to stretch to his size.

I allow myself a long inhale, remembering how he feels inside me and relish the first hit of pleasure. He eases out and slides in slowly, kissing my shoulder.

I circle my hips to goad him on. Sexual pleasure is what I need before my body starts to crave *him*.

His thrusts speed up. With every breath, I allow myself to take everything he gives, feel every thrust, and enjoy the way one hand works my clit and the other massages my breast. He places a hand on my shoulder. He's close. His breathing switches to deep, rapid panting. His rhythm speeds up, and he pounds me from behind. My body jingles, my breasts bouncing with every thrust until they are composing a dance of their own.

Small orgasms build and release as his hips collide with my ass. He rides me hard, all the strength leaving my body as I struggle to stand. With a hand on my neck, Byron pushes my head lower, my hips rising for him. The sweet side of Byron slips away as he fucks me into the next orgasm. Arching my back, I lift my head against his hold and moan with the ecstasy rushing through my body as I come, the joy of an orgasm ripping through every part of me, overriding every thought.

Byron groans loudly, shuddering with a final thrust as he empties himself inside me. He slumps onto my back and kisses my shoulders and wraps his arms around my waist. It's not to support him. I feel him wanting to be with me as much as I need him. For a few minutes, we linger in the afterglow of sex until I realize what I have done.

He gave me what I asked of him, yet it feels too familiar.

This is the first time he hasn't worn a condom with me.

I felt all of him. I broke the rules by giving myself to Byron without him having to chase or prove he won't hurt me again. Byron isn't to blame—I initiated the intimacy from the moment I asked him to touch me in the pool.

"Are you okay?" he says gently from behind me. The loss of his touch hits me hard.

"Of course," I say quickly.

He picks up the towel and hands it to me. "Would you like to use the bathroom, or... we could go to my bedroom?"

No, no, no. Not his bed.

"The bathroom, please. I really should be going." I tie the towel securely around my chest, and he picks up my wet bathing suit. "You can hardly put this back on."

"It will be fine," I say quickly, holding out my hand.

"I'll grab you something. You can freshen up. There are clean towels in the cupboard."

"Thank you, Byron, but my bathing suit is fine."

Byron walks into his house. I pad behind him until he stops and points to the bathroom. Again, it's all marble and brass with a hint of black accessories. He has exquisite taste.

I shower, pouring the citrus-scented gel over my body, and dry off with the softest towels I have ever used.

Who does his laundry? I need them in my life.

I emerge still towel-drying my long hair, the other towel wrapped around my chest. Brushing can wait until I'm home.

Walking into the kitchen, I note Byron has washed the saucepans while I showered.

"I never knew you were a clean freak."

He laughs. "Structure and neatness is key, Giana." He eyes me carefully. "It's routine." He comes to me and wraps his arms around my waist so we are standing barely a hair's breadth apart. "Tonight, you were the best distraction."

I stare at his lips. We could easily pick up where we left off. "While I enjoyed it, I also need to get home."

His brow pulls tight with disappointment. "We don't have to do anything else, just sleep."

Sleep...

"But you don't like anyone in your bed."

"You're not anyone." He stares at me for too long.

As much as I want to, I need to slow this down. "Maybe next time," I say gently. "I have to get changed." I look around for my bathing suit.

He hands me a LA Sharks T-shirt and his shorts. "Wear these. For our *next time*, bring a change of clothes with you."

The following morning, I'm sitting outside painting while Dad works in the garden. Mom comes to sit beside me. "This piece is coming along nicely."

"Do you like it?"

"I do." She smiles at me, and the lines around her eyes grow deeper. "Did you feel inspired after last night?"

"A little." I meet her curious gaze. "It's easy with him. Too easy."

"I know. He's familiar and safe."

"He's not safe. Not for my heart."

Mom's smile is softer. "Keep painting, Giana. It will guide your thoughts to what you want. When it's time for you to decide where your future leads, then you can assess how you feel about Byron."

"I already know how I feel about him."

"You told me you were keeping your options open and not falling in love here because it will affect your decision."

I let out a sigh. "Dad and you are my priority here."

"But you also need to have fun, and you enjoy being with him."

"I do."

"So, date someone else. Enjoy your young life. Don't let Byron be the only one to own your heart."

"Maybe." I keep painting, adding more color to the petals.

"Have you heard from Isabella?"

"Not recently. She's waiting for me to finish a few pieces, then we'll discuss another contract."

"Does it mean traveling back to Italy more frequently?"

Dipping my brush in water, I take a break for a moment. "It does. But if Dad or you need me, I can catch the next flight home."

"Do what you need for your career. We'll take whatever time you can give us." She kisses my cheek and stands. "I'll go make us some lunch."

"I'm packing up now, Mom. Let me do it so you can spend time with Dad."

My cell vibrates, and my chest warms as I hope it's from Byron. I haven't heard from him today. I'm not disappointed to see it's from Paige, but I also want to hear from Byron.

It can't be like the last time.

Hey, what are you doing now?

I tap a quick reply.

No plans yet. I would love to catch up.

After borrowing my mother's car, I meet Paige at a café. She greets me with a hug.

"How are you settling back in?"

"It's nice to be back at home. I missed my parents."

Paige coughs.

I laugh. "And my friends."

"From what I hear, Byron missed you as much as you missed him."

"What?"

"Nothing." She pulls a cheeky face.

"Just what did you hear?"

"That you spent time with each other at the beach."

I sigh. "We did."

"Mason said all he talks about is you."

"We've spent one day together."

Paige places her Gucci bag on the chair beside her. "He said he's happy you chased your dream and is amazed at everything you've achieved."

Her words warm me. Byron is the one who encouraged me never to give up on my goals.

"I had a fabulous time in Italy and was lucky to secure the design work."

She pushes short strands of blonde hair behind her ears. "Luck had nothing to do with it."

We all need friends like Paige. She is the one person I kept in contact with during my time in Italy. I didn't share a lot of details, but we did talk.

"What's next for the famous Giana Monroe?" Paige asks dramatically.

I laugh. I am *not* famous. "Don't famous people drive fancy cars and live in luxury houses?" Like Byron.

"You had a villa."

"Still do. I never sold it. But I'm back driving my parents' car and living with them. Does that sound famous to you?"

She narrows her eyes. "Don't pretend you're poor."

"I'm not. I have savings. I'm the world's best procrastinator. Do I buy a car? A condo? Because if I do, it means I'm taking a step toward staying in LA."

"Buy a car, Gigi. It's independence. You'll use it on return visits." She's right. "But you don't need a condo when you have your studio above your parents' house." She pauses. "Unless you need more privacy..."

"Stop it. What about you? How are you and Mason?"

"We went on our third date last night." She beams her big smile. "Why did we wait so long?"

"Why do any of us wait? The future holds no more safety than today."

Her eyes round. "Right?"

We order coffee and chat some more, laughing a lot.

"I've missed you, Gigi. Jessica is nice, but she seems to be in competition whenever we go out. Oh, and don't be surprised if she ignores you. She has a thing for Byron."

"I'm not fighting her for him. I'm not planning on staying. Besides, we're just having fun."

By the way she eyes me, she isn't convinced.

"We should go on a double date," she says with excitement.

"Paige, the problem with that idea is *Byron and I are not dating*."

"You will be soon enough."

And that is a colossal future problem. My heart would dive right in to loving Byron. But it's still raw, and I'm not ready for the hurt when my future is so unclear.

My cell vibrates on the table with a text message from Byron.

Do you want to catch up tonight?

8

BYRON

THE BALL HITS THE RING.

Fuck.

Ninety-eight foul shots.

It's the third time I've missed right before making my goal of one hundred straight. My focus is off. My thoughts wander.

Wiping sweat from my brow, I walk to the foul line and bounce the ball before I settle into a stance.

Breathe out.

Swish.

I'm ready to go again. I grab the ball and settle my feet.

Breathe out.

Twang.

The ball hits the ring and bounces back to me. I'm stunned, staring at the ring.

What the fuck is wrong with me?

Excuses flood my brain. It's not the absence of Brandon. It's her.

To hell with this.

I jog off the court and head to the locker room to shower.

Walking the tunnel to my car, I pass Lorraine from the office.

"It's supposed to be your day off training, Byron," she shoots over her shoulder as we pass.

"No such thing," I call back.

Inside my car, I check my cell. Giana has replied to my text. I asked to catch up tonight. It's two in the afternoon but, hell, I need to see her now. I drive directly to hers, jog up the steps to her front door, and press the button.

"Hello."

I look at the camera. "Hi, Mrs. Monroe. It's Byron Hendricks. Is Giana home?"

The door unlocks, and Mrs. Monroe gives me an uncertain look.

"Hello, Byron. Giana is upstairs in her studio."

"Is she painting?"

"She is. Can I get you anything, maybe a drink?"

I rub a hand over my forehead. There's a smear of sweat, and my face is probably glowing from training, despite my shower. "That would be great. Thank you." I follow her into the kitchen, where she is about to pour an iced tea. "Water is fine, ma'am."

She hands me an iced water. Out the window, I catch a glimpse of Mr. Monroe pruning a tree.

"May I take it upstairs with me?"

Her eyes soften. "Certainly."

Taking the stairs two at a time, I knock gently on Giana's door before peering in. "Hey."

"Hey." She stops midstroke and smiles. Her smile could win over the hardest of hearts. "I thought you said tonight?"

"Is it bad timing? I wanted to see you."

She looks at her canvas, then back at me. "I've just started as I had coffee earlier with Paige. But I can stop."

I stand beside her and study her art. "No, don't stop. I'm happy to watch. It might clear my head."

"Your head?"

"I trained like crap. Nothing was going right. I had to get outta there."

"*You* stopped training early?" She feigns shock. "What's concerning you?"

I shake my head. "It's just one day." A comfortable chair with a sloping back catches my eye. Does she sit in the chair to ponder her work? "May I?" I ask, pointing to the chair.

"Be my guest."

Giana continues to paint with gentle strokes and her wrist action smooth. Each flower looks perfect to me. She retraces her work, adding deeper shades and more color, perfecting something that is already perfect.

We are more alike than she realizes. Our best is not good enough. What one person sees as complete, we continue, feeling the need to refine our skill even more—an unreachable perfection. Giana stands back, studies her art, and adds a few more strokes. She tilts her head, the dent between her eyebrows creasing ever so slightly. Those long lashes flutter. She mixes more color. With my hands behind my head, I lean back and close my eyes, allowing the contentment in watching Giana ease the tightness in my muscles.

"Byron," she whispers.

I open my eyes and sit straight in the chair, my neck tight. "Jesus, how long was I out?"

I look at her painting, and it's been replaced with a portrait. *Is that me?*

"Long enough for me to finish this piece." She angles the canvas. "Do you like it?"

I push up out of the chair and study the lines of my face. I look... relaxed.

"Is that what I look like when I sleep?"

"It is." She steps up to me and reaches to kiss me on the cheek. I loop an arm around her waist. "I hope you don't mind. Some people are offended if they are unaware I'm painting them."

"When you make me look like I've just had sex, I'm not complaining."

She giggles. "You have a beautiful face. It has all the right angles for a portrait."

"I'll take that." I move hair out of her eyes. "Especially coming from the woman whose beauty leaves me breathless." Our eyes meet, and our gazes lock. "Can I kiss you, Gigi?"

She responds by pushing up on her toes to kiss me—a peck, nothing more.

She pulls away and flashes an innocent smile.

"Not what I meant."

Pulling her toward me, I kiss her in the way I intended. Our lips move together, our tongues meeting in an all-too-familiar way. I want this woman to myself and to feel like this with only her. I tighten my hands around her waist to stop me from touching her in other places.

Her parents are downstairs.

When I was younger, I didn't show her that respect.

Her hand goes under my shirt, and she rubs her fingertips over my back. I pull away. Giana has that look in her eye that says I could take her here and now.

"Hey," I whisper.

"Hey," she repeats, her voice raspy.

"What do you want to do tonight?"

"What do you want to do?" By her sultry expression, I know what she has on her mind, and while I want Giana in my bed, I want us to do this right. Date first.

"We could go to..." Fuck. There are not many places I can go without people intruding on my privacy. "We could dine at Bloom? My brother could get us a table." If he was in the freaking country.

"I was extremely happy with the chef last night. I'd like to try that restaurant again."

This woman knows compliments are key. "I'll make the reservations. Shall I pick you up around six?"

Giana glances down with a coy look. "That would be perfect."

GIANA SITS ON A STOOL AT THE COUNTER, WATCHING ME COOK linguine with a combination of seafood and a light rosé sauce. Tonight, she drinks the Chardonnay I imported from Burgundy.

"Would you like some help?" she purrs. "This dish is my specialty."

"Not at all. Enjoy your wine."

She raises her wine glass. "I like this... you cooking. It's sexy."

I turn and stare at her. "It's the least sexy thing I do. You should see me clean. Naked. *Dancing.*"

She eyes me over the rim of her glass. "I can picture it."

I laugh.

"Wait, don't you have a housekeeper?"

"I do. They come once a week. I like to clean and cook. It's therapeutic."

"Said no one ever." She shakes her head at me. "Though cleaning this house, I understand it."

"I'm a private person. You, of all people, should know that."

"Who is also a disciplined clean freak, which I didn't know."

I raise a brow. "We were the same at school."

"You were not like this." She stands and comes around to me. She wipes a finger over the counter and inspects her fingertip. "Nothing." I fight the urge to wipe her finger smudge off the marble. She opens a drawer. And another. And another. "You're next-level, Byron. You would hate living with me."

I still. For days, I have imagined living with Giana as a perfect life. "I highly doubt that."

"My studio is tidy..."

I laugh. It's like a tornado ripped through the room.

"... for me." She stares at me. "I tidy occasionally. I prefer to have fun and paint, go out and meet people, eat all the food and drink all the wine, swim in the ocean, and paint some more."

"It sounds like a vacation."

She narrows her eyes at me. "I work hard, but in my downtime, I have fun. I didn't waste time cleaning and tidying."

"You were in another country. I'd probably do the same."

She shakes her head. "No, you wouldn't. How could you relax? You'd be out running, watching your diet, cleaning up my messes. Did you ever leave your dishes for the morning because you had a great night and were too tired to clean up?"

"It takes two minutes to stack a dishwasher."

"You're missing the point."

I spin around. "What point, Gi? That without even trying, you can't see us being together?"

Fuck.

"Settle down, Byron. I was merely pointing out my faults." She twists her long hair on top of her head and secures it with a tie.

I turn to serve up dinner. "I apologize."

"Accepted. And since you don't require my help, I'm going for a swim."

She walks outside and slips out of her dress and bra, then slides her G-string over her thighs. I stare at the bowls of pasta, ready to eat.

What?

I can't take my eyes off Giana's body as she steps into the pool. Her skin still radiates from the Italian sunshine. Her sexy curves are fucking perfect. This woman is going to kill me.

Giana glides through the water to the far edge of the pool and stares out beyond the sprawling city to the sun setting over the ocean. I carry our plates and forks outside, then return to get her wine, pour myself one, and take them poolside.

I dangle my legs in the water, eating my pasta while Giana is on the other side of the pool. My gut tells me she needs a minute.

"We both love this view," I say.

She turns, studies me for a moment, and understands what I'm saying. "We do." She paddles back to me, picks up her wine glass, and takes a sip. "You're having a glass?"

I nod. "If I'm with you, then the rules need to change."

"I don't want you to change." She picks out a prawn and drops it in her mouth. Water drips from her hand into the pasta.

"Jesus, you're killing the taste and texture."

She giggles. "It's worth it to be in a pool eating my favorite food and drinking gorgeous wine." She picks out another, and more pool water drips into her bowl.

"Stop." I take her bowl, twirl the linguine around the fork, and hold it in front of her mouth. "We'll compromise."

As she takes the bite, she closes her eyes and makes a noise that makes me want to jump in with her. She flutters her lashes. "I like this compromise."

"If I jump in to silence you, I'll be throwing the pasta in the trash."

"Don't you dare. I'll be a good girl." She opens her mouth for me again.

A low growl escapes me. I have plans for those plump lips later, my *good girl*.

Giana finishes her pasta, and before I can join her, a strange ringtone sounds from inside.

"Oh shit," she says, jumping out of the pool with urgency.

"Is that your cell?"

"It is." She grabs the towel and quickly dries off before striding inside. Her phone rings out, but she makes a call, and I remain by the pool to give her some privacy. I turn when she stops talking and see her getting dressed.

I spring up and go to her. "Is everything okay?"

She stares at me with tears pooling in her eyes. "My father had a fall. He tripped and cut his head. The ambulance is taking him to the hospital for observation and to check he doesn't have a concussion."

I pull her into my arms. "Hey, hey, it's going to be okay. Do you want me to go with you?"

Giana shakes her head. "Thank you, Byron, it was a lovely night. I'll catch a cab home."

"No, I'll drive you. I may be of assistance."

"Thank you for the offer, but I think it just needs to be family for now."

How is your father?

I STARE AT MY PHONE, WAITING FOR GIANA TO RESPOND. IT'S just past nine o'clock.

Hi Byron, my dad required sutures. We need to observe him for concussion. I'll talk to you tomorrow x

I want to go to her.

Sitting on the couch, I tap my cell on my thigh while my leg bounces. I'm powerless to help her. There is no chance I'll sleep with this kind of energy pumping through my veins. In a few minutes, I've changed and am jogging down to the basement to use the weights in my gym.

Within half an hour, sweat drips from my forehead. My biceps and shoulders ache. The music cuts out on my phone with an incoming call. I dive on it, hoping it's Giana.

Strange. My mother never calls me this late at night.

"Hey, Mom."

"Darling, Penelope has gone into labor."

"What?"

"She is eighteen days early." Her voice is hoarse. "Franklin is on his way home now."

Shit.

My thoughts scramble. "It's Sunday in Australia. BJ's mom's party was last night."

"Yes. Their flight left four hours ago. As soon as Penelope told Franklin she was feeling strange, he organized for them to leave earlier than arranged. I really hope he makes it home in time."

"Where is Penny now?"

"Her mother is with her. I'm on my way there now. We'll

drive them to the hospital and be there with her until Franklin arrives."

"Which is?"

"Hopefully, in eleven hours."

"Woah." I pace the hardwood floor. "Do you want me to come up and keep you company? It's going to be a long night for you both."

"You need to sleep, darling. Lacey and I will be fine."

They absolutely will be. My mother and Penny's will have the staff bending over backward to keep her comfortable. "Okay, call me if you need any help."

"Royce will be ready when the jet lands to drive Franklin directly to the hospital. Maybe you could be there for Brandon and Charlotte?"

"I'll take my whistle. By the time they land, they'll need a referee."

"Don't be too hard on her. Charlotte wants what is best for Brandon's career and yours."

Hard on her? Does she know how hard Charlotte is on us *to supposedly keep us in line?*

My mother wears rose-colored glasses when it comes to Charlotte.

"Sure. Keep me updated with Penny. I'll message Lottie to see if she needs a lift home."

9

GIANA

My FATHER SITS QUIETLY, watching the television.

I barely slept last night, waiting for him to go to the bathroom. I heard him stumble. Mom didn't hear him as he gets around the house in stealth mode. She was upset when she heard our voices outside her door. For the remainder of the night, I listened out for every noise, every painful groan that came from him in their bedroom.

I reach over and squeeze his hand.

"How is your pain, Dad?"

He tentatively traces a finger near the wound. "My head throbs."

"You hit it hard. Do you want some more pain meds?"

"I can get them." Mom stands and leaves the room. It's the first time since his accident that we've been alone.

"How are you really feeling?" I whisper. He stares at me with wide eyes. His pupils look fine, which is reassuring.

"How do fools feel?"

"Dad," I say gently. "It was an accident."

His brown eyes glaze over. *Please don't cry.* I won't be able to hold it together if my dad cries.

"I know I haven't been myself." He shakes his head. "Your mother worries enough about me. I don't need you getting worked up too."

I link my fingers through his. "I want what's best for you."

"The time will come when I can't stay here, but until then, I'm grateful to stay in my home."

"You're decades from going anywhere." It might not be true, but it's what I feel in my heart. If my dad wants to live here, then I'll do everything I can to get him the care he needs to remain here so he never has to leave his garden.

"Gigi, I know I'm becoming more forgetful, and your mother covers for me. I trip more times in a day than I did a year ago. Most times, I gather my balance before I fall. Not this time."

"I'm getting rid of all the rugs and mats on the floor," I tell him. "Even I've tripped on the one in the living room."

"I told your mother to get rid of it years ago," he snaps.

"It's fine, Dad." I pat his hand. His mood swings will become more frequent as his dementia progresses, and it's not surprising, given the stress of his fall.

"I worry about you just as much as you worry about me," he says.

"Why is that?"

"In a different country living with strangers. I can't protect you when you're that far away."

"Oh, Dad." I hug him. "Thank you for wanting to protect me."

"I have to keep my little girl safe." He squeezes my hand. I stare at his wrinkled skin, tanned all year round with white spots along his arm from sun damage.

I swallow before saying my next words. "I'm home now. There's no need to worry about that any longer."

Mom enters the room and hands Dad a glass of water and some pills. "You should go paint, Gigi. You're on a schedule."

"I will later." I squeeze Dad's hand. I love having this time with him.

"I'll come and sit outside with you," Dad says. "There's nothing on the box I want to watch."

Dad prefers to be outside, so I leave him to set up my easel and add an extra chair for him in the shade.

AFTER LUNCH, DAD GOES BACK INSIDE SO HE CAN HAVE A NAP. The breeze lifts and carries the leaves in small gusts, so I move my art to the studio upstairs.

My piece is almost finished, and I have ideas for another. Unfolding my second easel, I set it up next to the canvas of painted bougainvillea in a rainbow of color. I take a shot and send it to Isabella.

> My ideas for the next spring/summer fashion line. The second canvas will be gardenias on a cornflower blue background. The third will be blue hydrangeas. What do you think?

I need her to love it so I can get another contract. It's close to midnight in Southern Italy, and Isabella will be dining on the streets, drinking wine. I can picture her laughing and can see the wine glass always in her hand. There will be pizza, bread, and all the things I miss.

I take a step back to look at the outline I drew while my

thoughts ran away. It's not bad. The gardenia petals need more detail.

Mom is adamant I fulfill my dream and return to Italy. She knows if they need me, I'll be on the next flight home. I want to spend this time with Dad. How many years do I have while he remembers me? It's quality time I won't get back, and I've already lost five years studying and living in Italy.

And then there is Byron.

Falling for his charm was not part of the rules of coming home. The way I wanted him, yearned for him the moment we were together, it lacked class.

The plan was to play hard to get. To slowly uncover the man he has grown to become. My heart is still stuck on the guy I loved in my teens. I am no longer that girl, so there's no reason he would be the same guy. While I loved the guy who knew all the answers in class, he wanted to be a jock and known for his athleticism, not his intelligence. With it came years of rejection and ridicule of not being good enough on the court—too skinny, not tall enough, not strong enough.

I remember his pain.

Byron Hendricks has great genes. His family did not inherit their wealth by luck. They are all geniuses and have a good work ethic and determination. Everything the Hendricks family touches turns to gold.

"It's perfect, Gi. Stop frowning."

I turn at the sound of Byron's voice.

He comes to stand beside me, resting one hand on my shoulder. "You don't need to change a thing."

"Thanks. I was thinking about something else."

"Do I want to know what?" I study him for a moment. Those beautiful blue eyes flick over my face, his pink cheeks a clue he recently finished training. His forest scent with a hint of lemon wafts around me, informing every cell in my body that Byron is standing close to me.

"I was thinking about getting to know you again... how you've changed and how you feel now about the old Byron from school."

His eyes don't leave mine. "And... did I pass some test?"

"It's not a test," I emphasize. "More an understanding of everything Byron while I'm coming to terms with unfinished business between us. I'm asking myself if you're still the Byron I knew in high school or this guy who is just as hot but with more muscles and an even bigger attitude than the younger version?"

Byron grabs a chair and drags it close, then sits on it backward so he is facing me. His arms fold and lock over the back. Resting his chin on his hands, it's his turn to study me. "Your painting offered you answers?"

I laugh. "I was looking blindly at it while I was deep in thought."

"The notion of you thinking about me is pleasing. However, if there is something you want to know, I'd rather you ask than come to an assumption where I can't defend myself."

"There's nothing to defend."

"Not entirely true if you're comparing the old me to the now."

"We've both changed. I'm not the same girl from high school."

He reaches out and cups my face. I lean into his touch and close my eyes momentarily.

"You're beautiful, Gigi. Inside and out. While I adore this womanly version of you..." His eyes lower to my breasts, and damn my nipples for reacting to his attention. "I'm also attracted to the girl I knew in school. I simply like you for you, no matter how you change. While there's physical attraction, we also have a connection I've never felt with anyone else. *You* understand me."

There is no denying I crave attention from Byron. Is it a deep-rooted craving from wanting him to want me, or is it more? "Do we have the same connection now as we did then? That is what I was pondering. I guess time will tell."

"How much time do we have?"

The big question.

"I like how we can discuss things openly, ask questions, and not be afraid of answers that might hurt us."

His brows crease with concern. "Is this your way of saying there is an expiration date?"

My cell buzzes before I answer Byron. I check the caller. It's Isabella. "I have to take this." I turn to my painting to focus on what she is calling about. "Hi, Isabella. Did you get my message?"

"I did, my *stellina*, and I love the new piece. I can't wait to see all the color." I smile while staring at my art. Isabella has called me her *little star* since I arrived in Italy.

"I'll start on it this afternoon and send a picture when it's complete."

"When do you expect to finish it?"

While I'm not painting as often as I would if I were living in Italy and not distracted by anything in Isabella's studio, I'm not prepared to leave home just yet. "In a few days."

Byron stands and knocks the leg of the easel. "Shit." He stops it from falling.

"Who is with you? Is it a man you're not telling me about?" Isabella probes.

I stare at Byron, and his eyes are fixed on mine. "Maybe." He fails to mask his curiosity. "I should go. I'll message you when it's done."

"Giana, we need to discuss your return. When you complete the five pieces, I need you here for the next stage."

"Of course." The last time we were at the stage before printing my designs on fabric, the lead-up time was about a month. For the celebrations and the fashion show, I can always come home in between unless Isabella demands otherwise. "Enjoy your night, Isabella. I'll message you soon."

"Paolo and I are opening another bottle of vino. The night is young. Ciao, my *stellina*."

I laugh before ending the call.

Byron's eyes do not leave me. "Isabella owns Leto Designs," I tell him to ease his curiosity. I do not tell him how I dated her nephew, Dante, for over a year and that when he hurt me, I decided to come home. "Isabella oversees my work for the fabric print of the new fashion line. Each piece is reproduced on a variety of styles... dresses, pants, formal wear. She's the reason I'm invited to fashion shows around the world." I wait for him to catch up. "You saw her at the fashion parade."

He grins and looks somewhat bashful. "I didn't notice. I only had eyes for you."

Our gazes lock, and something passes between us.

"You're a big deal," he says in a husky voice that envelops me in his warmth. "I'm proud of you."

"I appreciate your kind words, but I'm really not. Unlike you, there is no need for me to escape the publicity of being famous. My life remains pretty much the same."

Bowing his head, he waits a few seconds before he meets my gaze again. "I do my best to maintain a private life, which meant mainly staying in. I'm boring compared to the life you experienced in Italy."

To obtain his dream, Byron has had to give up what most of us take for granted. He possibly was lonelier than me, as we both know one-night stands for a physical connection never cured the loneliness we felt inside.

I wrap my arms around him. "Byron Hendricks, you were never boring to me."

Byron wraps his muscled arms around me, hugs me tight, and kisses me the way every girl dreams of being kissed. It's how I've always dreamed of being kissed by Byron, the man, no longer the kid out of high school.

His tongue finds mine in a slow dance, not desperate, all passion. He's taking his time tasting me. My hands run through his hair, gripping and holding his face to mine. His lips soothe me, chipping away at the rock-hard ball of worry in my chest. He makes me feel special, as though he is here for me.

I have missed him, and I still want him. This thought makes me realize we should discuss what we want from each other.

"What is it?" he murmurs against my lips.

I shake my head. "Nothing. Keep kissing me."

He repositions my long hair to the other side of my neck, gathering it in his hands in a loose ponytail. Those soft lips trail from my ear down the side of my neck, caressing my skin, and his name leaves my lips in a whisper.

"What's on your mind?" He licks a trail to the front of my neck, then replaces his lips with a hand. It's a hold of protection, authority, and security, but not threatening. He stares straight into my eyes, his expression unwavering. "I want to claim this neck, but not until you tell me what's on your mind."

"I want you to touch me."

His eyes narrow a little in warning. "Is it the phone call? Do you need me to leave so you can paint?"

I step forward so his grip tightens around my neck. "No. I want you."

He assesses me a moment longer. "While I'm happy to kiss you, nothing else will happen with your parents downstairs. I disrespected you once. I'm sorry, Giana. I won't do it again."

I take his face in my hands and guide his lips to my breasts. With one hand, I slide the strap of my dress over my shoulder. "I need you, Byron."

I groan when he pushes my breast up and out of my bra so he can caress the nipple, sucking and nipping. It would be so easy to turn around and allow him to take me from behind, a burst of pleasure to quiet the noise in my head.

His cell buzzes on the table behind us.

"Fuck," he says against my skin.

"I'd hoped we were leading to that."

He groans, straightens, and stares down at me as though his resolve is weakening, then turns to his cell. He checks the screen with part of a message displayed.

"Penny had the baby. The family can visit tonight." He looks at me as though he has an idea. "Come with me?"

I laugh, flattered he wants me there. "It's too early. It's a special time for your family." His eyebrows pull together. "I'm not saying I don't want to. I'm saying there is a right time, and tonight is not it. It's not like I'm meeting them for the first time, although they mightn't remember me."

"You're unforgettable, Gigi."

I smile at him in a goofy way. "You need to be with your family. We'll continue this..." I circle a finger between us, "... later."

10

BYRON

THE VALET GREETS me when I arrive at Franklin's penthouse residence. I hand over the key to Thomas, the doorman. "Afternoon, Thomas."

"Afternoon, Mr. Hendricks. The LA Sharks are looking good this season."

I shake his hand. "We are. Remind Frank to get you some passes to the game. You've earned it, putting up with my brother."

He chuckles. "I'll leave you to discuss those matters with him, sir."

"I'm on it."

The building entrance is through rotating glass doors opening to an all-marble foyer. Franklin resides here during the week, then on weekends he and Penny stay at their beachside house.

Inside the equally fancy elevator with brass panels, I punch in the code for the penthouse.

A baby.

The sliding doors open, and I pass the security camera. A guard stands outside the door of Franklin's penthouse. It seems Franklin isn't taking any chances.

"Hi. I'm Byron, Franklin's brother."

"I know who you are, sir." He stands aside and allows me to pass. I punch in another code and push open the massive double doors almost twice my height.

My mother is in the kitchen. She smiles the moment she sees me. "Byron." She gives me a tight hug.

I jab a thumb over my shoulder. "What's with the extra security?"

"You know your brother. He won't miss an opportunity to protect those he loves." She holds my shoulders and leans back to assess me, her broad smile meeting her blue eyes. "I'm glad you came. Come and meet Summer."

"Summer? I thought they'd choose a traditional name."

Mom's lips purse. "Darling, maybe keep that opinion to yourself. Your brother is very touchy at the moment. His protectiveness is off the chart." She leans in and hugs me again.

I pat her back. Mom has always been the hugger in the family. I'm smiling at how she described my brother. "And you're surprised by this?"

"Not surprised, just considerate with my words." She leans back. "You look well. And for the record..." she whispers, "... I thought Caroline a more suitable name." She winks at me. "How is Giana?"

"Good. I asked her to come, but she didn't want to intrude on the family."

Mom pauses. "While I always welcome your friends, your brother is only allowing immediate family to visit. He is stressed already, and for God's sake, if you hold Summer, *do not* kiss her."

"I'll do my best not to breathe."

Mom grins and continues making iced tea. "Please go and wash your hands before we go upstairs."

"But I—" She gives me one of her looks. I head to the restroom, all black and white marble, and return to the kitchen. "Okay. Let me help you." I follow her up the curved staircase, carrying the glasses. "Where is his housekeeper?"

Mom turns and tilts her head, looking for understanding. "It was Franklin's decision to have minimal people in the house. Sally comes in for three hours in the morning to prepare some meals. Ingrid comes once a week to clean. They have hired two nurses to stay around the clock so Penny and the baby could be discharged early and be home with Frank, but Penny insists on doing everything for Summer at this stage. They're completely besotted, and who can blame them."

"I was wondering about her being home this soon, and I'm beginning to understand what you mean by Frank's stress levels. He's a little over the top."

"He'll do what is best for his family. And he wanted his wife and baby home with him, not risking catching germs in some maternity ward, private or not."

"I thought that would be the least likely place to catch anything?"

She holds my gaze a moment longer. She has the same eyes as Charlotte and me. Franklin and Jobe have our father's dark brown eyes.

"Please don't antagonize your brother. Not today."

I follow her into a large formal room where the family has gathered. A bassinette is near Frank's chair. Frank's three-level penthouse is impressive, and if city living ever appealed to me, it would only if I could live here.

"Congratulations," I say and walk toward Frank to shake his hand.

He points to a door on the side. "Thanks, Byron. Would you mind washing your hands?"

I open my mouth to comment.

"He washed his hands right before we came up, darling," Mom interjects.

Frank stands, shakes my hand, pulls me in for a hug, and pats my back three times. My brother is never this affectionate.

"Where is your little princess?"

He grins at me, and pride oozes from him. "Penny is feeding her."

A solid wood door to our left leads to their bedroom. I peer into the empty cradle at white sheets with a pink ribbon design dotted over the white.

"I don't have a gift. Is there something she needs?"

Franklin's brow pinches slightly.

"Not *needs*," I correct. "I know you have thought of everything. More what can an uncle give his first niece?"

"That we know of," Jobe jokes.

"Unlike you, I have been careful my entire life," Frank snaps.

"Stop." Mom presses her finger to her lips. "This is not the place for that talk." She glares at Jobe. "Babies need calm. They can pick up on emotions, and the last thing Summer needs is to sense her father is angry."

Well, this is going to be fun.

"Do we just sit here and smile lovingly at each other?" I ask.

"Yes. In the presence of my granddaughter, that is exactly what you shall do."

I roll my eyes at Jobe.

The internal elevator dings, and the door slides open. My father steps out. "Sorry I'm late."

"Carson, please take the stairs." Mom shakes her head.

"There is no need to use the elevator. The noise is a disturbance." She points to the bathroom. "And wash your hands before you touch anything."

My father looks behind him to the elevator, and a bewildered look crosses his face. Franklin shoots Mom a small smile of appreciation. Dad says nothing and does what is asked. When he returns, he heads straight to Franklin and shakes his hand.

"Congratulations, son. I'm glad you made it back from Australia in time."

"Only just," he says, holding onto our father's shoulder. "I wanted to pilot the plane myself."

Dad muffles a laugh. "I bet you did." He scans the room. "Where is Charlotte?"

Mom takes his hand for him to sit beside her. "They went home to freshen up. She will be back here in an hour or so."

They?

"How was Lottie and BJ's bickering?" I ask Franklin. "She declined my offer to drive them home, so I haven't had a chance to speak with her."

Franklin looks at the door as though eager for Penny to appear. His forehead creases before he answers my question. "I didn't see them until the flight home. They laughed a lot, which annoyed the fuck out of me, so I spent most of the time in the bedroom. I tried to get some sleep, but my stomach was in knots worrying about Penny."

Charlotte and Brandon didn't fight?

Before I have time to ponder his words, Penny emerges from the bedroom in a strapless, flowing, white dress. We stand as though royalty has entered. Penny smiles at Frank before peering down at the bundle in her arms. "She's sleeping."

Mom approaches Penny and peers over her shoulder. "She's perfect."

Penny continues smiling while gazing at Summer, the joy of being with her daughter written all over her face. "Franklin, do you want to hold her?"

He looks at his father, then Penny notices me. "Hi, Byron." She tentatively walks toward me. "Would you like to hold Summer?"

The baby is hours old, and Penny is still recovering from labor. I look at Mom and then Penny. I shake my head. "She's too little. I'm scared I'll drop her."

"Jesus." Franklin groans. "Imagine she's a basketball, and Kirk is trying to make a steal as you head to the basket."

"Well, when you say it like that." I hold out my arms.

Penny gestures to the chair. "It's easier if you sit."

I take a seat in the leather armchair, and Penny leans close.

"Hold your arms like this." Mom demonstrates for me, but it doesn't make it any less awkward.

Penny places Summer in my arms, swaddled tightly in a pink blanket. I peer down at my beautiful niece. "She's so tiny." Her little lips are damn cute with her bottom lip tucked under her top one. Her eyes are closed, and she looks so peaceful. I cannot imagine ever being this relaxed.

Something comes over me—a warm sensation.

Unexpected joy for Franklin and Penny.

I've never felt so much happiness for someone else. On instinct, I want to kiss Summer, but I remember my mother's words. If I ever have anything as precious as Summer, I'll give my all to protect her too.

"May I?" Dad comes to stand beside me. I push up from the chair with extra care not to startle Summer. Mom takes her from my arms. Dad takes a seat and sits like a statue while Mom places Summer in his arms.

I grin at my father, sitting awkwardly. "Have you forgotten how to hold a baby?"

Dad steals a look at Franklin. "It's different when it's your grandchild and the father is watching my every move."

Quiet chuckles sound around the group.

Mom pours the iced tea and distributes it around the room. "I can make more if anyone needs a refill."

"Thank you, Sophia. I appreciate your help." Penny reaches out to squeeze her hand.

Penny's screen lights up on the table, and she checks her cell. "Mom and Dad will be here in the morning. The guest room is set up for them, right?"

"It is." Franklin takes her hand, pulls her onto his lap, and wraps both arms around her waist. He kisses her cheek before looking lovingly toward his daughter.

"Heard any news on the Grace takeover?" Dad asks Jobe. He looks at Franklin. "Any updates?"

Hendricks Capital Management put in an offer to take over a construction company in London. It's all on the hush for now though it's a career boost for Jobe to expand his company into international commercial real estate. While it might be Jobe's business, it also falls under the HCM umbrella by partnering with Franklin.

"Carson, please discuss all business matters tomorrow," Mom says quietly. The room falls quiet.

"I best be going," Jobe says. "Congratulations again. I'm glad everything went smoothly."

I also stand. "I'm extremely happy for both of you. I'll head out with Jobe. Can I come back tomorrow after training?"

"You can visit anytime," Penny says in a gentle voice. Penny rises off Franklin's lap to kiss my cheek, then steps to Jobe to kiss his cheek. "Thank you both for coming to see us. We appreciate it."

We say our goodbyes and head out past security.

"Imagine Frank's anxiety when Summer is older," Jobe says as we take the elevator.

"They should have named her Rapunzel."

He huffs out a noise. "How are the helicopter lessons?"

Earlier in the year, I began studying to become a pilot. "It's interesting enough. First practical flight is next week."

"I'm not sure why you need to fly it. You bought the helicopter. Just pay a pilot."

I pop a shoulder. "It's fascinating. And I can hire a pilot if I need."

I open up my cell and text Giana.

> Do you have plans for tonight?

Jobe looks down at the screen. "So, Giana and you are a thing?"

"No labels, brother. But we are enjoying each other's company."

He laughs. "Yeah, there's a label. You couldn't wait to text her."

"How many women do you text a day? None of them have a label."

He straightens his designer shirt's collar. "The only notable labels are on my body."

I shake my head. My brother is five years older than me and not the slightest bit interested in monogamy.

He gives me a pointed look. "Frank and you are more alike than you care to admit," he says. "It comes with obsessive control and an organized life."

"Your business controls your life as much as ours."

His dark eyes are full of humor. "Yes, but I keep the fun in my life, and no one tells me what to do or how to behave. Hendricks Capital Management runs Frank's life, and now he is consumed by his little family. Your coach and the *game* utterly consume you to a point you have become someone you might not have otherwise grown to be. Watching our father and brother's behavior when we were teenagers led us on different paths to them. While we still have a desire to live the high life, neither of us saw success in the same light. Fortunately, we inherited the same determination to succeed in whatever path we chose."

The elevator doors open.

Jobe maintains the same stride as me, even though I'm taller than him. "So, you don't think I'm in control of my future?" I can't see his face, so it's hard to read him.

"What happens if your coach decides to bench you? Or he leaves and the new coach replaces you? Regardless of how hard you train, your future depends on someone else, whether they like you or not, and whether they think you're a good fit for the team."

"I spent my entire life trying to fit in, and I've perfected my ball skills. If Coach shows any signs of being unhappy with my game, I'll work on it and prove myself on the court."

He pulls up once we are on the pavement and stares at me as though I have missed a crucial point. "The game controls you... you don't control it. What if you get injured? Think of the repercussions if a new guard replaces you, proves themselves on the court, and Coach is hesitant to bring you back on the team. What if our father didn't own the team? What if your injury is—"

"I get it," I snap.

He pats my shoulder. "Have a backup plan in place because distraction is another factor that will affect your game. And like Frank, I bet you fall hard." He pats my shoulder again and leaves his hand there for a moment longer as though he wants to say more. His chin dips before he strides toward his driver.

I'm momentarily stuck on the spot. It's as though he looked into a crystal ball and predicted my future. A coach who didn't understand what I could bring to the game. Being benched. Injuries. Being forced into a line of work I hate. I usually box away all those fears in a dark place in the back of my mind.

I bet you fall hard.

It won't happen with Giana undecided, if she even wants to stay in the country.

11

GIANA

BYRON WALKS into the restaurant wearing a burnt-orange button-up shirt. The color suits him. Not many people get away with that color, but with his tanned skin and the way the sleeves follow the contour of his powerful arms, he could wear anything and still look good. Behind him, a man in a black suit enters and remains near the corner. He scans the room, then returns his gaze to Byron.

Unseen but near if he needs him.

Byron lifts his chin as he sees us at a table at the back of the room at a table he requested. Before he manages another step, Jessica obstructs his path.

Did she dine in this restaurant?

"Jessica and her sister are here." Paige sounds as surprised as me. I go to wave at her, but she turns to Byron, hugs him, and leaves one manicured hand on his shoulder. It appears she is introducing him to her sister. Is there something between them?

"Oh dear," Paige murmurs from behind me. There's a part of me that is concerned. Eyes forward, I watch to see what happens next. Byron lifts Jessica's hand and drops it off his shoulder. Then there is a deliberate step back to add distance between them.

I can just make out what they're saying. He is not rude but tells both girls in a strong voice that he is late for his date.

Date.

I breathe out a long, slow breath. I shouldn't be worried since we're not together-together, more getting to know each other again. But shit, I had a *hands-off-my-man* moment, and I have no right to think of Byron as mine.

"Hey, man." Mason stands and shakes his hand. "What was that about?"

He kisses Paige on the cheek. "Jessica being Jessica."

"She can come on fast and be overfriendly," Paige says. "But I'm sure she is harmless."

"I disagree." Byron rounds the table to me. From behind, he wraps both hands around my shoulders and leans his chin on my head. His affection is the answer to my misplaced insecurities. I squeeze his arm that lingers around my chest, then he kisses me before taking a seat.

"I think Jessica is lonely. She likes you, so it's not a bad thing."

"Gigi has a point," Mason quips. "Remember when she tried to ruin you at school?"

"No, you have it wrong," Paige interjects. "She liked him and was trying to garnish attention."

"Likes me, hates me, I'm doomed either way," Byron moans.

"All the attention on the poor NBA star." Mason pokes fun at him. "Where's a decent violinist when you need one?"

"What? You think my life is easy?"

Mason huffs out a laugh. "No one's life is easy, but you have it easier than others with money being thrown at you," he ribs.

"Millions. Kazillions," Paige adds and laughs.

Byron shifts in his seat and straightens his back. "All right then. Let's start with ever since I was a teenager, I've had to train every day to the point where sometimes I'd lie in bed and wish the pain away. I can't eat what I like because I need to stay in shape and maintain peak fitness, so I've been on a diet for the last ten years."

"Oh yeah, I couldn't do that." Paige shakes her head. "If I stick to a diet for six months, I celebrate as though I've won the lottery."

I giggle at Paige. "And I've just eaten my way around Italy, indulging in pizza and wine for the past six *years*."

Mason pulls a face. "Still not good enough to earn any sympathy."

"Game on," Byron begins. "I've never had a girlfriend since Gigi left me."

I widen my eyes at him. Paige giggles.

Mason coughs. "That by right, was all your doing."

"Thank you," I say with a smile and like how we are making light humor about this. It's airing dirty laundry.

"I can't have a normal life without a fan wanting to get in my face with tips about how to win the game, improve my shoot, or why am I such an idiot, every time I go out." I look over his shoulder, and his security guard is now only feet away while stopping three girls from getting closer to us. Not once does Byron turn to his security guard. He keeps talking as though it happens all the time, and he simply ignores it.

Mason's gaze lifts and watches the girls for a few moments. They request a selfie. I look over my shoulder and flinch at their raised cells, even if it means getting a photo of the back of his head.

"Being popular is hard. Very hard. All those girls..." Mason shakes his head. "What do you do?" he asks incredulously.

Oh shit. I stifle a laugh.

"You, my friend, do not have one empathetic bone in your body."

Mason pops a shoulder.

"Take my place of work. On the court, I am abused with every cuss word imaginable, screamed at to work harder, only with more colorful adjectives, or if they're being nice, they say to pull my finger out and stop being a crybaby when I'm knocked to the floor. After falling into the crowd, I've had popcorn poured on my head, and these are *fans.* Someone spat on me when I walked down the tunnel to the locker room on an away game. Not a fan."

"Eww," I moan.

We all stare at Byron. "I could go on." He adjusts his shirt collar as though it screens him from the scrutinizing eyes waiting for him to make a mistake. "The fame is not as glamorous as you might think."

"Until you receive that paycheck," Mason adds and grins. "Good try, big fella. You almost had me feeling sorry for you."

Byron lightly thumps the table. "Points for trying, though."

I giggle because I didn't know if he was serious or not.

Mason raises his knuckles, and they fist pump. "Anyway, how's your new niece?"

"Tiny. I barely recognize my brother."

"Did you take a photo?" I ask.

"No. We were barely allowed to breathe around Summer."

I smile at his dramatics. "But it's understandable, right? She's just two days old."

His arm rests over the back of my chair. "Yeah. I held her, though. It felt awkward holding something that small and fragile."

"Fragile," Mason repeats. "There's understanding right there." He turns to Paige. "We'd be the same."

We?

"Already thinking about a family?" Byron asks the question on my tongue. "What have I missed? A decade?"

Mason laughs. "Paige and I know what we each want and decided to plan a future together." Paige stares at him with starry eyes as though he just asked her to marry him.

It takes a moment for me to catch up.

"So not a proposal, but... more an understanding of a future together?" Byron quips. He looks at me, a dent between his brow.

Is he thinking about us?

"Do you want to order any drinks?" the server asks.

A timely interruption. "An Aperol spritz for me, please." I turn to Paige. She agrees. "Make it two."

Mason stares at Byron. "I'll have some water." It's as though he knows his friend isn't going to drink alcohol because of his training schedule.

"What's our choice in bottled water?"

"We have Evian, Antipodes, and we just received an order of NEVAS," the server says.

"The German water?"

"I believe so, sir." The poor server isn't educated on water like Byron.

Byron grins at him. "I'll have a bottle, please."

The server leaves us, and Mason groans. "It's more expensive than whiskey."

"Not my whiskey."

"You're paying for the water to have special packaging and for the bottles to be recycled at an acceptable level."

Byron shakes his head. "It's premium water and the unique fine bubbles tingle my taste buds."

"Now you have my attention."

He raises a brow at me. "It comes from two artesian springs with natural mineralization and is sealed with a cork so it gets to us in pristine quality."

"Like champagne, and probably the same cost, but without the desired effect." I can't help but smirk at Byron. "You're so fancy. I'll stick to basic spring water."

"It's not being fancy. It's healthy, Gigi."

"I know." I pat his thigh, all solid muscle. He frowns at me. "I understand." I lean in close. "You don't get legs of steel from being complacent like me."

His lips quirk. "Do you want to feel them later?" he whispers.

I do.

"Depends on what time we finish here," I whisper. "I have to be up early to paint."

"Okay, it was great seeing you two." Byron pushes up from his chair.

"Stop it." I slap his rear, and my fingers sting. In six years, Byron has transformed to having a freaking superhero body. It's like having my own Thor.

He sits and leans in to kiss my neck. "I love your neck."

I giggle. "Why?"

"Because it leads me here." With one finger, he turns my face and kisses my lips. "And here..." His head lowers, and before he gets a chance, I nudge him to behave.

"Do not give this man anything other than water, please," I say to Mason. He grins, shaking his head at his friend. Paige is staring at Byron wide-eyed. "He's a breast man," I whisper.

"I believe so. You two best get a room."

"Yes, we will," Byron says in his low, sexy voice.

"Okay." I push Byron's cheek so he is looking forward. "What are we all going to eat? And I mean food."

Mason and Byron groan as though I'm a fun-killer.

"I forgot to mention that we're planning a trip to The Bahamas," Mason announces. "Why don't the two of you join us?"

Byron rubs the side of his jaw. "Unless it's in the offseason, I can't go anywhere."

"If it's between my trips to Italy, I might be able to meet you both there for a couple of days."

"I would like that," Paige adds. "Maybe we could do it around Byron's schedule when he plays Miami in Florida. Get a few days off to meet us?"

Byron stiffens beside me. It's hard for anyone to understand the level of commitment it takes to be an elite player in the NBA.

Mason is aware. "It sounds like fun, but Byron can't drop everything just for us in the middle of the season," he says gently to Paige.

Eyes wide, she mouths, *Oh.*

"While you're at the top of my list of importance..." Byron begins, "... my list differs from Coach's. His list includes my shooting consistency, which relies on extra trainings outside of team trainings, my ball handling drills, and my defensive drills so I'm one of the best point guards in the league. He wants other teams to fear me so we have an upper hand on game day."

"Do they... fear you?" The words are out before Paige can recover.

"Do you fear me?" he asks in a serious voice.

Paige giggles. "No, because I know you. You're a big softie."

Opposite the table to Byron, I watch Mason's eyes round.

Byron remains quiet. All his life, he has worked to be respected on the court, and that does not include being known as a big softie.

"What we know and yet cannot see behind his handsome face and big heart is an undeniable determination larger than Mont Blanc. Byron is unstoppable, and that should be feared."

Byron's eyes narrow at my comparison rather than appreciating the compliment. I realize my mistake. I could have compared him to any massive mountain—Mount Everest or K2—but my mind went straight to Italy, and Byron noticed.

"Right." Mason leans forward. "The high school final when you were a junior was a game I'll never forget. I bet that game was a turning point for your basketball future. All thoughts of robotic engineering were put on hold."

I gape at Byron. "You wanted to study robotics?" I shake my head. "Of course. You were the math whiz." Byron and I were not in many classes together as he focused on math, physics, and all the numbers while I was in the creative units.

"I thought robotics was cool." He pops his shoulders, and it confuses me as to why he's being dismissive. "But while I love math and physics, the adrenaline rush on the court was more addictive and a bigger challenge."

Mason snorts. "Only you'd say that. You're a freak of nature, physically and intellectually. You could do either with equal perfection."

Byron stares at his friend. He looks down and shifts in his seat before glancing back at Mason. "Perfection. It's a hard word to live up to."

I need to lighten the mood again. With a cheeky smirk, I say, "There has to be something you're bad at."

The drop in his shoulders is subtle, but I see it before the slow blink. "There's a long list. The latest addition is holding a baby. Do you know how awkward that is?" He raises his large hands slightly in the air. "Two is shopping for said baby. I haven't a clue what to get a little girl that has everything before she's twenty-four-hours old."

I rub his thigh. "I could paint something for her bedroom."

A smile grows on Byron's face. "Gigi, you're the real genius. It's perfect."

I laugh. "Well, if you want to first go baby shopping, I can help you. It will take me a couple of days to finish the art."

Byron kisses me on the cheek. "I'll pick you up tomorrow. Thanks for saving me a world of embarrassment at the family dinner next weekend."

I appreciate his excitement. It's the gentle kiss on my cheek leaving a tingle that I shouldn't read into. He picks up my hand from under the table and squeezes it. *Thank you,* he mouths.

Two words and warmth expands within—a sign it's safe to lower my guard because this feels right. Physically, I allowed Byron to penetrate my walls. His touch heals me in ways no one else can. And I understand sex can be without strings. The stolen glances where I catch snippets of how he feels warns me there is hope. Maybe it's appreciation of being part of a friendship. We were friends, after all.

"You're welcome," I whisper. "I'm sure you'll return the favor one day."

My cell chimes with a sound I set specifically for Isabella. "Excuse me. I should take this." I push up from the table and head outside. "Hello." The background music makes it hard to hear. It must be after three in the morning there.

"Giana," she says, dragging out my name. "Austin Cisterna is here, and he requests you come to Italy next weekend." Her slight slurring is not missed.

Isabella has had far too many glasses of bubbles. "The filmmaker?"

"*Sì, stellina.*"

"Why would he request my presence?"

"Because our designs are being worn on his biggest star."

Oh my God.

"Are you messing with me?"

"Why would I do that? I love you, my *stellina*. I'll call you tomorrow, but I couldn't wait to share the news. Clarissa Carrington will be wearing Leto Designs in three scenes!"

"Congratulations!" I shout. My lips hurt from a tight smile. "That's amazing."

"It is. Ciao, Gigi."

My cell turns blank. I spin around and look up to the twilight sky, hoping to see stars, but it's too early and harder to see in the middle of the city. I'm looking for a sign. Do I rush over and be with Isabella or allow her to make the decision since it is her designs? I love that she wants me involved. I also know she wants me to return to Italy, and while the excitement is still bubbling in my chest, I need to assess everything before I make a rash decision. When the enthusiasm settles, I know my anxiety will rise. The fear of leaving Dad will overwhelm my rational thinking. I'll be forced to choose between making a life in LA or returning to Italy, where my career can thrive and also feels like home.

Dante. I won't be able to escape him. I remember how convincing he is and also how much he hurt me. But Isabella offers me a future no one else can.

I stare through the glass to the man who is slowly

stealing my attention away from Italy and more toward staying in LA.

I spin around to the sound of car horns and sirens. The sound messes with my thoughts, and I suck in a deep breath. No decision will be made tonight.

"Hey, are you okay?" A protective hand rests on my waist.

I look up to Byron. "I just received some exciting news."

"Yeah?" His eyes sparkle. It's a tiny thing, and my chest flutters that he wants to share in my joy.

"Leto Designs will be in Austin Cisterna's upcoming movie. The main star will wear our designs in three scenes. Isabella wants me back there soon."

His brow furrows. "There as in Italy?"

"Yes."

"So the movie isn't being made in LA?"

"He's an Italian producer." My frown matches Byron's.

He takes both my hands in his. "This is big for you?"

"It's *my* artwork on the designs." I hope he understands the importance. Pride grows in my chest as the realization settles in, and a tear wells in my eye. I laugh once and swipe it away. "I'm supposed to be happy."

"You're overwhelmed." He rests both hands on my shoulders and waits until I look into his soothing eyes. "What's worrying you? I'm sensing something other than excitement."

I close my eyes, then slowly open them. Byron will see through any lies. "Leaving my father." He waits. "And... going back to a country I love. Isabella will try to convince me to stay."

His breath hitches. He takes a while to answer. "Do you want me to go with you?"

He would go with me?

"It's fine. It's for a few days to be present at the meetings before the final shooting begins." Then it dawns on me. "Imagine if I'm invited to the red-carpet screenings?"

"Then, if it's okay with you, I'd be honored to be your partner for the night. I'll drop everything to share a special moment with you." He pulls me in for a hug. "Congratulations, Gigi."

"Thank you," I whisper. While the film release won't be for many months, possibly a year, my thoughts whirl as to where Byron and I will be then. We are together now as if no time has passed, and while being with Byron is easy, my heart warns me it's not ready to be hurt again so soon. He is trying to make amends for past mistakes, yet basketball still controls every decision he makes.

"Do you think you could get the time off to come?"

He nuzzles my neck. "Is it within the next four weeks?"

I close my eyes, enjoying the tingles shooting over my skin. "I believe so."

"Then yes. If you need me to be alongside you, I can. Oh, and forget the artwork for Summer's room. You're under too much pressure. I'll get Mom to buy something from me."

"No," I say, pulling away. "I want to do this. I'll have it finished within the week." I already have ideas using soft pastel colors.

He takes my face in his hands. "Only if you have time, Gi." He kisses my cheek. "And I don't want to upset Isabella, so I'll get you home now." Hoping Byron would take me to his for the night, I had caught a ride in with Mason and Paige. He kisses my lips. "Coach called early-morning training anyway. We could both use an early night."

I let out a breath of disappointment. "Sure."

He takes my hand, leads me to his sports car, and opens the door for me. The moment he closes the door, I'm hit with the scent of new leather seats. While Byron is excited for me, our careers in terms of financial rewards don't even come close. And he is married to a game that rewards him with riches.

The initial silence on the drive home fails to hide the tension.

"I'm only away for a short time." I reach across to lay a hand on his thigh. His strong muscles flex beneath my fingers.

"I know." He doesn't take his eyes off the road. The bright lights of his fancy dash reflect onto his face. His expression is tight, giving me nothing.

"I'm not going to see him," I say quickly.

He jerks his head, giving me a quick glare before turning back to the road. "See who?"

"Dante. I thought maybe the idea of me seeing him again concerned you."

"I wasn't concerned, but I am now," he murmurs.

"Why were you quiet if you weren't thinking about my ex in Italy? When I mentioned him at the beach, you told me you wanted to know 'everything about your opponent'."

"Is he my opponent?"

"No. That's why I said I wouldn't see him."

Byron makes a growly noise from his throat. "Then why bring him up?"

"Because he is Isabella's nephew, and he'll want to see me. I just want you to know that while I am nervous, I am not interested in him."

"Why are you nervous, Giana?" he asks matter-of-factly.

I shake my head. "It doesn't matter. If it wasn't about him, then why the silence?"

"First, it does matter. And second, I was thinking about what my brother said about how I'm not free to make my own decisions." He takes my hand in his lap and squeezes it. "But I'll move heaven and earth to accompany you to Italy."

12

BYRON

BRANDON PULLS UP beside me in his BMW. I jump out of my car, lock it, and walk with him into the gym. We take the tunnel to the locker room, ignoring our teammates' banter.

"How was the land Down Under, BJ?" Simpson asks, his tone lined with sarcasm.

"Oh, you missed us at the game," I throw over my shoulder. "I didn't see any triple-doubles on your stats."

He grumbles something as we walk past him to reach our stall. I toss my bag onto the leather chair embossed with the LA Sharks logo near the headrest. It rolls from the force and hits the cabinetry behind the chair. *Byron Hendricks #19* is printed on the overhead cabinetry. I hit the number in superstition like I have every day since the first time I entered this room. Retrieving my Air Jordans, I take a seat and prepare for training. I glance up at Brandon sitting opposite me in the room. He pulls his jersey over his head and taps the number seven on his chest, then touches his temple.

Each one of us has a ritual.

Brandon has barely mentioned the trip to Australia, and now I'm curious as to why. He's mentioned how his mom was overwhelmed with happiness when he surprised her, the weather, and the party, but not much else. Nothing about Charlotte annoying the fuck out of him. He's been quiet since he returned.

I took it as sadness at leaving his family and friends. We all make sacrifices to play the game we love. Now, I'm wondering if Charlotte made the trip almost unbearable, and he's staying quiet so as not to offend me. I know what she's capable of—she is my sister. And I have not been hanging with him as much as we used to due to being distracted by Giana.

Springing from my chair, I jump up and down on the spot, testing the fit of my Air Jordans.

"You playing in the training match?" Simpson snickers. "I thought Coach was playing Trax." What is he talking about?

Leroy leans close. "Ignore him. He's pissed because Holden Hayes hit on his sister."

Holden Hayes is my main opponent and plays for the LA Stars.

"Hey, Simpson. Remember the last time I owned Hayes? You should take a page out of my playbook."

"Fuck you, Hendricks." His eyes dart to Brandon, who is focused on tying his laces. The bastard better not start with Brandon. "You wouldn't be so smug if you knew—"

"Hey, hey." Jye pulls at Simpson's jersey. "Let it go, man."

"Who's ready to crush it?" I yell, bouncing up and down. We jog out of the locker room, along the tunnel, and toward the court.

Leroy is beside me. "While Simpson pisses me off..." I tell LeRoy, "... I understand his anger. If anyone in the team touched my sister, I'd destroy them." Not them, but their career. "I'd make sure they never got to play another game with the LA Sharks."

Leroy slaps my back. "Calm down, tiger. We all know the bro code. Even Simpson wouldn't lay a finger on Lottie."

For a few seconds, a possessive emotion rips over me. I would tear them apart. Family is off-limits.

"Gather in," Coach calls out as we file onto the court. "Before training begins, I want to discuss rosters over the next couple of preseason matches. This weekend, Byron and Brandon will start. The following weekend, I'm giving the four rookies a chance in the player rotation. Brandon, Byron, Leroy, and Jye will sit that one out."

I nudge Leroy. "Should I read anything into this?"

Leroy shrugs. "I'm not complaining. It's a rest before shit gets serious."

"You're expected to be here every day for training, twice a day for some of you. Every player will have one weekend off, so use the time wisely and spend it with family. They're not going to see much of you over the next six months."

AFTER TRAINING ON FRIDAY, I HEAD TO MY PARENTS' PLACE for dinner.

Franklin, Penny, and Summer will be there, so I drove past Giana's home since she texted earlier to say Summer's painting is ready. Giana was heading out with Paige, but we spoke briefly about catching up on Sunday after I train.

Tomorrow is a training game, and Coach hasn't revealed our opposing team's lineup. It messes with my head not planning my game around a player, but for what it's worth, I remind myself it's still preseason.

It's not reason enough to lower my competitive guard.

I park my car on the massive horseshoe entrance. While my parents have a basement garage large enough to house most of our cars, I don't see the need since I'm not staying long.

With the framed canvas tucked under my arm and covered in pink paper, I nod to their security, then greet their house butler who is standing stiffly by the open front door. "Evening, Finn. I trust you're well?"

"Evening, Mr. Hendricks. Extremely well, thank you. Your mother awaits you in the upstairs formal family room."

"Thank you."

Laughter echoes out into the lobby. I take the stairs two at a time and enter the room, which is more like a miniature ballroom, where everyone awaits my arrival.

"Byron. How was training?" my father asks in a deep voice.

"Fine. Coach is rotating a few of us. I don't need the rest but understand it helps develop the rookies." I shake his hand, then kiss my mother's cheek while she rocks Summer in her arms. I stop and stare at her.

"Does Summer do anything other than sleep?" It sounds dumb, but I have only visited twice.

Penny giggles. "She doesn't sleep much, actually. I have bags under my eyes from being awake half the night." She hugs me.

"This is for you. Summer, not you." I wink at her.

Franklin comes over and stands behind Penny. "Do I need to remind you we have a nanny who will attend to Summer's every need?" Franklin says with displeasure. He shakes my hand. "It's good to see you, Byron."

"I know, but I treasure every moment I get with her,"

Penny coos. She pulls the paper from the canvas, and it reveals the back of the frame. "Oh, what did you choose?" she asks excitedly.

Franklin hitches his trousers gently before kneeling beside Penny to help tear the paper away and reveal the painting. I'm hit with a wave of embarrassment at not knowing what Giana created. She hid it from me, saying to trust her.

"Oh, Byron, I love it." Penny stands, and Franklin helps her hold up the framed canvas. "It's beautiful."

Franklin gives me a look of approval. "Very thoughtful, brother."

"It's from Giana and me." For a moment, everyone stares at me. My words came out as though we are a couple.

Franklin turns the canvas for us to see, and *wow*. I can't hide my surprise. *Giana, you are one hell of an artist.*

"It's beautiful," I murmur.

"You didn't see it before?" Penny asks.

"No." I can't take my eyes off the fairy garden, the array of colors, and the tiny golden horse on its hind legs in the middle of the flowers. "Giana painted it for you. She told me to trust her," I say, pride choking my throat.

"Please thank her. It's perfect." Penny flashes a smile.

Charlotte stands to take a closer look. "Gigi is talented," she says gently, directing the compliment at me. While I appreciate her praise for Giana, I'm hit with confusion. She didn't once query me about training when I entered the room. Something is off.

"Byron, sit and hold your niece," Mom says.

I take a seat beside my sister, smiling sweetly at Summer. "Hold out your arms," Charlotte says gently. I look at her for a moment, expecting a taunt about being clueless with babies, but it doesn't come.

With my niece in my arms, content in her sleep, I can't

help but feel a sense of contentment of my own. But I know peace never lasts.

LATE SATURDAY AFTERNOON, I DRIVE TO BRANDON'S HOUSE before the game. It feels like any other game, except it's an internal game—purely for our team's benefit since preseason doesn't officially start until October. Yet it's different because this time, Giana is watching me play. My body tingles with nerves, more excited than ever. Not a good thing when I'm trying to level out my thoughts and focus on the game.

"You ready to prove we're the best guards on the team?" Brandon says after closing the car door. It might be a training game, but we're both wearing trousers and a white button-up with the LA Sharks logo on the left side of his chest.

"You bet." We do our shake—back of hands, palm to palm, smack, smack, then a light punch. "Did I mention Gigi is coming?"

He turns to me, wide-eyed. "Serious?"

"It's been years since she saw me play."

Brandon grins. "And live. She could have watched the game on TV."

I shake my head. "She's not like that. She doesn't love the game. But she'll watch to support me. It's what she did in high school."

I veer into traffic.

He thrums his fingers along the armrest. "You've never talked about her."

"She was the one who got away, so I did what I could to forget." I give him a quick glance. "Fate." I shrug. "She's here, and I know I want to try with her again. So, while she is home, I'm proving I'm not the guy I was back then."

I see Brandon staring at me in my periphery. "Who were you back then?"

I tap my finger along the steering wheel to the beat of the tunes pumping out of my speakers. I should be listening and motivated. "I did what I had to do and made basketball my priority. Some considered it selfish. I thought of it as focused. Remember when things didn't go my way in my freshman year? I was... reckless."

He wipes the palm of his hand across his mouth. "Yep. You took some convincing to calm the fuck down."

I shake my head to dispel the images in my mind. Not just the night with Giana, but on other days when I was so drunk at parties I passed out.

"Your toxic trait was when shit went down concerning basketball, and you acted like it was the end of the freaking world. At least now you sulk for a day or so and then your mind is back and focused to prove them wrong."

I chuckle. "So what you're saying is I've grown up. I wasn't selfish, just immature."

He laughs. "Wait. Where are we?"

"Picking up Gigi."

His eyes go round. "She's coming *with you* to the game?"

"Yep. And you need to move your ass to the back seat."

Brandon peers into the back of my Porsche. "My legs won't fit in there."

I grin. "Then you best ask Gigi if she minds."

Before I turn off the engine, Giana is closing the front gate. She is wearing a pink floral maxi dress with a small bag in the same material. She looks fashionable, classy, and sexy. Her long, dark hair is pulled back into a ponytail and has a curl to it. My mind is on where she'll sit tonight, as I don't want her next to just anybody.

"Hi." She waves. I'm out of the car and around her side instantly, ready to open the door. Brandon steps out of the car. "Oh, you must be Brandon."

He takes her hand and kisses it. "I am. And you must be Gigi. It's nice to finally meet you."

I step between them. "You can drop her hand now."

Giana's hand goes to her chest. She looks up at me. "You've never kissed my hand." I step close, take her face in my palms, and kiss her lips slowly before flicking my tongue out to taste her. I pull back and stare into her beautiful eyes. "That's because I'm busy kissing your lips. And BJ here is sucking up to you, hoping you'll allow him to sit in the front."

She giggles and places a hand on his arm. "Of course."

Brandon hugs her, and the urge to push him away surprises me. Now I'm making mental notes about kissing Giana's hand and hugging her when I appreciate the little things instead of thinking about my opponent for the game.

I'm in the middle of traffic when Giana asks her first question. "What time will the game finish?"

"Around eight thirty," Brandon answers.

"Are we going for dinner after the game, or do we eat there?"

I laugh. "It's not high school, Gi. Food is available, but you have access to the VIP area and the restaurant during the game." I meet her gaze in the rearview mirror.

She offers a warm smile. "Any chance we can go for pizza after instead?"

"I like her," Brandon says.

"Unlike many in LA," Giana continues, "I eat gluten. People act like I'm robbing the place if I walk in holding a bagel."

Brandon chuckles. "I'm up for pizza after the game."

"If we invite you."

"Of course, you can join us. Can I call you BJ..." Giana asks, "... or do you prefer Brandon? And how did you get the name BJ?"

"It's not what you think," he adds quickly.

"Bullshit," I cough, and Giana laughs.

"For fuck's sake, Hendricks." He shakes his head. "My birth name is Brandon Johns, and being from Down Under, that nickname was always going to stick."

"Right," she says. I keep an eye on her as she gazes out of her window. "I've always wanted to visit Australia."

"Well, if you do and I'm home, I'd be happy to show you around."

Not without me.

We arrive at the LA Sharks' special parking lot for players. I take Giana's hand and lead her past security. I stop at reception and introduce her to Kirsten. Her eyes round in surprise, as I've never introduced anyone to her. Kirsten acknowledges what the introduction implies. She'll be seeing more of Giana, so she needs to organize a pass to allow her entry whenever she needs to visit. Taking Giana's hand, I lead her toward the office where Charlotte will be dealing with last-minute business.

"I'll see you in the locker room," Brandon calls out over his shoulder.

Giana squeezes my hand. "Where are we going?"

"To see Charlotte so she can escort you to our family seats."

"Oh. I thought you were taking me to the storeroom. I've heard about what happens in those rooms."

I stop walking and stare at my beautiful, sexy girl. Is she my girl? All I can think about is whipping up her skirt and recreating her fantasy.

"You'll be the death of me tonight."

13

GIANA

We pass multiple offices, and I read the signs on the doors in my head as we walk. Director of Mental Health and Wellness. Team Nutrition Manager. Director of Legal Operations. Accountancy. Security. Director of Information Technology. Human Resources Manager. Chief Executive Officer. General Manager. Assistant Coach. Coach. Chief Financial Officer. We stop outside the door labeled Owner.

Byron knocks, and Charlotte opens the door.

"Byron. What's wrong?"

"Nothing's wrong. I was hoping you could show Giana around."

I step out from behind Byron and give a small wave. "Hi."

Did he really need to bring me here? It's been years since I have seen Charlotte. She is blonder than before but with the same blue eyes as Byron. She wears a classic navy suit jacket and pencil skirt to match. Her heels match too, and she looks every part the businesswoman and not the teenager I remember, who loved her tiny denim shorts.

"Gigi," she says affectionately, coming in for a hug. "It's been a while."

"It has. You've grown up," I say and laugh, not knowing how to explain how quickly the years have passed.

"Well, I'll leave you two to catch up." Byron kisses my cheek. "See you after the game."

Watching his sexy ass as he strides away could be my new favorite pastime. My man looks damn fine in a suit.

"You look beautiful," Charlotte says, distracting me. "And you've barely changed."

I laugh once, knowing her kind words are not true. "While I recognize the Lottie I used to know, I now see a professional businesswoman."

Charlotte closes the door behind me. "Thank you. Sometimes, I think Byron still sees his little sister. If I point out something he disagrees with, he retaliates like he would if we were home bickering like teenagers." She points to a lounge chair by a coffee table. "Take a seat."

"Oh, I don't want to keep you from your work. Honestly, I could have found my way around and am rather embarrassed Byron brought me up here to be babysat."

Charlotte grins. "If I know my brother, you're here so other guys aren't looking at you." She opens a cupboard door that reveals a hidden refrigerator. "Champagne?"

"God, yes. Thank you." I take a moment to look around Charlotte's office. There are three office desks, a lounge area, and a massive bookcase. Trophies don each shelf, and on the walls are framed jerseys of, I assume, famous players. "I don't think Byron is the possessive type."

"Are we talking about the same Byron Hendricks?" She grins as she hands me a crystal flute.

I laugh. "Oh, I know how particular he is about

everything, but we're not at that stage where I'm his, nor will we ever be. I've always considered a relationship to be a partnership."

Charlotte clinks her glass with mine. "I agree."

I take a sip. It tastes expensive. I take another sip and another. "Is there anyone special in your life?"

Charlotte runs her finger along the outside of the crystal. Her expression is pensive, as though she is considering her words. "There is, but we're not official if you know what I mean."

"I do."

"We've been seeing each other on and off for a few years, but we've never been exclusive until recently. Now I'm ready, but I sense he's not ready to put that label on our relationship. It's not that he doesn't want to be with me but more about other people knowing our business."

"Ah."

She toys with her long, blonde ponytail. "We're happy, so it shouldn't matter what other people think, right?" Her eyes scan mine as though she seeks understanding.

"It shouldn't, yet we all seem to allow others' opinions to control us in some form."

"What about you and Byron? Do you see a future together?"

Oh. I take another sip and allow the cool liquid to ease my throat. "It's too early to make assumptions. We're barely past being friends again." Charlotte's eyebrows rise. Has Byron told her otherwise? "While I'm home for a while to be with family, I'm also not sure if my career will lead me back to Italy."

Charlotte beams her big smile at me. "I did hear about your art and fashion and how famous you are now. Actually, I was told by a certain someone to purchase every past issue of *Vogue* that features you."

I look away as heat travels to my face. "He didn't?"

"He did. He's very proud of you."

I take another sip. "I didn't realize he'd asked you to do that?"

Charlotte shakes her head. "While I enjoy helping him with certain requests, he often acts like I'm his PA. He's always had a little sister who will get things done for him. But now, there is a whole team that needs shit done. And yes, we have people employed for these roles, but the guys like to ask me because apparently, I'm like a little sister to all of them."

"All of them?" I say, exasperated for her.

"Well, not all of them..." She laughs. "If you get what I mean."

I laugh with her but don't get it unless she means there are players she has hooked up with. Of course she has. What am I thinking?

Charlotte drains her glass. "Come." She stands and refills our glasses before leading me to a glass window that overlooks the court. I stand alongside her, watching the players warm up.

This is not an official game, and yet a crowd is starting to fill the lower stands. I find Byron and watch him dribble and dunk the ball through the hoop.

She eyes him over the rim of her glass. "He'll pull out all his best moves tonight to impress you," she says, her tone flat.

"Is that a bad thing?"

"No, but he should stick with the coach's plan and not show off. The rookies are waiting for an opportunity to snatch his spot, and as much as I want what's best for the team, I want what's best for my brother first and foremost. He is our family's priority."

"Did your father buy the team for Byron?"

She spins to face me, her brow heavy over blue eyes. "Who told you that?"

"No one, but Byron mentioned it was a rumor."

Her expression softens, and she takes another sip of her champagne. "Byron was always going to play in the NBA. He's really that good. While his determination equals his talent, my father was gutted he didn't want to continue in business to add millions to the billions my father already owns." She rolls her eyes. "Byron was never going to forgo his basketball dream, so my father decided the family could also profit from the sport rather than Byron earning a fortune for himself."

"I remember Byron telling me about his father's plans for him when we were in high school. Recently, I learned he wanted to study robotics."

"He did?" Charlotte asks. I nod. "It does not surprise me. He was always intelligent. I didn't get Frank's or Byron's mathematical brain. Like Jobe, I'm diligent and will work toward setting up a future in a business that is right for me."

"Is the team your future?"

Her expression changes to contentment. "It is. One day, I hope all this will be mine."

The way she says it, I believe her.

"My father is rarely, here and he trusts me to handle the organization's business."

I don't miss the passion in her voice. I glance down to the court, and Byron looks up and sees me at the window with Charlotte. He grins before receiving a pass and then setting up a play for Brandon to score.

"BJ appears to be a good friend."

"He is. They met in college, and he's been part of the family ever since." There's an affectionate sound in her tone. While her family may have welcomed the Aussie into their lives, I'm curious if Brandon is more to her and possibly one of the *not all of them* she referenced earlier. I track her gaze to Brandon. She watches him closely, even though he doesn't have the ball in his hands.

"Do you think Brandon will return to Australia when he retires from the NBA?" The way Charlotte's eyes round and her lips part, I think I've managed to surprise her.

"His retirement plan has never come up in our conversations. I hope he plays out his days with our team, but if he sees the need to go elsewhere, or even to Europe, I guess we can't stop him." Her voice fades with the last words. "There was talk of him returning to Australia for a few months next year if he makes the Olympic basketball squad. While we'll miss him during that time, I would also be extremely proud of BJ. None of our other players have made the USA squad, so it would be great recognition for our team."

All her talk of the team and what might be best for it is evident when it comes to Byron, and I suspect Brandon too. Secretly, I imagine her loyalties will always lie with them first.

"We should head down and take our seats. It's getting close to tip-off."

I take my handbag from the table and follow Charlotte to the elevator. "Are any of your family coming tonight?" I ask when the double doors close.

"No. They rarely come for the preseason games and never for internal games."

I don't pry further. I'm relieved not to be seeing the rest of the family tonight.

Charlotte leads me along what appears to be a hallway for the VIPs until we come out of a door near the tunnel leading to the locker room in one direction and the court in the other. We walk courtside, so close to the players now huddled around the coach, and take a seat in the third row behind the players' bench in the stands.

I only have eyes for Byron, watching his intense expression as he listens to the coach. His brow is heavy, and he nods several times while the coach speaks. The intensity in his eyes almost steals my breath, and I wonder if it deepens when it's a season game. Or is his concentration always like this? I expect the latter, as I have always known his extreme passion for the game.

The players place their hands in the center of the huddle and shout something before breaking apart. Byron bounces up and down on the spot, and his eyes find mine. He jogs to the stairs, takes all three in almost one leap, then leans in and kisses me quickly on the lips. It takes me by surprise.

"Wish me luck?" he says with a grin.

"Good luck," I whisper.

He jumps down to the court and runs into position.

Charlotte stares at me. "He has never done that."

"What?"

"He has never brought a girl to the game to watch him, and he kissed you. Byron never deviates from his routine. They're all superstitious about their pregame routines."

"Oh." I smile at her. "I like that I'm the first he's kissed before a game."

"You know how I mentioned superstition? Like, they eat the same thing for breakfast, wear the same underwear, say the same chant in their heads before every game. If he plays well tonight, he'll take that kiss as something he needs to do before *every* game." *What?* "He'll want you here every home game, in this same seat, so he can kiss you before tip-off." I look over to see if she's joking, but Charlotte is serious.

"I'm not sure that's possible."

"Then pray he plays less than his best tonight."

Byron didn't play bad. In fact, he played outstanding,

and as Charlotte predicted, he did all the fancy tricks for me. Brandon and Byron proved why they are the team's best guards and not to mess with them. Even from my inexperience, I could tell how well the two work together, as though they know the other's thoughts.

After the game, Charlotte and I wait outsider the locker room.

"What are your plans tonight?" she asks.

"I hope we're heading out for pizza. What about you?"

"Who is we?"

"Byron and me, though BJ came with us to the game, so I assume he is also coming."

Charlotte rolls her eyes. "They take best friends to another level. I've never had a best friend who had my back like these two do for each other." She shrugs one shoulder. "Sometimes I wish I had a best friend, but then I would have to cancel catch-ups more times than not. Work always comes first."

I touch her arm. "I can relate. I have friends, but not like Byron and BJ."

"Half my friends are in New York. The guys are lucky they share the same interest, and it took them in the same direction from college to their current career goals. Surprisingly, they never argue, though BJ would agree with whatever Byron suggests." She eyes me for a moment. "I could give BJ a ride to give you two some privacy?"

Boom. I knew it.

"Or you could both come with us? I don't need privacy while eating pizza and drinking wine." While I'm happy for them, my gut tells me Byron might not be as understanding as I am if they are a secret couple. One thing I remember about Byron is that he despises secrets and dishonesty.

THE FOLLOWING MORNING, I WAKE IN AN EMPTY BED. I crashed at Byron's after consuming far too much wine. The last thing I remember is him refusing to touch me the way I wanted to be touched because I'd consumed too much alcohol, but he did kiss me a lot.

I spread my arms out on the while linen of his massive bed and stare up at his high ceiling and the grand light overhead. It is quite remarkable in its design. I wonder if Penny helped him choose it since he mentioned she helped with the interior design and decorating. I'm looking forward to meeting her.

I roll onto my side and groan. What am I saying? My thoughts are racing ahead to meeting his family and being part of his life. I need a shower to clear my head. Pushing up onto my elbow, I see a note on the bedside table. He left me a note before leaving for his training session. *Cute.*

Morning Gi,

I kissed your cheek and whispered goodbye, but you were in a deep sleep at four thirty this morning, so I didn't wake you. If you need to leave before I get home, take one of the cars in the garage. After training, we have a strengths session and plyometrics. I'll be home to cook you lunch.

B x

A warm sensation rolls over me. I fold his note. Before I make it to the shower, my ringtone sounds in my bag. *Isabella is calling.*

"Hello." Thank God it's not FaceTime, as I'm wearing one of Byron's T-shirts.

"My Gigi."

"Morning, Isabella."

"Yes, good morning. I forget." I check the time, and in Southern Italy, it's an hour before midnight. "I'm glad you're awake, as I have fabulous news. I need you here for the weekend."

"This Friday?" I croak.

"Sì, but only for a few days, my *stellina*. We have meetings. Saturday, we have to attend a... hmm, what do you say in America... a gala? Then you're free to go home."

"It's late notice, Isabella."

"No. Not late. First, let's discuss your new artwork. While I love the colors, we want something to pop."

"A brighter background color for a more vibrant contrast? We could do yellow and burnt orange or hot pink? Vivid backgrounds make me think of summer."

"Bellissima, my *stellina*. I can see it now. And it's perfect for our next project."

"We have another project?"

"*Sì. Cibo Creativo* wants your designs on their appliances. Their mixers, toasters, kettles... all in the kitchen will have your beautiful artwork. *Arrivederci noiosa cucina*," she says grandiosely. *Goodbye boring kitchens.*

It takes me a while to comprehend it's not a fashion contract. I laugh and shake my head to unravel my thoughts. "Their appliances will be bright yellow and orange, covered with my flowers and nature art?"

"Sì."

"This is exciting." My lips are tight with a wide smile.

"We will discuss the terms, and you can meet the *direttore generale* at Cibo Creativo on Saturday." *CEO.*

"This weekend?" I hesitate.

"Yes. Stay for four days. We have much to discuss."

"Okay."

"I'll book your flights. Dante will be happy you're coming home."

Although Italy felt like home for a while, I've come to realize it's not. Comfortable, yes, and safe. Then there's Dante. He is her nephew, but it is an uncomfortable conversation. I repeatedly drag my foot along Byron's cool bathroom tiles.

"It's nice Dante feels that way."

"He misses you. He is sorry for what happened between you."

Why is he not telling me this?

"Sometimes things happen for a reason. I've met someone, and I'm happy."

"*Stellina*, you know Dante. When he gets something in his head, he acts like a bull with a red muleta."

Certain types of fixations annoy me, and bulls have dichromatic vision—they can't even see the color red. I struggle to hide my irritation. "Byron is *also* a determined man." Though the last thing I want is for these men to come face-to-face, and I refuse to be a trophy.

I spin around, thinking. If Byron is with me, maybe Isabella will ask Dante to leave me be. "May I bring someone to the gala?"

"We can discuss it later. I need to go, *stellina*, my ride is here."

"Of course." I shake my head. I do not want to step on Isabella's toes, especially since this will be a great career advancement. Who knew I would come this far?

Byron. He always believed in my talent. But we both have careers we need to focus on, and neither one of us is ready to give that up for love. I'm still getting to know the man, not the boy I loved who broke my heart.

"I am excited to see you, *stellina*."

"I'm looking forward to seeing you, too, Isabella." It is an

144

odd feeling not seeing her most days anymore. I do miss her vibrant personality. "Bye."

My thoughts are all over the place. What do I say to Byron? If he cares for me, he'll be equally excited. I need to see him. At least he is easy to track down. I never knew where Dante could be or with whom. Byron's second home is on a basketball court, and I'm happy to sit in the stands and watch him train. Who wouldn't when his muscles glisten with sweat, contracting with every movement.

I shower, then call a ride, deciding not to take one of Byron's cars. As soon as I'm home, I race inside to find my parents at the dining table.

"I have wonderful news." I sit beside Mom and pour iced tea from the jug filled with ice on the kitchen table. "I might have a new contract with an Italian company for my designs to be on their kitchen appliances." Mom's eyebrows pinch as though she is trying to imagine it. It's far different from the chrome appliances in our kitchen. "And Isabella wants me to return to Italy this weekend."

"Why are you so calm, Gigi?" Mom places her hand over mine. "You should be shouting from the rooftops."

I laugh, and my smile broadens. "I am, though I'm hesitant about something she said. Dante is excited to see me. Apparently, he misses me."

Mom shakes her head as though she is processing. She understands he hurt me, but she has also always believed in second chances. "Do you still love him?"

I take a sip of iced tea. "I don't think I was ever *in love* with him. I loved feeling wanted and being treated special. Being Isabella's nephew had contacts in high places, and we experienced fun times on yachts and cruises and were often treated like royalty."

"Are you scared to see him? Afraid you might want to go

back when you are building a new life at home, a place where you feel safe?"

My mother can always see through me. "Maybe."

"Nowhere is safe when it comes to having your heart broken, my darling."

I take another sip of my tea. "While he hurt me, I didn't upset Isabella or any of her family or business contacts. If I hurt him by rejection, I hope it doesn't influence my business relationships."

"It sounds like it's not Dante that scares you but your relationship with Isabella, both personal and professional."

"Yes." I gulp more tea. "I'm happy being with Byron and want to try again. I also want to be here for Dad and you."

Mom pats my hand before pulling it away. "Never put us before your career. It will work out. I need you to do what is best for you."

"I agree with your mother. We'll be here for you, Gigi. Always."

I swallow hard, knowing that might not be true.

"Your father is right. When the time comes, you need to make the decision that is best for you at that particular time."

I let out a long breath. "I will."

Mom pats my arm. "Are you heading out today?"

"I'm going to watch Byron at his practice session and then tell him my news."

Mom's eyes widen. "You'll sit in the stands, alone?"

My lips quirk into a grin. Mom knows I was never into sports.

"I guess that's what girlfriends do."

And just like that, I decide what's right for me at this particular time.

14

GIANA

THE ARENA IS NOT AS busy as last night. In the entrance hall, I walk up to the reception desk and talk to the security guard on duty. I recognize him from when we were here watching the game. He points to Kirsten as soon as she finishes taking a call.

"Hi, Kirsten, I'm looking for Charlotte. Well, Byron, actually. Are they around?"

"Miss Monroe. Charlotte should be in her office, and I think Byron has left, but you're welcome to head to the locker rooms and check. You know the way?"

"I do. Thanks."

I take the elevator to the basement and walk the long hallway, admiring the framed images of basketball greats who have played for the LA Sharks. I hear Charlotte's voice. It's faint, but I know it's her. I'm walking toward the locker room, apprehensive about whether I should enter. What if other players are showering or getting dressed? Charlotte is used to being around the players.

"Brandon," she says playfully, but in a gentle way. Are they flirting?

I assume Byron is with them, and I can picture the three of them sitting around chatting. I never imagined I would be comfortable hanging out in a locker room, but with Byron, I would be comfortable anywhere. I slow my steps. Charlotte's voice is off. Is she moaning? I reach the locker-room door and stop. *Oh my Lord.* Her moans are of pleasure.

With one foot inside the door, I see her clinging to the cubicle wall, Brandon's name above her head. Her legs are wrapped around Brandon's waist, his bare ass clenching as he pumps into her.

I stumble back, my hand covering my mouth. Scanning the halls, I make sure no one else is around. What if someone sees them? What if Byron walks in on them? Jesus, they have a death wish. I spin around and rush back toward the elevator.

My heart is racing. I'm so nervous for them. I know how Byron hates secrets, and I am aware of how protective he is of Charlotte, especially regarding his teammates. When I'm far enough away not to be heard, I pull out my cell and call Byron.

"Hey," he answers. "Where are you?"

"I'm at your second home, hoping to watch the end of your training." I'm panting, slightly out of breath.

He chuckles. "Serious?"

"I am." I look along the hallway. Still no sight of anyone.

"We finished early. I came straight home hoping to find you here."

My heart thumps hard in my chest. "I'm sorry." I hesitate and decide my news can wait.

"I'll meet you at yours, Gigi. I'm taking you out."

"Out? Like on a date?"

He laughs. "Not on a date. We are dating. I'm not sharing you with anyone."

My heart swells. While I want to add that I'm not sharing him with the hundreds of women who would like one night with Byron, I clamp up, remembering my meeting and the offer of my art expanding beyond the canvas and the fashion world.

"It sounds perfect. See you soon."

WHEN YOUR FAMILY IS BILLIONAIRES, IT HAS PERKS, LIKE A last-minute lunch booking at Bloom. It also helps if your brother is the owner of said restaurant.

I'm learning more about Byron's family than he ever shared with us at school. Sure, when we were teenagers, I knew he was wealthy, but the extent of that wealth was never discussed, nor did he care. Byron cared for basketball and trained in classic athletic wear. While I remember he wore a suit well at prom, it was probably Armani, Dior, or Gucci, but he complained about it all night. He never spoke about their riches, and apart from the polite pitch in his tone and the fact he could speak different languages, he didn't act rich. But I guess that's the thing with wealthy people—they never talk about their fortune.

Sitting in one of the finest restaurants in LA, I'm surrounded by classy people. It's evident not only in the way they dress but in the way they conduct themselves—low voices, articulating words slowly and with deliberate pause, every word holding meaning. While I am kind of wealthy—not like Byron—and I'm wearing a beautiful Leto Designs dress and matching purse, I feel like an impostor in a millionaire or billionaire's world.

"You choose the wine," Byron says, bringing my thoughts back to the table, red roses in a crystal vase between us. "I'll order the food."

"I'm paying," I tell him. "We're celebrating today."

He closes the menu and grins. "Gigi, my brother is paying today."

"That doesn't feel right. It was kind of him to secure us a last-minute table." It's at the back of the restaurant and more private than the others. If you wanted to be seen here, then you wouldn't choose this table. Our table is the best for privacy.

He leans close. "This table is reserved for last-minute bookings for family or close friends."

"Oh." I inhale sharply, understanding the privilege, only to be hit with his fresh, citrusy scent.

"You smell good," I whisper. "It's a shame Byron Hendricks is not on the menu. I could—"

He raises an eyebrow. "Are you trying to get me excited in a public place?"

"Are you easily excited?"

His eyes narrow. "Around you, yes. Easily. So please, let's focus on food so the owner's brother doesn't get kicked out for indecent exposure."

I giggle. "We can always go back to your pool."

He sighs loudly. "Now all I'm thinking about is you in my pool. You'll be the death of me, Giana." The way he says *Giana* sounds like he wants to discipline me later, and I'm here for it. "I also think you're trying to distract me from whatever it is we're celebrating."

Byron unbuttons the top buttons of his pale-yellow shirt. The server arrives, and I order a white wine to complement our pasta dish. While we differ in many ways, he enjoys the pasta and the carbs for his energy as much as I love it. And

I've been thinking about the glorious food and wine I will have this weekend.

"When our wine arrives, I'll tell you." We don't wait long as the waiter returns, opens the bottle, and offers us both a taste of the fine Pinot Grigio.

"It's perfect," I tell him. He pours the wine into our glasses and places the bottle in an ice bucket beside our table before leaving us.

Byron holds up his glass and clinks it against mine. "To..."

"A new contract in Italy." His expression sags. "Isabella called this morning..." I add quickly, "... and Cibo Creativo wants my designs on their kitchen appliances. Can you believe that? My bright colors and floral designs will be on kettles, toasters, stand mixers, and state-of-the-art cookware. Isabella said *Arrivederci noiosa cucina*, which means *Goodbye boring kitchens*." I smile at Byron, still overwhelmed every time I think about it.

He blinks a few times. "Wow. All this from you painting for fun at school. Do what you love, and the world is your oyster." He stands, rounds the table, and leans in to hug me. His thick arms wrap around my shoulders as he squeezes tightly. "I'm so proud of you, Gi." He kisses my forehead slowly and deliberately before resuming his seat at the table. He adjusts his shirt. "We should have ordered champagne."

"I love Italian wine, and it is fitting since I'll be there this weekend."

His glass freezes halfway to his lips. "This weekend?"

"Mm-hmm." I take a sip of wine, avoiding his intense gaze for a moment. "While I was to return on Thursday, Isabella has a grand opening for Leto Designs in a new store, and she wants me there for photographs. The rest of the weekend will be about meeting with Cibo Creativo, except for Saturday night, when I'm invited to some gala."

Byron takes a slow sip of his wine before placing the crystal on the table and meeting my gaze. "The last time we spoke about your returning to Italy, you sounded apprehensive. I said I would go with you. The offer still stands."

I reach across the table and take Byron's hand. "Thank you. While I would love for you to come and share this with me, allow me to check with Isabella first."

Byron's brow pinches. Oh shit.

"Isabella doesn't make the rules. Frankly, if I want to be with you, stay in your room with you, it is none of her business what happens after hours. While you're in meetings, I could explore the city. At the grand opening, I could be an anonymous customer in the crowd. I could also be warming your bed, waiting for you to come home from the gala. Isabella doesn't have to know I'm there. I could be your secret."

I giggle at him. "Okay, I like the sound of your plan. Let me check first, though, in case I can get you a ticket to the ball." I tilt my head at him. "Can you get time off training?"

"I'll train. Mostly in your bed."

Someone, please pass me a fan.

Every step from Byron's garage to the kitchen, I'm thinking about what comes next. Something has changed. A familiarity. When we are together, it feels right. Natural.

The way my hand fits neatly in his. The shooting side-look of him checking on me. While he's breathing normally, I'm a little out of breath. My excited heartbeat doesn't help.

"I'll fix us a drink," he says. He lets go of my hand and

opens the refrigerator, pours cold water into two glasses, and adds ice. I stare out at his pool, which beckons me to strip and cool down. Suddenly, Byron is behind me, shifting my hair away from my neck and kissing my skin with a tenderness that has me closing my eyes.

"Do you want to swim?" he whispers, his breath sending tingles along my spine.

"Hmm." I tilt my head for him. "With wine, maybe." The caress stops, and I feel cheated.

"I need you to drink some water." He hands me the cold glass.

"You're the athlete who needs to hydrate more..." I take a sip, even though it's not my drink of choice.

"And I don't want you drinking until later."

"Later?" I take another sip.

Byron removes the water from my hand and places it beside his half-empty glass on the bench. He takes my hand and turns me to the staircase leading to his bedroom. "We have unfinished business, and I need you to remember everything."

Sex in his bed. A big step forward. He has given me some great orgasms, and we have fucked by the pool in a moment of lust. Heading to Byron's bedroom could mean he wants to make me his.

I want this. *I want him.*

Our lives are not woven. If anything, our careers are leading us apart. In a few days, fate will decide if I am to return to Italy. But we have this moment in time—one day and one night for each other. I stop at the base of his sweeping staircase and follow the railing.

His gaze flicks over my face. "What is it?"

I take his cheeks in my hands and pull his face to mine. "We can swim and fuck," I say against his lips in an attempt to play the moment down.

Suddenly swept up in his arms, I let out a scream. With my arms around his neck, I study his amused expression as he takes each step. Not once does he struggle while carrying me.

"If this is a romantic gesture to win points, then I give you ten out of ten."

"By the time I'm finished pleasuring you, Giana Monroe, I expect fifty out of ten."

I giggle. "That's not a thing."

"It is, and I'm about to prove it."

15

BYRON

My PLAN of taking my time kissing every inch of Giana's beautiful body gets lost the moment her desperate mouth takes mine.

Our bodies ignited immediately. Giana spins me toward the wall and rips open my favorite shirt, popping two buttons. My fingers make light work of the rest to rid the shirt from my body and toss it to the side. Giana runs her tongue along my chest, down my abdominal plane, and hovers there while she unfastens my trousers.

Jesus, I'm so hard for her.

She yanks my trousers down and takes my dick in her mouth.

Leaning my head against the wall, I remember the last time her mouth was on my cock. *God, I've missed this. Missed her.* My hands are in her hair, assisting her rhythm as I build. It wasn't part of my plan. It was supposed to be about her and damn Giana for flipping the script and taking the power.

But fuck, I'm so close to coming, I'm handing the control to her. She squeezes my balls as her tongue glides over the shaft, and I shudder, so damn close. Grabbing my ass, she pumps those lips over my cock, sucking harder and faster, and I lose control when the orgasm hits with a force, and I come in her beautiful mouth.

Pulling away, Giana wipes her mouth and gazes at me with the sultriest look in her eyes. She sits back on her heels, and I slide down the wall and kneel in front of her. We stare at each other for a moment.

"You still taste good," she says demurely. My lips mash with hers, my cum still on her tongue, and suddenly, our mouths are wrestling. I'm overwhelmed by the lust inside me. She falls back and laughs as we untangle our legs. My face is close to her breasts—a perfect starting point. Reaching around, I unzip her dress and slide the straps over her shoulders until her breasts bounce free.

No fucking bra.

I take one nipple in my mouth to toy with, kiss, lick, and suck before moving to the other. Her moans goad me on while her neck arches in pleasure.

"I need this dress off you." I tug it down her thighs and slide it off before throwing it aside. "And these." Returning the favor, I take the thin strap of her thong and snap it with my fingers and teeth.

Giana gasps loudly. "That was my favorite."

"As was my shirt."

I spread her legs and bend each so I get a good look at her glistening folds. She is so wet for me. I give myself a moment to ingrain the memory in my mind, as it's been far too long. I run one finger over her opening, then take it into my mouth, closing my eyes as I remember her taste. I insert one finger inside her and find her sweet spot.

Giana's hips buck, her hands flying over her head as she moans in pleasure. I insert two, then three, and work her, using my other hand to hold her pelvis to stop her from moving about. She is close to coming, so I bury my face in her and suck her clit, licking and sucking as my fingers work her harder. She lifts her hips against the force of my palm, her arms thrown wide. She smacks the hardwood, which is killing my knees.

"Byron," she moans. I love the sound of my name on her lips. "Byron," she says in a higher voice.

I need to watch her beautiful face as she comes for me, so I slide to lie alongside her. "Why are we on this fucking floor?" I whisper, grinning when her eyes flash open momentarily and close again as my fingers pump harder.

My erection is pushing against her hip. I thrust against her, and she moans my name in a whisper as her cheeks flush with the beauty of her orgasm.

Her body softens. Her legs sag, one sliding straight. Her rapid breaths slow.

I remove my fingers. With her orgasm coating each one, I write *always yours* on her stomach, then proceed to suck each finger clean.

"What did you write?" she whispers.

"The truth." I lean down and kiss her lips with all the gentleness I feel for this woman. "I need to get you off this floor." I pull her to her feet, carry her to the bed, then lay Giana in the center and lie beside her. "Are you ready for more fun?"

Her long lashes flutter as she peers up at me. "Today, my body is all yours, Byron."

My dick jumps to attention as all my fantasies of Giana

flood back to my brain, but her saying *today* messes with my thoughts.

Frustration ripples over me, like in any situation where I have no control. It's why everything around me is tidy, and routine is king.

I breathe out and count to four, trying to release the need to want her here with me and love her every single day. But Giana is not mine.

However, today, *her body* is mine.

Body, mind, and soul, I need all of Giana, not just the sex, and I need to prove it. If she needs time, then I'll honor that. So I tear myself away and say the words before I regret it.

"Do you want to take that swim now and recharge? I'll grab your favorite bottle of wine."

Giana has been gone two days.

Yesterday, I spent most of the day reading the aviation notes for the week before spending three hours on flight practice. The buzz of being in the air distracted all thoughts of Giana and dickwad in Italy.

Today, I hit the courts at four thirty in the morning because I couldn't sleep. Between trainings, I scrolled social media, searching Leto Designs' and Giana's accounts for any image of her. *What the fuck is wrong with me?* We're now in between weight repetitions, and I have my cell in my hand, scrolling again.

"Byron?" Brandon points to the bench. "Want me to spot?"

I guzzle the energy drink and choke.

"Jesus." Brandon jumps out of the way before spots of the orange liquid hit his prized Nike shoes.

"The fucker," I murmur.

"Who?"

I turn my screen toward him. "Gigi's ex."

"Man, this is not like you. You have to trust her."

"I do," I grunt. "It's him I don't trust." I stand from the bench and run a hand through my hair. "I should be there to protect her from this asshole."

Brandon lays a hand on my shoulder. "Mate, Gigi is capable of looking after herself. I saw the two of you together. She's not going to do anything stupid." He takes his towel and wipes sweat from his brow, his blond curls still wet.

I don't want *him* anywhere near her. And I don't give two fucks if he is her boss's nephew. I add extra weight to the bar.

Brandon makes a click sound in his throat. "Okay, here we go. I got you... I fucking hope because this is a lot, mate." He stands with his hands under the bar, ready to assist. He counts each rep, and I only get to ten with the added weight. I pause to catch my breath.

"Go again," he tells me. A vision of Dante with his arms around Giana and Isabella on a stage somewhere is stuck in my mind.

I do not want him touching her.

I groan with the final two reps before Brandon helps me steady the bar on the support beam. We finish with squats before we shower and head to a team meeting.

The meeting room is newly decorated and state-of-the-art. It's one of the things Penny helped my father design. She acquired single leather chairs to accommodate all players and staff in rows like a movie theater. Each chair is like a professional gaming chair in soft gray leather, designed for comfort while watching videos of our opponents or meetings and professional speakers.

I lean back in the chair, and it tilts enough to relax my mind. I close my eyes and imagine Giana's smiling face as she receives the admiration she deserves, except I want to be there to share in it with her. It's the first time I don't want to be at a basketball arena, doing what I'm told. My eyes fling open at the sound of Coach's voice.

"Saturday night," he begins. "I have a team named for the preseason game. My report states everyone is available and fit."

I raise my hand. "Coach." I cough to clear my voice. "I'm not available this weekend."

Coach stares at his tablet, then looks to his assistant. His assistant shrugs one shoulder. "News to me."

Coach eyeballs me. "Since when, Hendricks?"

"My hamstring pulled up tight after the session, and I'm getting a massage after the meeting. Just thought maybe I should sit this one out."

The team therapist pushes off the wall and walks over to me. "Why didn't you say something?"

"I felt it tightening in the weights session."

"Right. Come and speak to me after the meeting, and I'll take a look."

Coach nods his head. "Hendricks is out. BJ, you can take Byron's position, and Jye can play the number two spot."

Usually, Brandon plays shooting guard but never point. The way he replaced me with Brandon doesn't sit well with me. Coach didn't fight me on playing. It's as though he was already thinking about it. I expected a rookie to take my place to give him a chance in the preseason.

If it were another time, I would dwell on it and train harder to prove I'm not replaceable and the best damn point guard on the team, but not when I'm distracted by how the fuck I can get on a flight to Italy *tonight*.

As soon as the meeting ends, I send a text to Penny.

An angel sleeps in my arms. I peer down at her cute little nose. Summer purses her lips as she sleeps. Already, she has sass, and the thought of her as a fiery teenager giving lip to Franklin makes me grin. I walk with her in the nursery, admiring Giana's painting on the wall as I rock Summer gently in my arms.

"You sounded anxious on the phone," Penny says as she returns to the room. She takes Summer from my arms and places her gently in her crib. "Come, I'll get you a cold drink." She closes the door and activates the baby monitor on her phone. "We'll hear her if she wakes."

I follow Penny into the sitting room, where she pours iced tea. "Thanks." I take a sip. "I need your advice."

"Fire away," she says with an easy smile.

I just come out and say it. "Frank doesn't need the jet, right?"

"No," she says, curiosity in her tone.

"Do you know if Jobe needs it?"

"What's going on, Byron?" She takes the hair tie from her wrist and pulls her hair back into a ponytail. Fuck, I'm inconsiderate. Penny has shadows under her eyes.

"Am I intruding on your rest time?"

"No." She places a hand on my knee to stop it from bouncing. "Talk to me."

I let out a long breath and consider my words not to sound like a fucking fool. "I need to be in Italy tonight. If Franklin thinks I'm being rash, he'll say no, as it's mainly Dad, Frank, and Jobe's business jet. I considered buying one of my own, but I can't buy one that fast."

"Oh my God, you *are* being rash. Your family does not need any more private jets," she says, sounding annoyed. "If you want to get on a plane, then book it. Is your passport up to date? Visas?"

"Yes, but the only seats available on flights leaving tonight are in coach." My knee continues to bounce in a steady rhythm.

"Byron." Penny stares a moment longer than usual as though she is waiting for an explanation. "Why does it need to be tonight?"

Dragging my palms down my face, I rub at my jaw for a second before picking up the tea and taking a mouthful. "It's Giana. I want to be there to support her. There is an event to showcase her new art on appliances, and it's important to me to be there so she understands how much she means to me."

Penny crosses her legs and sits back in the pale-pink designer chair. "Don't underestimate a woman's intuition. I'm sure she already knows."

"Maybe, but her douchebag ex is hanging around, and I don't want to give him an inch."

"Ah. There it is. The jealous part of the Hendricks men always pops out when you least expect it." She giggles as though she's reflecting. "Byron, if you need to go, then go. I'm sure someone is on call to do your approvals ASAP. Ring Frank, and he will help you out."

"He'll loan me the jet?"

"No. We're being conscious of emissions when it comes to the jet's usage. Jobe and Frank are being more practical. Buy the seat that's available on tonight's flight."

I stand. "Coach? I don't think I've ever—"

"Go and pack, Byron, and stop being entitled. If you want to see Gigi, then do it."

16

BYRON

Colton, my security guard, is losing patience with me.

"I'll be fine. I doubt anyone will even recognize me."

Even over the phone, I can tell his laugh is mocking. "You're known worldwide, Mr. Hendricks."

I tug my cap lower to shade my eyes. "I'll be incognito," I tell him. "Besides, I only booked one ticket, so you'll have to trust me on it. I'm already at the airport."

"Part of my job is protecting you from yourself," he mutters. "Book me a ticket, even if I have to sit in the luggage compartment. Why does your family have a private jet if no one will use it?"

"A great question that my sister-in-law can answer." I grin as I recall my conversation with Penny. She wanted to kick my ass when I considered buying another private jet. "I'll be gone a couple of days and don't intend to be in busy places." The hotel bedroom with Giana is my only destination of interest.

"Fine. If you feel threatened while you're over there, call me. I'll contact a friend to come to you."

"Deal."

I hang up and keep hold of my cell as I stand in the longest freaking line to board the plane. Christ, I could age years waiting to board.

The airline employee checks my name, then hesitates. He stares at me for a few seconds before reading the seat allocation.

"Is there a problem?"

"No, Mr. Hendricks. Next."

Filing along in the line, I walk at a snail's pace to the back of the plane. Travelers shove their overhead luggage into compartments, others groaning as they hold up the line. I'm in the back section of the plane, near the restrooms and kitchen, and already, the smell is nauseating. I fold myself into my seat, despairing at the lack of space between my knees and the seat in front of me. I won't be able to stretch my legs without coming into contact with the feet of the person in front.

"I can't wait," the girl sitting opposite me says to the guy sitting beside her.

"You have to wait until the plane is in the air," he snaps.

"I can't." She stands and when no one is looking, disappears into the restroom.

Fuck me. Are we there yet?

Minutes later, she emerges, and a waft of a putrescent, rancid smell assaults my nostrils. I hold back the urge to heave and try to discreetly cover my nose and mouth with the material of my shirt.

Keeping my eyes forward, I watch the other passengers find their seats and pray no one takes the seats on either side of me. I'm not so lucky.

A teenage girl chewing gum pushes past my long legs,

the words "Excuse me" apparently not known to her. She flops into her window seat, clicks her belt, and then gives me a side-eyed look. "Hi."

What I wish to say is, "Could you please stop chewing like a cow eating grass?" but instead, I say, "Hi."

She pushes her feet up onto the chair in front to stretch her legs. The passenger in front groans and turns to look between the seats.

"Sorry," she mutters, munching away. She curls up in her seat, on her side facing the window, and shuts her eyes. Her Doc Martens push into my thigh.

Don't choke on your gum.

The flight attendants assist passengers, and before I ask to sit in the spare aisle seat beside me, a guy with long hair and an equally long beard slides into it.

Terrific.

"Hey, man. You traveling the world?"

"No. Just in Rome for a couple of days."

"Business?"

"Yes." I'm on a mission, and Giana is my business. "You?"

"I'm traveling to Venice. My flights have been rerouted more times than I can count. I was lucky to get this seat."

"Some of us are lucky," I mumble.

"Seriously, I've been in the same clothes for two days." He lifts his arms for emphasis, and his body odor hits me.

"You must be dying for a shower."

"A change of clothes would be good. My luggage was lost on the flight from Vietnam to Miami."

Trust me, it's not the clothes. Pushing away the thought of giving him the shirt off my back with the hope it would dull the smell, I process what he said. "Vietnam? How was that vacation?"

"I reside there for most of the year." He grins at me, his dried, cracked lips almost splitting. "I teach English and tutor children, then travel for a couple of months every year. It's the best life."

While I can't imagine it, I like this guy. "It sounds like an adventure."

He raises his arms again. "The stories I could tell." His long arms fall safely by his sides, and I let out the breath I was holding.

"Keep the stories for the other end of our flight, when I need to stay awake. Like our friend here." I jab a thumb toward the girl whose shoes are leaving a tire-like imprint on my thigh. "I need to catch some z's."

"Well, I'm Vince." He holds out a hand. I stare at his long, potentially germ-covered fingers. Where has he been the past two days?

"Byron." Out of an abundance of politeness, I shake his hand and almost immediately regret it. I subtly wipe my now moist palm on my pants.

As I close my eyes, I'm vaguely aware of the plane taking off and then leveling in the air. A voice interrupts my dozing with an offer of food.

"Man, I am starved," Vince comments.

"You can have mine," I tell him. "Do you drink whiskey?"

"Do pigs fly?" He laughs. I shake my head. So, it's a no? "Sorry, I'm delusional."

"Yes or no, Vince?"

"Yeah. I could do with one."

"Then I think I'll order us enough to get through this flight."

Three hours later, I regret ordering the whiskey.

Vince's head is tilted back on the seat, his mouth wide open as he snores louder than a freight train. The man needs a mandibular advancement device. Every time he winds up, I give him a gentle nudge, and he makes a gargling, choking sound before stopping for a few minutes.

And emo girl beside me now has those fucking boots stretched across my thighs. I need to piss, and yet, I don't want to move either one of them. While I don't know their stories, I'm not oblivious to the fact they both clearly need to rest.

An hour later, I remove my cap and scratch my scalp. I have to move. All I fucking need is a blood clot in my calf. "Hey," I whisper to Vince. "Sorry, man, I need to get up." There's no way I can squeeze past him. Vince nods wearily and stands so I can slip past. I lift the girl's legs slightly, and they drop back onto my seat. Great. I stare at the soles of her shoes, wishing my eyes could shoot lasers into them.

Praying for patience, I take one last clean breath and open the door to the lavatory, twist to step inside, and close the door behind me. *Christ, how does anyone fit in here?* I'm forced to hold onto the walls as turbulence hits. My stomach somersaults, and I narrowly avoid painting the seat with its contents. It reeks in here. I have to get out. Outside the cubicle, I take what I expect to be a clean, deep breath, only to be hit with hundreds of musky armpit odors.

There is no safe place.

As I hold onto the back of a seat, a guy goes to step around me.

I look at him to wait as the aisle is only wide enough for one.

"Hey." His eyes go round. "You're Byron Hendricks."

"I think you have me confused with—"

A girl pops out from behind him. "Oh my gosh, you *are*! Can we get a selfie?"

Before I have time to answer, her cell is turned, and they lean into me. I force a smile because the camera is in my face.

"Why are you traveling to Rome?" the guy asks. "Don't

you have a game? Wait, is Jye or Brandon playing your spot?"

This dude knows our roster.

"Both will rotate."

"Selfie? Can we have a selfie?" More people ask from the aisles beside us. "Can you sign my T-shirt?" A girl yells, "I love you!" and then giggles. Someone pushes, and the couple standing with me stumble.

"Everyone, please return to your seats," the flight attendant says from behind me.

I am fucking trying.

"If it's okay with you, Mr. Hendricks, I can get them to form a line..." the steward says, "... and I wouldn't mind a picture with you myself."

Fuck me.

For the next half hour, I pose for photos and sign freaking anything the girls can get their hands on, but I flat-out refuse to sign their chests.

"Okay, that's enough," Vince says, standing beside me. He's surprisingly tall. "Let the guy get some sleep."

"Thanks," I whisper as I slide into my seat. "Any chance you want to stay near me at the airport?" Now, I regret saying no to Colton.

After going through customs, I say my goodbyes to Vince and wish him luck traveling. While waiting for my ride, I send Giana a text.

> You looked beautiful onstage. I hope you are having a fabulous time.

She responds almost immediately.

> I am! How was training?

> The usual. What's on your agenda today?

Today we are in the studio, and then I'm
going to relax before getting ready for the
gala tonight. I hope to get to my villa
tomorrow.

Giana mentioned the hotel where she is staying before
she left. While the nine-hour time difference has messed
with my sleep, not getting any sleep on the flight over was
torture. I have a newfound respect for coach-class travelers.

But it's all worth it to see my girl.

As I sit in the back of the chauffeured BMW, my playlist
sounds in my ears for the next forty minutes—a distraction
so I stop thinking about Giana's reaction. I wipe my palms
on my trousers. It's hotter than I anticipated.

"Excuse me," I ask the driver. "Would you mind turning
up the air conditioning?"

"Of course, sir."

We pass weather-worn stone pillars, historical
monuments, and the architectural-pleasing piazzas. I
understand why Giana fell in love with Italy.

After tipping the driver and thanking him for the
tourist-like commentary, I grab my suitcase before the
concierge greets me. At first, they speak in Italian. I catch a
few words and offer a friendly smile. "American."

"Sì." They take my bag and follow me to reception. As I
look around me, I'm graced with the hotel's beauty. I speak
with the receptionist and ask her to call Giana to the foyer,
telling her it's a surprise. She points to a lounge to wait.

My heart skips a beat every time the elevator doors
open. I check my watch. Three minutes. *What is keeping her?*

17

BYRON

My leg bounces with the unwelcome ideas springing to mind. Fuck this. I stand and turn toward the sweeping staircase. Giana stands on the third step, frozen.

Our eyes meet, and her lips part.

She grips the rail before taking the next step.

I stride to meet her before she takes the final step. At this height, she can look me in the eye. Her hands fall over my shoulders as I bring her in for a tight embrace.

"Mr. Hendricks," she whispers. *Fuck*. My dick reacts to her calling me that. She leans back and stares at me, her thoughts whirling behind those pretty brown eyes. "You're full of surprises."

I push flyaway strands away from her beautiful face. "This was a good surprise, I hope?"

She kisses me once. "Yes, it is."

I kiss her hard, tasting her, and tighten my arms around

her waist as she falls into me. All I want to do is scoop her into my arms and carry her up the stairs to her room.

"*Mi scusi, signore.*" Excuse me, sir. The concierge stands to our side with my bags. "*Quale stanza?*" What room?

Giana speaks in Italian to the concierge. The way she uses her hands as she speaks, one wouldn't know she is American. I hear her mention her name, and the way *Giana Monroe* rolls off her tongue with an Italian accent hits me hard in the chest.

So fucking sexy.

She smiles at him, and he bows with a nod.

"Shall we?" She takes my hand, beaming her beautiful smile for me, and I take the first step by her side—the first of many steps I'll take to be by her side this weekend.

Giana unlocks her door, and once inside, I flick it closed with my foot as I take her into my arms.

"I've missed you," I say against her lips.

Her hands cup my face as if she never wants this kiss to end. We walk backward, our lips locked.

"I've missed you too. I can't believe you're here," she whispers, then pulls at my shirt. "I need this off."

"With pleasure." Giana sits on the bed, watching my hands as I unbutton my shirt. "What time are you expected in the studio?"

"Soon," she says casually. Her eyes lower to my trousers. "Something just came up." Her eyes meet mine with a hint of playfulness.

"Something?" I continue to strip for her. First, I undo my buckle, then I stall to bend and slide each foot out of my Amadeo Testoni shoes.

"*Testoni?*" Giana asks in a higher voice.

After learning of Giana's love for Italy, I bought the fine Italian leather footwear. "Have I impressed you?"

Her gaze flicks over my face. "You're full of surprises, Byron Hendricks."

I unzip my trousers and slowly push them down my thighs, watching her expression as I do.

Giana licks her lips. "Wait." She springs from the bed and peers up into my eyes. "Allow me," she purrs.

Her delicate finger slides under the band of my underwear, our gazes still locked. I see the yearning in her eyes, matching the lust pumping to every inch of my body. She slowly slides the elastic down until my erection bounces free. Her gaze lowers. Giana falls to her knees and takes my cock in her hands, assessing the thickness. Her lashes flutter. She looks fucking perfect from here. Her lips part as she takes me in, and all the blood leaves my brain, heading south. In seconds, I'm heady, and the fatigue from the trip is lost as excitement rips through my bloodstream.

Christ.

Her lips suck, and her tongue swirls as she tastes me all the way to the base.

Fuck.

I grip her hair, rolling a handful around my hands. I'm unable to keep my thrusts in sync with her mouth. This woman is everything to me, and my body knows it, emotion and passion ripping through every inch of my body.

"I'm going to come," I murmur through the delicious haze clouding my thoughts. Her mouth pumps my dick at a speed where I'm struggling to focus on anything except the pleasure. "Giana..." I breathe out hard, then inhale deeply, and she takes me deeper into her throat, faster, with more pressure from those perfect lips.

Eyes shut, I imagine her standing naked before me, touching her rounded breasts, fingers spread, her hand gliding down her stomach toward her pussy.

"Yes," I murmur. In my vision, her fingers slide inside,

and I lose every coherent thought as I find my release. The orgasm rips through my core, overtaking every thought as I empty into her pretty mouth. She releases my dick, which is still hard, and wipes her mouth. Her brown eyes look sexier than ever.

"Thank you for coming, Byron."

Best fucking pun I've ever heard.

I fall to my knees, resting my forehead against hers. "My pleasure." The words come out hoarse as I catch my breath. I soon find the energy to stand and carry her to the bed, as I initially intended when we entered the room.

I kiss her mouth. My hand finds her breast, and I trail my lips down her perfect neck.

"Byron," she whispers. "As much as I want to stay here with you, I have a hair and makeup appointment." I caress her nipple with my tongue. "I was on my way when I received the message from reception," she says, sounding breathless.

"Cancel it. You're already perfect."

She giggles. "We can finish this later." She takes my face in her hands and guides my lips to hers. "I'm so glad you came."

I grin at the pun.

"So am I."

Two hours later and no sign of Giana. After showering, I sit on the balcony and watch the streets come to life. Church bells sound in the distance, and the tangy, sweet scent of basil, tomatoes, cheese, and pizza cooking in wood-fired ovens fills the air.

As I wait, I listen to an Italian app to give myself more than the basics of the language, kicking myself for only studying French, German, and Spanish in college. Closing the ivory and pink curtains of the balcony, I plop onto the lounge opposite the bed. The room is ivory, dusky pink, and jade, with splashes of red. The framed painting behind the bed spans wall-to-wall, a tropical setting where a river enters the sea, emphasizing the green rainforest. The huts and the boats on the river highlight the softer tones in the room. I feel like I'm inside one of Giana's paintings. A blue-green ocean and the green foliage complement the jade throw over white bedsheets and the carpet. The carpet is enough to send one crossed-eyed—ivory diamonds with pink and red centers and a jade background. The couch has stripes of ivory, jade, and pink. My eyes go back to the painting, to the people with bare bums waving to the boats on the lagoon from grass huts. The uplifting color draws you into a beautiful landscape with the simplicity of life.

I dream of it yet cannot imagine it.

My knee bounces.

It's been over twenty-four hours since I sweated in a gym. *Since I touched a ball.*

What was I thinking, coming to a foreign country where I can get high just sitting in the hotel room staring at the décor, with barely enough room to do pushups?

I'm out of my comfort zone. My thoughts shift to Giana's boss declining a plus-one to the ball, and I'll be damned if her sleazy ex gets a chance to touch her again.

I need a drink.

I head out of Giana's room to the elevator and hit the button. A man and woman come to stand with me. After a few words, I hear Giana's name and do my best not to turn around. The doors open, and we enter the elevator. I go to the back while they stand in the front.

Fuck me.

It's Isabella and her dickwad nephew, Dante.

My hands ball into a fist.

Words are spoken fast, and while I don't understand most of it, I hear Giana's name, and it pisses me off. He has curly, dark hair and my height. His trousers, shoes, and crisp pale-pink shirt scream designer. Isabella's hair is styled to perfection, not one strand out of place. I recognize her floral dress—it's one of Giana's designs, and her shoes and handbag match. Between her eau de parfum and his aftershave, I'm doing my best not to inhale his fucking scent, but it's one I will remember, and I'll never wear the same.

The elevator stops at level two.

"Excuse me." Pushing between them, I advance toward the bar, ready to down a bottle of whiskey. I don't turn to give them a chance to see my face before the doors close when I'm already twenty yards away.

I don't trust the bastard.

As I stride through the doors to the bar, a few heads turn my way. I keep moving and find a stool, ignoring the hum of a foreign language. The mirrored wall behind the bar is lined with some of the finest wine on the planet.

The bartender, I assume, asks me for my order.

"Blanton's. Double, on the rocks." I pause. "Doppio."

"*Sì.*" He pours the whiskey on ice and slides the glass to me. "American?"

"*Sì,*" I repeat.

"East or West Coast?"

"West. Los Angeles."

"Ah. Are you charging to your room, signore?"

"No." I pull out my card, ready to pay. There is a quarter of the bottle remaining. "I'll pay for the rest if you could leave it here."

"Certainly, signore. What brings you to Rome?"

"A story similar to others." He slides the glass to me, and

I take a sip, relish the burn as the liquid slides down my throat. "A girl who owns my heart."

He watches me for a moment. "Does this girl know you're here?" he asks in broken English.

I peer into my glass. "She does."

"Then why the sad eyes with such a handsome face?"

I choke. I should be flattered.

"There's an ex trying to win her back." *Win.* What the fuck is wrong with me? I hate losing, so I need a game plan to make sure I don't fucking lose. "What's the most romantic thing to do in Rome?"

He considers my question. "Serenade her beneath her balcony."

I cough and inhale my whiskey. "Sing?" I choke out, wiping my mouth. "I don't want to scare her, or anyone, for that matter."

"*Sì.*" He wipes his hands with a towel. "Walk with her, always holding her hand. Buy her flowers along the way. Take her to dinner and pay for a private violinist."

Giana has lived here, so tourist places are out. "Do you recommend any specific restaurants?"

"*Sì.*" He pauses and glances over my shoulder. His lips part as though he is transfixed by something. I swivel on the stool just as a gentle hand lands on my shoulder.

"I thought I would find you here," Giana says in a soft voice. "Whiskey?" Her brows pull together. "You know we're in Italy, right?"

I lean in and kiss those lips, pulling back to admire my girl. Her hair is swept off her shoulders and pinned on her head with a loose curl here and there. Her makeup is perfect, her brown eyes capturing my attention as well as the attention of every other person nearby.

"You look stunning." I kiss her again and, with an arm around her waist, pull her close to me.

She flutters her long lashes and lowers her gaze. "Thank you."

She doesn't believe it? "Giana, you're the most beautiful woman I have ever seen. I can't take my eyes off you."

"Stop it." She leans on my shoulder playfully and smiles at the bartender. "How many has he had?"

"One glass, signora. He does not lie." He looks at me. "Bellissima."

"She is beautiful," I agree with him and kiss her forehead.

"As much as I would love to stay and chat, I need to dress. Isabella and Dante are waiting for me. The limo will be here soon."

"Is there a ticket for me?"

Giana tilts her head. "I'm sorry, Byron. But as soon as the formality is over, I'll leave. I don't need to eat. I'll come straight back. I'd love to take you to see my villa, but it's almost a five-hour drive from here..." She pauses. "So please don't drink any more if you intend to drive."

Nothing would please me more than to get her far away from Dante.

"I'm sorry," she says, "I haven't even asked when you're leaving?"

"Monday. Three in the morning." I take her hand. "I don't need to sleep between now and then." Thank fuck I have a first-class seat on the return flight. I turn to the bartender. "Can I take this?"

He hands me the lid to the bottle. *"Godetevi tutto."* He flashes a smile at Giana.

"Lo farò," she says and beams her killer smile at him. She takes the bottle and places it in her handbag.

"Grazie," I tell him, and slide off the stool, taking Giana's hand as we head toward the elevator. "What did you say to him?"

"He said for you to enjoy it all, and I said he will." She bumps her hip with mine. "If you'd finished the bottle, you might have ruined my plans for us." The elevator doors close.

Us.

"I'm sorry I have to rush away," she says. "I'll throw some things in a bag when we're upstairs. I'll call you after the formalities, and when you arrive, I'll come out, and we can go on a road trip tonight." Her voice is filled with excitement for just one night to share with me where she has lived for the years she was missing from my life.

"Throw what you need on the bed. I've plenty of time to sort out a suitcase, although..." I kiss her on the lips before the doors open, "... you won't need to wear a damn thing."

She giggles against my lips. "Byron. We need to eat. I want to show you some of my favorite places, and we can't do that naked."

The doors open, and Giana quickens her pace toward her room. She opens the door and heads to the cupboard, throwing multiple pieces of clothing and a bathing suit on the bed. She then strips, and fuck, I wish we had more time. She changes into a navy thong and removes her bra. *What the fuck?*

Giana steps into a navy gown.

Strapless.

Large, white magnolias cling to her every curve from her chest to her toes. She holds the dress to her breasts. "Could you zip me up?"

I zip up her dress, watching her golden skin disappear beneath the fabric. She adjusts her breasts to fit under the material with enough flesh protruding over the top in perfect molds.

I cannot take my eyes off her.

"Do you have to leave now?"

She runs a palm over her long, bare neck. "Byron," she whispers.

I clear my throat. "Go and have fun. Kill it, Gigi. You deserve this. My dick will get over it."

She laughs. "Just a few more hours, I promise." She sprays perfume on her pulse points. "Can you arrange our plans for tomorrow night?"

"It will be my pleasure."

She slips on her heels, grabs her purse, reaches up and kisses me, then rushes out the door.

I have twenty-four hours to make this romantic. Before packing up our belongings, I google florists close to the venue. While I have a list of things to do before we meet up —securing a rental car should be a priority, not freaking florists—I'll go crazy waiting, knowing Dante will not be able to keep his eyes off Giana.

I stare at the bottle of Blanton's. *Fucking hell.*

18

GIANA

Iᴛ's the final presentation of the night.

As I stand onstage with Isabella and Dante, the applause is music to my ears. While the gala was a fundraiser, and an elite line of Leto Designs was auctioned, along with luxury holiday destinations and sailing vacations from her wealthy friends, I don't see the need for me to be here. While I am an employee and business partner when it comes to my designs, the gala was organized by the Leto family. Isabella and Dante are the stars. I'm just on the sidelines. For years, I felt part of the family. Now...

"Now we dance," Dante whispers in my ear.

I stare up into his brown eyes, pools of chocolate that once melted my heart. "Dance?"

"The formalities are over, and the fun begins."

Isabella waves to the crowd as Dante and I leave the stage. He is handsome and full of class in his designer suit, but there is nothing that makes me want to be with him anymore.

"I can't. I'm driving to my villa tonight. I need to check a few things before I fly out in a few days."

He takes the first step and turns to take my hand to assist me down the stairs. "Are you listing it for sale?"

I shake my head. "It's why I want to oversee some things." I take his hand and look up before the final step. The large wooden doors to the ballroom are open, with some guests exiting the room. A tallish man in a suit stands by the door, and his heated gaze meets mine.

"Do you need me to accompany you to your room?"

I let go of Dante's hand and tear my gaze from the man who has my heart to focus on Dante. "Thank you, but I am with someone. He is here, and we are leaving tonight. Tell Isabella I'll speak with her at the next meeting on Monday."

Dante turns and easily spots Byron standing by the door waiting for me since his eyes are locked on us.

"I want you to introduce us," he says with authority.

Not a good idea!

"Perhaps another time. We're in hurry."

He rests a hand on my shoulder. "Go to him, and I'll fetch your purse and bring it to you."

"Okay." My voice breaks. Dante sounds genuine, so maybe I'm overthinking this.

Lifting my dress a few inches, I move toward Byron, remaining on the edge of the crowd.

"Hey." I reach up and kiss him. "You're overdressed for a road trip."

His brows are tight. "I arrived an hour ago hoping to sneak in and stand at the back. I wanted to see you onstage."

"*Sneak in*?" I rasp. "It's not a sneak-in type of event, and you're not that person."

"No. And my status holds no sway here. Security didn't

care. Though I did get a glimpse, and I saw the last few minutes."

I giggle. "Wow. They didn't fall to your charm."

A gentle hand rests on my shoulder. *"La tua borsa, bella signora."* Your purse, beautiful lady. Dante speaks in the sexy Italian accent that caught my attention the first time we met. His words are not a threat to Byron, but he says it in a way to make Byron feel just that.

Dante smiles down at me for a moment too long before looking at Byron. *"Ciao, sono Dante Leto, un buon amico di Giana."* Hello, I am Dante Leto, a good friend of Giana.

Dante has spoken to me in English all night, and *now* he chooses to speak in Italian?

Before I can translate for an informal introduction, Byron speaks first. He holds out his hand, and I'm sure he wants to crush Dante's fingers. "Byron Hendricks. *Sono il ragazzo di Gigi.*" Byron Hendricks. I'm Gigi's boyfriend.

I stare at Byron, surprised he knows more than ciao and arrivederci.

His girlfriend. It rolled easily off his tongue. I push it out of my mind and glance down at their hands, still locked in a fierce handshake.

I press a palm to their locked fingers. "Byron, we have a long drive ahead of us." I stand between them. "I'll see you on Monday, Dante." I place a hand on Byron's back and head out of the ballroom.

"That wasn't awkward at all," I say sarcastically as Byron and I reach the foyer.

He glances down at me, his expression taut. I sense he wants to say more about what just happened. Instead, he remains tight-lipped, takes my hand, and walks briskly toward the doors and hands the valet his card.

"Do we need to return to our room?" I ask.

He shakes his head. "I have everything in the car."

"I need to change."

"Later."

His gaze focuses on each car picking up guests and driving away.

His car arrives. Byron opens the door for me. "Thank you." He closes the door, and I look over the seat to see some clothes and...

My hand goes to my throat. Byron slides in and smirks when he sees what has caught my attention. He picks up the bunch of red roses. "These are for you." He hands them to me and leans in to kiss my cheek. "I am proud of you, Gi. You rocked it on the stage. You're a natural."

I peer into the petals and inhale the sweet scent, closing my eyes as joy fills me. I'm energized and equally calmed, filled with hope, and can see a future of contentment.

"Thank you," I say excitedly. "It's so thoughtful of you."

I never imagined Byron to be a romantic or envisioned us ever getting back together. It's why Mom always told me never to assume or rule anything out. While something might be wrong for you at a certain point in time, it may be the perfect fit in another.

The present always changes.

Our path in life fluctuates with every decision.

I believe in destiny.

Fate.

Maybe we are soulmates, and while our decisions affected our relationship years ago, we were destined to eventually end up together.

Or maybe we are destined to right our wrongs, forgive each other, make peace, yet not remain together.

I take another deep breath to be hit with the dopamine of happiness from the roses, engraving the memory of this night into my brain. The present is what we have, and I'm going to enjoy every second of it with Byron.

I keep hold of the flowers until we are on the highway heading toward Pescara and then making our way south along the coast.

Even with the cool air blowing on my face, I need to change. "We'll need to stop for coffee and so I can get out of this dress."

Byron glances at me, his gaze lowering to my chest. "I like you in that dress... though it would be better if you stripped out of it now."

"And then we wouldn't arrive by tonight."

A smile grows on his lips while his gaze returns to the road. "What's wrong with sleeping in the car?"

I shake my head.

"Judging by the way you're perving at my boobs, we wouldn't be sleeping."

"I can't help it if I'm already planning what I want to do to each breast. To all of you."

"There'll be plenty of time for you to have me all to yourself."

LAUGHTER IN THE DISTANCE AND THE QUIET HUM OF MUSIC invades my brain. Slowly, I wake and realize where I am.

I swallow and sit up straight. "I'm sorry. I must have dozed for a while." As I stare out to the lit-up streets, my thoughts catch up.

"For the last hour," Byron jokes. "Not even the potholes or bumpy roads woke you."

"You get used to them." I adjust my seat as my senses catch up. Byron is driving at ten miles an hour. Stringed lights shine over restaurants, and chairs and tables line the walkway. There is barely enough room for the car on this one-way road, which isn't much of a road but more like a cobblestone path. "Isn't it beautiful?"

"It's not what I expected," he murmurs as the street narrows further.

I'm bursting with excitement for him to see my villa. "That's a good thing, right?" We slow to almost a walking pace. "Park anywhere here. We need to walk the rest of the way."

The look Byron gives me makes me giggle.

A few minutes later, we collect our bags from the trunk. I grab my flowers from the back seat, hold my heels by the straps, and walk barefoot the few hundred yards along irregular alleys to my villa.

It's after two in the morning, and the alleys are pumping with romantic music, laughter, and song. While I love LA, I feel most alive here in a small historic town in Northern Puglia.

"We have to take the stairs," I tell Byron. Patrizia, the elderly lady who oversees my villa, is usually asleep as soon as the sun goes down. Byron carries our two small suitcases, and I have my roses and purse. His gaze lifts to the façade—an ancient, weathered limestone wall facing the street with yellow halos from the lamp-shaped wall lights. From here, I see what has caught his eye and assume his thoughts. Above us, a wooden balustrade is nailed to the wall over arched wooden doors. "The balustrade is for safety, so they can open the doors for fresh air."

"Not a balcony," he murmurs. His gaze roams the wall encompassing the minute, compact residences as though they were a single building.

He follows me to the terraced alley behind the building.

"*Mi scusi.*" Excuse me. We bump and pass people on the stairs. I smile, excited to be here, as we weave the windy stone steps dividing buildings with terracotta potted flowers, pink bougainvillea creeping toward the sky like an abstract painting on the wall. Single chairs, blue or yellow, sit beside doorways. Lifting the hem of my dress so I can lift a leg, I lead Byron to the second level, where the stairs level out to a string of balconies with a low stone wall. We stop at my entrance, which has dead leaves scattered over it.

What was I thinking, bringing Byron here to impress him? It's been empty for months and is far from perfect.

"It needs a sweep," I say apologetically.

"Not the first thing to come to mind."

I lean over and place my flowers and purse on the ground before easing my rear onto the stone wall and lifting my legs over, groaning as the dress restricts my movement.

"Shit." My dress.

"Giana, allow me to help you," Byron says, dropping the bags over the ledge and almost scaling it like a hurdle.

"I have done this many a time. Double back to what you said. What's the first thing that comes to mind?" He watches me as I lift an upturned pot to retrieve a key.

"That anyone could easily break into your villa," he emphasizes, staring at the pot.

I love my caring man. "It's safe here. People respect each other. If anyone were to break in, it would be Patrizia leaving food, and she has a key."

"I suspect Patrizia is not a sexy young woman who has a smile that lights up a room and a body that sends men crazy with desire?"

I push the key into the lock and turn to Byron before unlocking the heavy wooden door. "No," I whisper. "She is not since she is a widower with no children and in her mideighties."

He was referencing me?

I turn the key, open the door, and touch the wall for the

lights. A dusty smell wafts around us. Flick. Flick, flick. No power. *Shit.*

"Maybe I missed a bill. I'll pay at the post office tomorrow."

Byron pulls out his cell and turns on the flashlight. He shines it around the room.

"It's a little dusty," I say quickly. "I'll open the windows."

I stride to the other side of the room and push open the shutters that open against the exterior wall. A buzz of energy from the nearby streets fills my room. Excitement is in the air, along with shouts of laughter and the scent of herbs and pizza. Leaning over the ledge, I peer down into the alley below. Byron joins me, and his gaze lowers to the street instead of up to the stars.

"It smells divine."

I point to the opposite corner. "That's my favorite restaurant. The best pizza and pasta in the world. Do you want to head down and try it?" I ask, failing to contain my excitement upon hearing the vibrant chatter below.

He leans in and kisses my lips. "I'd rather stay here with you."

"Byron, we have the rest of the night. I want you to experience the culture *with me* while you're here. We're both dressed to party. Besides, you said you didn't need sleep."

He grumbles something before kissing me again. "Let's not eat our body weight in pizza, or we'll be in a food coma."

I grin at him. "I wouldn't dare do that to you."

Finding my purse and flat shoes under the light of his cell, I take Byron's hand and lead him down the dark stairs to my front door. "There's a tiny laundry, bathroom, and a bedroom where I keep my paint supplies," I say, pointing behind us. I open the huge wooden door with its iron frame. It creaks as it closes behind us with a clunk.

"Did you grab a key?"

"Patrizia has this door key. I have the balcony key."

His brow lifts slightly before focusing on the restaurant across the cobbled street. I take his hand and walk into the small restaurant.

"Giana," Roberto sings. *"Mi sei mancata."*

I tell him I have also missed him. Roberto is a jovial, round-bellied man with graying brows and receding hair. I order a margherita pizza, a dish of marinara spaghetti, and Roberto's famous monkfish dish. He tells me to sit at my favorite table—outside so I can people-watch. But tonight, I'll only have eyes for one person.

BYRON SHAKES HIS HEAD AS HE FINISHES A SHOT OF limoncello.

I giggle at his reaction. "It's delicious, right?"

"It's something else." He wipes his mouth as he eyes the last piece of pizza. "It's all yours. I couldn't eat another piece, even though I want to."

"I craved it every day, living with all the aromas that filtered into my room. While I was often alone, Roberto and others made me feel like part of their family."

Byron's brow pinches as I sense his thoughts whirling. "Dante wasn't here with you?"

"Sometimes. While I spent many weekends at one of his many homes or on the yacht, I needed my time here to unwind and clear my head. It's different here, more me than the bustling cities. I still love Rome and the vibrant street life at night, but I feel more at home here in my little villa. I have some fun art on the walls and decorated it in a way I like, not all designer pieces and expensive art. Dante is a collector of valuable things."

"My guess is he wants to add you to his collection."

"I cannot be owned, Byron. If I feel trapped, I'll panic." He smiles at me and lowers his gaze as though he is collecting his thoughts. While I want to be his and for him to be mine, it's more about trust, not ownership, and not like the way Dante wanted to control me. "For a long time, I allowed him to tell me what to do. It's why I needed to spend time here and just breathe. Be myself."

His lips press into a thin line, and I sense I hit a nerve. "Why did you allow him that control over you?"

I let out a long sigh. "I wanted to fit in." I reach over the table and take his hand. "Remember in high school how I never fit in with the *it* girls? I hung out with Paige, Mason, you, and a few others. I would often spend lunch alone to finish some art pieces as Paige could float from one group to another. She wasn't popular and wasn't a geek, but she could mingle with everyone. I felt lucky to be friends with you both. But when you trained most lunchtimes, I would be alone in the art room. I heard whispers, so I avoided people."

I thought his brow was pinched before, but now, it's like a porch over his eyes.

"You were the hottest girl at school," he rasps. "I never thought of you being lonely. Merely focused, like me."

I give him a warm smile. "I was glad I had you as a friend... most times."

"Friends..." He fiddles with his designer wristwatch. "I always wanted you, Gigi. But I needed to keep my eye on the ball. In a way, I always thought we would end up together somehow, and... here we are."

"Really? I'd hoped, but when I was here, I stopped believing we had a future."

He tilts his head back. "I was an idiot," he whispers.

"Byron..." I wait for him to look at me. "I don't regret a thing. We made mistakes, learned, grew, and became better people for it. It was a part of finding ourselves. While I loved being part of Dante's fancy world, I don't need to be lavished and worshiped with gifts and expensive playthings. It was fun while it lasted, but it wasn't me. It was too much, a distraction to finding myself, so I had to keep taking time out for me. And those times when I needed to be by myself, Dante thought it was okay to be in bed with someone else. The same old story... it wasn't love with them, just sex. He *loved* me."

"Why am I torn between wanting to hurt him and thanking him?" He squeezes my hand, his eyes searching my face for understanding. "I hate that he hurt you, Gi."

I smile at my beautiful, handsome man. "I allowed him to hurt me. I knew he was a playboy, even though he loved me. Deep down, I knew we had an expiration date." I glance at the ladies sitting at a nearby table, admiring my man. "I wonder how you would cope with all the attention here?"

"What do you mean?"

"The ladies at the next table can't take their eyes off you, and it's not about your status as an elite athlete. You're a sexy man. You'd probably be treated like a god. I'm glad you're wearing a shirt."

A smirk grows on his lips. "Thank fuck I can't read their thoughts."

"If you knew what I'm thinking right now..."

Byron stands and takes my hand. "It's time for us to go. I want to know *exactly* what you're thinking."

19

BYRON

SO MANY CATS.

Some sit beside doors and others on chairs, watching us with beady eyes. A gray one rubs against Giana's leg.

She leans down to rub its head. "Hey, Gray, you're still here."

I don't ask. She hums a tune as we take the steps to the back entrance. The heat hasn't affected her mood. Meanwhile, my shirt is stuck to my back in the ninety-degree heat with humidity that feels different from home. I wasn't planning on sleeping, but fuck me.

She opens the door and hesitates. "Thank you for coming and sharing this night with me. It means a lot."

"I wish I got to do it sooner." I lean in to kiss her, twirling with her in my arms as the weathered wooden door closes behind us, blocking out the light from the full moon.

Hot, moist air on musky, ancient limestone walls fills my

senses. Kissing a trail along her neck, I inhale her perfume and scent until only Giana is imprinted on my brain.

"You're hot," she whispers in the dark.

"You're not too bad yourself."

She giggles. "This heat is a lot. I think we could both do with a shower."

"If it means getting wet with you, then count me in."

She takes my hand and leads me through the dark as though she has done this a million times. I walk with a hand raised in case something smacks me in the face.

"Your cell, Byron." I pull out my phone and turn on its flashlight.

We enter a bathroom that's all terracotta and white tiles. She places two towels on a ledge.

"Can you help me with the zipper?"

I undo her dress and kiss her shoulders as the fabric pools at her ankles. Her skin is hot beneath my lips. I continue to caress her neck, her cheeks, back to her lips. "Get naked with me, Byron."

Through the small bathroom window, light reflects from the street. I pull my shirt over my shoulders, watching her face as I do. Animal instinct takes over as she helps divest me of the rest of my clothes, ungraceful and desperate. We turn under the water spray, and I imagine the sizzle of steam as it hits my heated skin. My attempts to be tender are lost in my desire, a yearning to have wanted this moment for what seems like a lifetime. Dark shadows fall over her face and tanned body, accentuating her curves and breasts. The whites of her eyes fail to hide the longing, and a deep ache settles in the pit of my stomach. I crave Giana like nothing else.

"I need you *now*," she whispers. She jumps into my arms, and her legs wrap around my waist. As I push her up against the cool tiles, she lifts her rear enough for me to slide inside her. Slowly, I rock into her, wanting to draw out the moment and be with her gently. Her hands run through my hair, over my face, and claw at my back. Every moan goads me to go faster until I'm thrusting desperately, ignoring my tight chest and racing heart. Our harsh pants sound out in the small room. She reaches out and hits the tap, and we lose water.

"Sorry," she moans. "We have a shortage."

What?

With water or without, I'm at the point of no return. Giana fists my hair, using it as leverage to ride me harder. I pound into her, desperate for release, and then it comes. I shudder, and she moans.

"Byron," she says breathily. She doesn't say anything else, and I'm perfectly happy hearing my name on her lips, knowing I'm the one who gave her the climax.

We slip down the tiles to the floor and lie there for a moment, our wet bodies sliding together as our legs untangle.

After a few minutes, I feel I can breathe and talk again. This hot, humid weather is ridiculous. "What happened to the water?" She lifts one arm and turns the faucet and the water sprays over us on the tiled floor. "Thank fuck," I murmur. I thought my head was going to explode.

She giggles and lies over me, sliding her chest over mine. "It's the best way to fuck in summer." And damn, it sounds sexy, the way *fuck* rolls off her tongue.

"Looks like we're spending the night in the shower," I murmur.

"Not possible," she says, flicking it off again. "We have to use it in spurts."

"Then I'm going to spurt with you all night long."

KNOCK, KNOCK, KNOCK.

What the fuck?

I force one eye open, though I don't remember falling asleep.

"It's Patrizia." Giana groans and rolls over. "When I'm here, she brings me breakfast and leaves it at the door."

I'd be all for it if I weren't still shoving food in my mouth at two in the morning.

"Can you text her and tell her we don't need it?"

"My cell is dead," she murmurs. "Ugh, can you bring it in before the cats get to it?"

I squinch my eyes, trying to focus with the harsh light shining through the open windows. Christ, I'm going to fry in here. I groan.

What the fuck is the time? Hell o'clock?

I roll over and kiss her bare shoulder. We are both naked with no covers and while I'm cursing the heat, I'm grateful to wake up like this with Giana. I think about last night. "If I do, then I vote for a repeat of last night in the shower."

Water shortage or not, my dick reacts thinking about it.

"Sure thing, babe," she murmurs. "Just grab the tray and bring it upstairs."

Forcing myself to move, I head down the stairs, waking more as I think of taking Giana in the shower again. I stroke my cock and open the door slightly. Jesus, this is one hell of a door. Heavy, and another three feet taller than me.

No one is around. I bend to get the tray, step forward to gain my balance, and—

The fuck?

My towel slips as I drop the yellow wooden tray and stumble forward. I manage to prevent our breakfast from spilling onto the pavement as the weight of the heavy wooden door pushes my rear, forcing me out into the alley before clicking shut behind me. I cover my package with my hands and look around. *Jesus.*

"Giana," I say, hoping she'll hear through the open window but not loud enough to gather attention. "Giana." I grumble a few choice words while looking around. This is not how I imagined serenading her.

A giggle sounds across the street. A young girl, a teenager maybe, is peeping out of the open window. "Mamma," she says over her shoulder, along with a string of words including *nudo*, and it does not take a genius to work out what she is saying. *Christ, I'm about to get arrested.*

I grab the tray, hold the edge above my cock, and run down the alley, the pastries bouncing all over the plate. A black cat crosses my path and threatens to trip me. I have no time to think about superstition and dodge it, so I leap. It hisses. A trail of giggles sounds behind me.

Voices shout. I don't stop running. I turn the corner toward the stairs and—

My heels skid on the rough stone as I come to a halt.

A group of old ladies sit in those blue and yellow wooden chairs outside their doors, chatting. I eye the stairs now yards away. I'm desperate to get there, like I'm about to score a touchdown. I decide not to run but to briskly walk past the first few ladies, hoping they are too busy to notice.

More laughter. More shouting.

I'm close to the stairs when one springs from her seat as though she suddenly has the energy of a twenty-year-old. She stands in front of me, and before I sidestep, she moves, blocking my way.

She eyes me, and I prepare myself for the abuse. I look around, and all the ladies are out of their chairs, walking toward me. A vision flashes in my mind of being struck down by walking sticks while the old ladies call me Satan, the ground burning my feet like I'm at the motherfucking gates of hell.

I lift one foot, then the other, almost hop on the hot cobblestones. The woman peers down.

"Mother of God, please no."

She lifts one of the pastries and sniffs it. "Patrizia?"

I nod, thanking the freaking gods she understands. Wait. *No, no, no.* I'm not Patrizia's toyboy.

"Giana," I clarify, averting my eyes and looking to the stairs.

"Giana," she repeats and grins before turning to her friends. "Giana," she announces.

She steps to the side like Gandalf allowing me to pass, takes a good look at my ass, then repents by making the sign of the cross over her body.

Fuck me.

My legs propel me forward, and I take the stairs two at a time, giving the audience below a terrestrial view of my butt and balls.

"*Bel culo,*" she shouts, and the women giggle.

I slow near the top to find Giana leaning over the ledge, elbows bent, her chin resting on her hand, watching me. An amused expression quirks up her lips. "*Bel culo,*" she says and straightens.

I pass the tray over to her.

She is wearing my white shirt. It's open, and she has nothing underneath.

"What the fuck, Gigi? Someone will see you."

She tilts her head and smirks. "Well, everyone has seen you. I heard giggling and something about a gorgeous naked man. I jumped up to look out my window and saw you running down the street with the tray. The ladies are right in saying you have a nice ass." She giggles, picks up a pastry, and takes a bite. "This is probably the most excitement they've had in a while," she says, with a mouthful of croissant.

I close the door behind us. Keeping my hand on the door, I bow my head. My heart is racing. I'm no prude, but that was mortifying, and the thought of being arrested in a foreign country—

"You know I can never come back, right?" I say to Giana.

Giana laughs so hard she holds her stomach with one hand and her croissant in the other. *That's it.* I stride to her and scoop her up and over my shoulder, smacking her ass as I walk into the bathroom. I lower her to the tiles and turn on the water, then push her under the spray until my shirt is soaked and clinging to her body.

I stroke my cock as I watch the water trickle down her beautiful face, snake down the middle of her stomach where my shirt isn't stuck to her skin, then roll down her thighs. "You're so fucking beautiful." I keep stroking my cock. Her hand glides over her stomach to her clit. She spreads her legs, watching me as I watch her touch herself. The first moan that comes from those plump lips has me on my knees, pushing her hand away so I can taste her.

She reaches over me and turns off the water.

"Best you save the water to cool down your pussy," I murmur. "By the time I'm finished, you'll need the spray to ease the throb."

I spin her around, grab the scruff of her neck, and bend her so her ass is in the air, then push inside her, and her hips roll back to meet mine in a steady rhythm. It's a beat of mutual understanding, one we easily dance to. We know the moves, understand our bodies' needs, and up the tempo until the song finishes. Except, I don't want this song to end and don't want to stop dancing with Giana. She makes everything right, and when we fuck, there is no better sound.

Holding her hips, I piston into her at a fast pace. My balls smack her ass, and her heavy sighs fill the air. Leaning over her back, I hug her. Her breasts bounce hard with every thrust. I'm building fast, and I hear her come, my name rolling off her lips and her knees buckling. I hold her steady, pump into her a few more times, and shudder as I empty everything I have into her. This time, I twist the faucet, and the water sprays over us as we slide to the tiles, my arms still wrapped around her body. I turn my head so the water sprays over my face, then catch my breath.

"Next time, call ahead. I'll pay the power bill before we arrive."

Giana laughs, pulls off me, and slides on top. She smothers my face with her kisses. "You can't deny it's been fun."

"If that torture is what you call fun, then yes, it's been fun." I laugh at her expression when her bottom lip drops. "No, seriously." I reach up and turn the faucet so the water shuts off again. "This is real fun."

She slaps my chest playfully. "You like it, admit it."

Giana is sitting on top of me while I lie on her shower floor. Her wet hair clings to her face and shoulders. Water droplets cascade over her beautiful breasts and along her tanned body. I massage her beautiful tits. Tilting her head back, she closes her eyes and moans. "I'm just drying you off," I whisper. "I hear there is a towel shortage."

Her eyes fling open and narrow at me. I laugh but continue touching her body. "Giana," I murmur. She stares at me and waits, though she gives me a look that suggests she doesn't trust what's about to come out of my mouth. I look side to side to make a point. "Here or anywhere, if I'm with you, it's going to feel like heaven."

She stares at me and realizes I'm being truthful. She leans down and kisses my lips, her tongue finding mine, her mouth telling me she feels the same way.

FROM THE MOMENT WE LEFT ROME, GIANA WANTED TO SHOW me around her coastal village. After Giana made a call about her villa and paid some bills, we walked hand in hand along the cobbled streets, finding the best espresso and admiring the architecture of churches and the way the village was built into a limestone mountain. We eat lunch at a sidewalk café. A soft breeze picks up her hair, stirring the strands around her cheeks, but it's not strong enough to cool my body from the balmy air that hangs heavy in the atmosphere. Giana leads me along a path, down two hundred and fifty freaking stairs to get to the beach.

Blue and white umbrellas are positioned in lines from the ocean to the stairs, each with its own beach chair. It's not a large beach, but it is divided at each end by rocks on the limestone cliff face.

Sweat is dripping from my brow, and all I can think about is diving into the sea. It's a turquoise blue, the water lapping the shore. We walk along the water's edge with our shoes in our hands as the gulls caw to each other over our heads.

"Are we swimming?"

She gestures toward the rocks ahead, blocking the beach at high tide. "Follow me," she says, climbing to scramble over the boulders.

I follow her, keeping close in case she slips, and walk sideways, then slide, scale some more, and descend onto a ledge where the ocean rushes in like a river.

It's a small cave-like pool.

I follow her along the stony ledge. She drops her sandals.

"You wouldn't."

She grins and pulls off her dress.

"Stop it."

She jumps in.

"Giana!" I shout. "Fuck." I drop my sneakers, rip off my shirt, and jump.

I come to the surface and look around.

Giana is wading, laughing. "Your face," she says, amused.

I swim over to her. "You scared the fuck out of me." I pull her close and want to spank her sexy ass.

"Scared I'd drown?" She pulls a face. "Byron, you need to live. Take a risk."

"I take risks every day, but not like this." Calculated risks beneficial to my game or to beat my opponent, sure. "How do you know it's safe? There could be a rip or some territorial sea beast in the water."

She tilts her head back as she laughs. "Like what?"

"A crocodile," I shoot back.

"We're a long way from Australia." She wraps her arms around my neck and kisses me. "Make love to me."

Love.

"Here?" I was thinking of soft, silky sheets and being surrounded by luxury when we made love.

Giana lets go and paddles toward the back. I follow her to where the water laps against some stony man-made steps.

"This is a thing?"

"Yes. Especially at night, during low tide. It's called Lover's Cove." She sits on the step and spreads her legs. "Allow me to initiate you." It's the first initiation in my life that I'm excited to be part of.

Giana spins and climbs the final step, strips out of her

bra and thong, and lies on the stony ledge. "It looks painful, Gi. I don't want it to cut you up."

"Byron," she says firmly. "I won't feel anything if it's love. All I want is to feel you inside me."

I rid the last of my clothing, fall to my knees, and settle between her thighs. I tuck my elbows near her shoulders and shove my hands under her to try and protect her skin, then lean down and kiss her tenderly. Her lips move with mine, slowly at first, speeding up as our tongues entwine and taste. "I want this to be my favorite memory of Italy," she whispers as her legs wrap around me, her heels digging into my hamstrings.

I kiss her cheek, ear, jaw, and forehead, then move to the other ear and whisper, "I love you, Gi." I feel her soften beneath me. I keep kissing her cheek and face, then find her lips again. While she doesn't utter the words, her mouth tells me everything I need to know. She kisses and devours me and, with one hand, guides my erection to her opening. I push in slowly, checking she is okay and not sore because we have fucked hard over the last twelve hours. I withdraw slowly, then slide in farther, and she gasps as her pussy adjusts.

"I'm okay," she whispers.

I quicken the pace, driving deeper yet still gently. I faintly acknowledge pain in my knees and elbows, but I don't stop, overwhelmed with desire and wanting to give Giana the orgasm she craves.

A new memory. *With me.*

We arrive back in Rome around nine thirty, and Giana books us in for dinner at a restaurant a block from her hotel. While she is in the bathroom, I inquire about a violinist, which took longer than necessary with the communication barrier. It's the last thing on my list to make the trip as romantic as possible.

I end the call as she emerges from the bathroom. She drops the towel near her suitcase, and my breath hitches. Not at the sight of her beautiful body but the scratches on her back. "Gi..." I go to her and kiss her shoulder. "I'm sorry I hurt you." I run a finger over the raised red marks.

She turns and smiles. "You ought to see the other guy."

I laugh. "Yeah. He's pretty cut up." I kiss her shoulder. "But it was worth every second with you."

"Byron," she says breathily. "Please don't regret anything because I'm enjoying every minute with you. My regret is we don't have more time. There is so much more I want you to see."

I kiss her shoulder again and rub my hands along her bare arms. "Next year, in the offseason, we'll plan a vacation here, and you can show me all the places. Make a list."

She smiles again. "Why don't you make lists?"

"I do, mental notes."

"I need to write it down. I'm not as confident as you, and doubt is a killer."

"Why do you question your decisions?" It's the first thing our mentors taught us—trust the process be confident moving forward.

She turns, eyes wide. "I have always doubted myself."

"Gi." I take both her hands. "Doubt is a waste of energy. It doesn't change the result or what you do tomorrow. We work hard toward our goals. I practice every day. If we lose, I practice the next day to be a better player. If we win, I still practice to be a better player." I move strands of hair away from those brown eyes that are searching for understanding. "If your art is not what you thought, you either improve it or create another. If a deal goes sour, you propose other ideas.

Doubting your ability gets you nowhere. Losing or winning is the same, just with different emotions. We get up and do it again, only *better*. Whether we fail or succeed, the process doesn't change."

"You're right," she whispers. "I've wasted so much time doubting and procrastinating."

"Now, get dressed so we can eat before I have to catch my flight."

"I'll be about twenty minutes to apply my makeup and style my hair." She grabs her makeup bag and retreats to the bathroom.

Twenty minutes. I'm not going to waste it by sitting around.

I strip off my shirt and trousers, then grab the books on the coffee table and pile them on the floor. Sitting on my rear, I place the books to the side, and bending one leg to my chest, I wrap my arms around my knee for balance. I lift the extended leg and over the pile of books, back and forth twenty times before switching legs. Then I repeat it but faster. Positioning the books behind and to the side, I go on all fours, extend a leg and the opposite arm, and lift my straight leg over the book pile, back and forth. Switch legs. Repeat it faster.

I roll my ankle, stretching it out. Standing, I utilize the desk chair by lifting one leg and lunging into it, keeping my back leg straight and pushing into a deep Achilles stretch. Then I do the same without the chair, with extra pressure through the ankle.

I hop side to side, quicker, higher, then switch legs. My ankles feel great.

While I missed training, the rest is what I needed, and mentally, I'm recharged. Not by being in another country on a mini vacation but by being with Giana and seeing her in her element. Kicking goals. Being rewarded and applauded.

It gives me a kick, even more than receiving my own accolades.

I finish up with jump lunges. It's not enough to call it a training session, but it's better than nothing, and I didn't sweat, so I redress, sit on the bed, and wait a few more minutes for Giana.

The bathroom door opens, and I push up from the edge of the bed.

Wow.

"You look beautiful." I lower my gaze, taking in her tight black strapless dress that clings to her waist before following her curves and ending midthigh. "Is it too late to cancel our dinner reservation?"

She smiles at me, lowers her eyes, and wipes her hands over the material. "It's my favorite little black dress."

"I don't care what it is. I want it off you."

She shakes her head. "Later, Byron. I still have a list for Rome I want you to see."

Fuck Rome. The best it has to offer is right in front of me.

She takes my hand. "Wine and dine me, then I'm all yours."

20

BYRON

ON TUESDAY MORNING, my energy is drained after sleeping fourteen hours straight trying to catch up on missed sleep.

"Move your ass, Hendricks," Coach yells at me. "You're running like your shoes are two sizes too big."

I hiss out air and sprint to the end line.

"Coach just called you a clown," Simpson says with a laugh.

"Fuck off," I say, quiet enough that Coach doesn't hear.

"Next time, don't leave the country without permission, especially when you miss two trainings and were rested for one game," Coach fires at me. "Everyone is sprinting for the next ten minutes, not just Byron. We're a team, and if one of you fucks up, it affects us all."

My teammates groan, some of them glaring at me. I wipe my brow. I've had my share of penalties for other players' fuckups. I feel like a piece of shit when I'm the cause.

"Go," he yells, clicking the timer. "Next time, consult

with the team before making an impulsive decision. And what did you do to your knees?"

"Rock climbing, Coach," I shout over my shoulder.

We sprint for a minute, then rest for fifteen seconds.

"Rock climbing?" Brandon says, mocking me.

"Shut up. How was your weekend?"

He walks in a circle to catch his breath. "Great... watched the AFL Grand Final."

"Yeah? Good?"

"Yeah, it was a close game. My team bombed out last week, so I enjoyed the game without the pressure."

"Go."

We take off to the other end of the court. By the end of the fourth minute, we're sucking in air as though all the oxygen has evaporated. Hands on hips and heads tilted back, we walk slowly around the base line before lining up again for the timer.

"Go."

I swear all the pasta and pizza have slowed me down.

"Time."

We are spread out on the court, some of us faster than the big guys.

"Go."

My legs burn. My calves tighten. Sprints are part of our program, but not at the end of a two-hour training, the second training session of the day.

"Time."

I slow to a jog, stop, and shake my legs and fingers. Two to go.

Some of the senior players send me sideways glances. Yeah, I'm an asshole.

When we finish the final sprint, I suck in as much air as I can and line up again.

"What are you doing, man? We're done," Brandon says, patting my shoulder, still out of breath.

"I'm not. It's my fault. I'll do another five."

"Sorry, mate. You're on your own. I'm heading to the showers."

"BJ, tell Byron we have hot and cold therapy waiting," Leroy shouts.

I raise a hand as I sprint. "One more," I shout back. I finish the last lap and walk the tunnel toward the new ice bath and sauna facility next to our locker room.

Coach waits outside the door. "We good?"

"Yeah, we're good."

His gray eyebrows tighten, the indents around his eyes deepening. "Don't make what happened last weekend a habit."

"No, sir," I say before pushing open the door.

I shower, then head to the ice bath. Leroy and Brandon are still in the bath.

"Fuck," I say, lowering myself until my shoulders are covered.

"Hurts so good," Brandon sings.

Wolf-whistles sound. I turn as Charlotte walks into the room, her heels clicking on the floor as she passes some of my teammates who have it all hanging out.

What the fuck?

I hate it when the guys walk around without their towels, but it all goes straight over Charlotte's head.

"I have a surprise for you all," she calls out. "You may want to thank me for getting us in at the Ritz-Carlton in Abu Dhabi," she almost sings. "Luxury at its finest. But remember, you are there to win games. It is *not* a vacation."

She walks over to Coach.

"Can I lie with you on the beach, Lottie?" Simpson calls out.

I glare at him, then turn to focus on the way she talks to Coach. Is that how he knew about the details of my trip?

"Ignore him," Brandon remarks.

"Coach?"

"No, Simpson. Don't let him get under your skin. That's his aim."

"Yeah, but when he says shit like that to my sister, I want to smash his face in." Brandon laughs, but there's a nervousness there that surprises me. "You know I wouldn't, though, right? It's just bro code. While he doesn't respect me, I respect him as a teammate and wouldn't do anything to ruin the team bonding this close to the season starting. Still, I can't help feeling pissed off."

"He pisses me off, too," Brandon mutters.

We hit our knuckles together.

"One week," he says.

"Abu Dhabi, baby." I can't fucking wait to play.

BRANDON THROWS ME THE BALL FRIDAY MORNING, AND I HIT A three-pointer closer to the center circle.

"Keep them coming," I shout. I practice these shots at the end of training to perfect a game-winning shot when the clock is in the dying seconds. The fans think it's luck and their prayers answered, but it's a shot we practice over and over, so when we're under pressure, I'm not relying on the paradox of luck—only the fact I've perfected a pressure shot by practicing it a thousand times before.

I shoot the ball. *Swish.*

"What are your plans tonight?" I ask him before catching the pass. *Swish.*

He pauses before throwing the ball. "None. Just hanging at home."

I clap my hands for the ball, then pause, breathe, and bend deeper at the knees. *Swish.*

"Frank and Penny have asked me to babysit. They think it'll be good for me to get to know my niece."

Brandon's eyes round. "You? Do you know anything about kids?" He passes the ball like a bullet, and if I hadn't caught his pass, it would have broken my nose.

"I've visited a few times. They said Summer would be down for her sleep and just to stay there. She has a bottle prepared in case Summer wakes before they get home."

"Where are they going?"

"To his restaurant. A date night."

Swish.

"Don't they have a nanny or something?"

"Yeah, but Penny is funny about the family getting to know Summer. I'm stoked they asked me before Lottie." I grin at Brandon before taking the next shot. *Twang.* The ball hits the ring and flies back into my hands.

I move under the net, and Brandon finds his spot to shoot.

"Do you want me to come and help out?" He claps his hands for the ball, his knees bent, ready in stance for a quick catch and shoot.

I bounce the ball before passing it to him. "You want to come?"

"Yeah. I could learn a thing or two."

I stare at him like he's grown six heads. "What the actual fuck?"

He laughs. "I'm not doing anything else. We could watch a movie or reruns of the finals from last year."

"The sound would have to be muted unless we watch it in the home theater. That's soundproof. And Gigi might come if that's okay. She stayed extra nights in Italy, so I haven't seen her since Sunday."

"Listen to you sounding all lovesick." He holds out his hands for the ball, and I send a hard pass. He catches it, grins, then shoots. *Swish.* "I'm cool with Gigi coming. She's gonna have to understand all our plays if she's going to the games."

I stare at him. "Yeah."

Giana is not invested in the game like other players' girlfriends and wives. I know she'll support me, but I wonder if she'll ever love the game like a fan.

PENNY HANDS ME A LIST OF WHAT SUMMER NEEDS, AND ONCE I read the first few lines, I stop reading. "I thought you said Summer would sleep the entire time?"

Penny looks at me, then at Brandon, and back to me. "I said I hope she sleeps, but if she doesn't, it's often a process of elimination to figure out why she's crying. It could be hunger pain, so there is breast milk in a bottle in the fridge. Just warm it up. Not too hot... body temperature."

"Eww."

Penny rolls her eyes. "Please. I'm not asking you to drink it."

Brandon chokes out a cough.

"This is good for you boys. It'll be you one day."

"I'll have a nanny," I add quickly.

Penny receives a notification there is someone at the door. She looks at me and checks the security camera. "Oh, it's Giana. You two are saved."

"Thank fuck," I whisper to Brandon. "Next on the list was change her diaper. I'm not ready for that shit yet."

"Literally, mate."

We laugh under our breath, although I know it's

something I'll have to do soon, but at least give me a few months to warm up to it.

"What else is on the list?" Brandon whispers. "Because now Gigi is here, I'm bailing if it involves puke."

I screw up my face. "You're not leaving me alone. What if Gigi has to leave? We work best as a team."

Brandon shakes his blond curls from his eyes. "Mate, you're bloody on your own for that." His phone dings in his pocket.

"Put it on silent. We don't want anything to wake her."

"Hey," Giana says, her brown ponytail swinging as she walks back in with Penny.

"Hey. Welcome home." I lean in to kiss Giana. "I wasn't sure you'd make it."

"I slept a few hours this morning, so I feel okay." She reaches up to hug Brandon. I'm busy admiring her in her white dress scattered with sunflowers. It ends midthigh, showing her shapely, tanned legs, and think I could let Brandon leave if it means Giana and I are alone. Then I remember Penny's list.

"Hey, Gigi. You'll have to tell us the story of how Byron slipped on the cliff."

"What?" She stares at me, bewildered.

Oh fuck.

I make round eyes at Giana. "When we were *rock climbing*... it wasn't bad. My *knees and elbows* suffered the worst damage."

"Oh," Giana says slowly, then shrugs her shoulders. "He slid a couple of feet. He really is being dramatic."

"Serious?" Brandon punches my shoulder playfully.

Penny takes the list from my grip. "I think this is safer with Giana."

"Okay." I hold my hands up in surrender.

She hands the list to Giana and waits for her to read over

it. Giana lifts her head and looks at Penny. "Did you really trust these two with all that?"

Penny shakes her head. "I hope she'll sleep, but if not, I wanted to explain everything. Eventually, I hope Jobe can help out. I want her to be familiar with her uncles' faces."

Penny is trying to bring the family closer, and I respect it. "What about Lottie?"

"She has already babysat three times, and she comes every second night to visit." She does? "I also mentioned to her that you might need help, so expect a phone call. But I wanted you to try first. If you can't manage, Frank and I can come home."

"No," Giana says quickly. "Enjoy your date night."

She checks the time on her cell. "Okay, I should go. Please call me if you need me."

"We'll be fine," Giana reassures Penny, then she waves before closing the door. Giana looks around the kitchen and picks up the gadget from the counter. "This is the monitor. Oh, it has a camera. How cute. We just take this everywhere we go."

"Summer can hear us?" Brandon asks.

"We can hear her if she wakes, and look..." she turns the gadget, "... you can see her sleeping."

"Bloody hidden cameras everywhere," I mutter. "It's so Franklin."

"Sweet. I vote Gigi to be in charge of the monitor. Now let's utilize your brother's big-ass TV and catch a game."

"I'll get us some drinks first." I open the refrigerator, and there is a food platter. "Penny knows us well." I grab the plate and hand it to Brandon, then carry a jug of iced water and glasses up the stairs to their home theater. It's a waste of space in their luxury penthouse with Franklin being so time-poor.

"This is next level," Giana exclaims. She looks around at

the black leather recliner couches, the navy carpet, and the circular overhead lighting.

"Wait till you hear the sound system," Brandon adds.

"Will it wake Summer?"

"Soundproof walls." I jump into the seat beside Brandon, leaving Giana to sit on my other side.

"I'm not watching a game." Giana gives me a look. "How about a nice romantic movie?" She takes my hand and squeezes it. I can't say no to those eyes.

Brandon leans forward in his reclined chair. "You've just *Eat Pray Loved* my friend. He's starting to go soft on me."

"And I agree with Gigi."

We all jump at the sound of the voice behind us.

"Jesus, Lottie, you scared the fuck out of me." I shake my head. I thought it was Penny speaking through one of their hidden cameras. "Did Frank ask you to check in on us?"

Charlotte stands in front of us. "No, but when did you last check on Summer?"

Giana holds up the monitor. "She's sleeping."

"Can I see?" Brandon holds out a hand, and Giana passes him the monitor. Charlotte sits in the chair beside Brandon, and they stare at the monitor together.

"It has sensors for breathing, motion, body temperature, and cough detection," Charlotte whispers, but I doubt Brandon is interested. He places the monitor between us.

"How about an episode of *Friends*," Giana suggests. "It's funny and uplifting."

Finally, we agree, and when the second episode finishes, Charlotte takes the monitor from between Brandon and me. "Fuck, she's crying. Look at her hands moving." She jumps up and fiddles with the monitor, and baby screams fill the room. "You idiots had it on silent." She runs out of the room with us in tow.

Summer is distressed. Her little face is red, and she's croaky.

"She has worked herself into a state." Giana strokes her forehead while Charlotte gently rocks her.

"Penny said she might be hungry or need her diaper changed." I stand back, as the last thing the kid needs is all four of us in her face, gawking.

Brandon retrieves her pacifier from the crib and encourages her to suck.

I shake my head. "For something so little, she has a good pair of lungs."

"Wait up." Brandon goes and fetches the backpack he takes everywhere with him.

Charlotte places her on the changing table and checks her diaper. "Her nappy is fine."

"I could warm up her milk," Giana suggests.

Brandon returns, takes the pacifier, and—

"What the fuck, man. What are you thinking?" I stand in front of Brandon and Summer. "You can't give that to her."

"Trust me. My mum has given it to me and my sisters and brothers. It works great."

"What is it?" Giana asks.

He walks past me and stands beside Charlotte, who looks as distressed as Summer. "Penny and Franklin have already had a heated debate about whether Summer should have a pacifier. If she reacts to Vegemite, they'll never trust us again."

"Lottie, trust me," he says gently.

"It tastes like tar off the road," I tell Giana.

Her eyes pop, and she stares at Charlotte. "For real?"

"Not to me." Brandon tickles her lips with the pacifier.

I am baffled why Charlotte doesn't push Brandon away. She is hardcore about doing everything right. Knowing Penny and Franklin will be infuriated, her allowing him to give Summer something surprises me. Wondering what has changed for her, I'm stuck in the moment and haven't noticed the silence.

"Bloody hell, mate, it worked," Charlotte says, ribbing Brandon's accent.

"Told ya." He leans a hand on her shoulder as he stares down at Summer, who is sucking away and falling back to sleep.

"You two should go," Charlotte whispers. "Frank and Penny will be home soon."

Giana looks at me with beckoning eyes. I know that look and would rather be alone with her than here when Franklin gets home, and Brandon tells him he gave his kid freaking Vegemite.

"Do you need a ride?" I ask Brandon.

He looks at Charlotte, then back at me. "I'll stay with Lottie. If Summer wakes again, I'd best tell Franklin what I did."

"Risking your life, man." I tap his shoulder and take Giana's hand as we head down the stairs.

"So... kids," she murmurs before we reach the door. "Do you want them?"

21

GIANA

One week later...

"CAN WE PLEASE ORDER ANOTHER BOTTLE," PAIGE ASKS THE server in her politest posh voice to disguise the number of drinks she has already consumed. Paige tidies her hair when he leaves, then looks around the table. "One more bottle."

"We've had three already," I add.

"I like this side of you," Jessica says. It's been years since I hung out with Jessica, and tonight, she is fun. Not as amusing as Paige. "But girl, I am not holding no puke bag on the ride home."

I giggle. "If it comes to that, I'll be your wing girl."

"Wing girl?" Jessica says with round eyes, her long fake lashes touching her brow. "Too late if she's already crashed and burned." We laugh together.

Tonight has been fun and exactly what I needed. With

Byron in Abu Dhabi for preseason games, I have spent most days at home, painting and spending valuable time with my parents. This is the second time Paige and I have caught up this week, and when she suggested a girls' night out, I screamed with excitement.

"So, how is life with a famous NBA player?" Jessica asks.

"It's fun with Byron. He's different. As for the fame part, we don't go out much, so I don't really see the fans."

"I heard he's boring now because he is so focused on the game."

"Who told you that?" Paige pipes up.

"He's not boring at all." I wink before turning to Jessica. "He has always been focused on basketball, even at school, so I guess he hasn't changed in that regard. He's... calmer. He trusts his intuition and doesn't care what other people do or think. He has his routine, and I've never met a more disciplined person. I am not that person..." I admit, smiling at her, "... but life is good with Byron."

Paige stares goggle-eyed at me. "You're a cute couple."

The waiter tops up our flutes, the liquid bubbles making us giggly. "I never expected to settle into life with Byron as easily as I have after coming home. When I first came back, I made a list of rules and decided to avoid him because I had sworn off his type for life. But he was persistent and... sweet."

Jessica smiles at me. "I'm really happy for you." She turns to Paige, who is already downing her drink. "I like that you all get to hang out together and do couple dates. I want that too. Anyone would think I was doing a dick detox."

Paige and I giggle. "Byron doesn't get to do much socializing, and now the season has started, I expect to see even less of him. Not a bad thing, as I have paintings to finish."

"So you're staying?" Jessica asks. "You're not returning to Italy?"

Paige slurs her words. "She bought a new car, so yeah, she is staying. An Alfa Romeo, baby."

I grin at Paige. "Part of my heart is still there, but I'm not going anywhere for now. I'm not sure how long, whether it's months or years. While I can spend time with my parents, especially my father, I'll only make short trips back to Italy."

Jessica holds up her purse, the fabric printed with one of my designs. "I bought this online and love it. You're extremely talented, Giana."

"Thank you." Heat rises to my cheeks. Jessica has never commended me on my work, and it means a lot. "Please, if either of you like the designs, tell me as I can get it significantly cheaper. It's the least I can do for my friends."

Jessica picks up her crystal flute and clinks it with mine. "Cheers to all the Leto Designs coming our way."

"Now drink," Paige says. She is sitting next to Jessica. Paige holds a finger on the base of the glass, forcing Jessica to down her champagne. "Keep going. Keep up the pace." She tilts the glass higher. Jessica's eyes pop with Paige force-feeding her. "Gurrll, don't waste it." She wipes the sides of Jessica's mouth. "This stuff isn't free."

I'm laughing. I can't remember laughing this much in months.

"Whoa," Jessica utters as she catches her breath. She lets out a burp that she tries to hold in, and we crack up at the weird animal noise that bubbles out of her throat.

Paige is still giggling as she refills our glasses. "Mason and I are talking about moving in together." At first, she sounds dismissive, but then her face sags and she downs a few mouthfuls of her drink. Finally, some answers to her behavior. We should order more food, or I'll be on puke duty for Paige.

"That's a good thing, right?" I say, signaling to the waiter.

She downs the rest of her glass. "So why am I scared?" She places her glass on the table and looks to us for answers.

"I think it's natural to be afraid. It's the next step in our lives, where we go from making decisions that are right for us to making decisions that are best for both of you."

"Right." She tops up her drink, then places the bottle back in the ice bucket. Something isn't right.

"Is it what you want, Paige?"

"Yes, but I'm not ready for babies."

Jessica splutters her drink. "That went from zero to ten. Are you pregnant?"

"Nooo," she groans. "Mason wants to get married and have kids, like yesterday."

"Then talk to him and say you want to slow it down. Move in together and enjoy each other first. Mason is the opposite to Byron. When I quizzed him about the future and kids, not that I want any yet, he looked like he'd seen his dead grandmother rise from the grave."

"See, I'm on the same page as him," Paige agrees.

Jessica turns to me. "What did Byron say?"

"Maybe in the future." I shrug. "It was a big maybe, but to be fair, we were babysitting his new niece, and he was spooked."

"I saw photos on Penny's Insta. She's sooo cute." Paige swoons.

"Paige, when the time is right, you'll make a great mom."

"Until then..." Jessica adds, "... I vote for more girls' nights."

We clink our glasses again.

Jessica peers over the rim of her glass. "Tell me about BJ. Byron and he are close, yeah?"

"They are. They met in college and have been friends

ever since. He's from Australia, so the Hendricks kind of adopted him."

"Single?"

Oh shit. How do I say he's unavailable without saying who he's with, as they know *I would* know, and yet his best friend has no clue.

"We went to his condo recently and hung out with him and a few of the players," Paige remarks as though it's nothing. "We watched a big game of Aussie football. I didn't understand much, but Lottie filled me in. She seems to know a lot about the game."

"Right." I look nervously at Jessica, then back to Paige. "She loves sports and is a lot like Byron."

"I didn't stay long. I left Mason and went shopping. He was in his element with all the players around him."

I let out a long, silent breath. "I prefer shopping to sports, so if I were there, I could have accompanied you."

Paige slurs her words. "But to answer your question, Jess, I don't think he is with anyone."

FOR THE PAST FEW YEARS, MY SATURDAY NIGHTS HAVE BEEN about wine, pizza, and late-night festivities. Tonight, I'm sitting in the VIP seats at the LA Sharks' sell-out home game —the first of the regular season.

Byron's parents are behind me. I've had little time to speak to his mother, and yet she has already invited me to their house for Thanksgiving. It's a kind offer, yet I'd prefer to have Thanksgiving with my parents, then visit the Hendricks later.

Sensing someone is staring, I turn and sneak a glance. Jobe gives me a nod. His eyes are serious, and I can't help but feel like he is assessing me. I understand he is looking out for his brother, but I am already nervous about being here, so I return my gaze to the front.

I'm sitting on the aisle seat, and Charlotte is next to me, Franklin and Penny on her other side. They got sitters for the game. I overhear Franklin and Penny discussing player matchups while the cheerleaders entertain.

The loud pump-up music ramps up, along with the lights. It's entertainment at an A-list level. Flashing lights shine erratically over the crowd, and my eyes are pulled to the circular multiscreen scoreboard high over the court. One of the screens shows the players in the tunnel, jumping and bouncing off each other as they mentally prepare themselves for the game. Then the players run out onto the court as screams and cheers echo around the arena.

"Good evening, and welcome to the home of the LA Sharks." The announcer continues to talk about player histories and the coaches and staff, and the cheers continue, but my gaze is stuck on Byron.

He is in the zone, his own bubble of concentration. I doubt he hears anything as he bounces up and down, runs fast on the spot, crouches low, then springs into a jump. When the announcer stops, he grabs the balls and bounces two at a time while focusing on something in the distance. He jabs and moves while his team gathers around the coach. Once the coach finishes, the team starts to take their positions. Looking up into the crowd, his intense gaze finds mine. He jogs over, up a few stairs, and kisses me, his lips lingering.

"Good luck," I whisper. There's a hint of a smile before he turns and bounces down the stairs to regroup with his team.

Charlotte nudges me. "Told you this will be his new routine before every game. Best book your flights now."

But what if I'm not here? I have an upcoming trip to Italy for Austin Cisterna's new movie. And then there's Isabella's new offer, which I have to consider without declining on instinct. Surely, after all his hard work, a little superstition of my absence won't affect his performance.

It's not a concern for tonight—the game is edge-of-your-seat fast, and we come away with a win.

The following morning, after sleeping at Byron's, I park my new Alfa Romeo in the garage beside Mom's Mercedes. Her car is now ten years old, yet still in pristine condition. I can't help worrying about their future, what with Dad retiring early and all their finances dropping significantly. Thankfully, Dad had good insurance, but it's a matter of time before he'll need better supervision, especially at night if he gets confused and wanders. With an uncertain future, I understand why Mom wants me to take every opportunity possible to advance my career. More than ever, I need to be financially independent and continue with new contracts to help my parents with their health insurance and my dad's ongoing needs.

"Morning," I say to my mother, who is prepping food in the kitchen.

Mom turns around. "How was your night, love?"

"Great. Byron won, and he mentioned getting Dad and you tickets to the next game. He thinks Dad would enjoy it." Mom doesn't look excited. "Only if you want to go."

This time, her eyes crinkle when she smiles. "We would, but the noise might scare your father. It could make him anxious and more confused."

"Or it could be a great night for him. There is a special glassed room if sitting in the VIP section could be too much.

The noise is dulled, but you can see everything, and it's private, away from the crowd."

"Byron offered to do that?"

"Yes. He's thoughtful, Mom."

She ponders my words. "I'll talk to your father first."

"Of course."

"Are you going to tell Byron about your offer to return to Italy?"

I sense my brow tightening. "Not today. I'll wait until after the next game." They travel to Boston, and Byron believes their guard has an edge over him in an away game. It's not like Byron to admit someone is better than him. He is all about the win.

She turns to the kitchen window to keep a watchful eye on my father puttering in the garden.

Before I take the stairs to change my dress, I stall, thinking about my dad. "Does he garden all year round? Even on the coldest days?" I should know this about him. While he did when he was younger as gardening was like therapy, even when I was at school, I'm concerned for his health. His immunity has weakened.

"I try to keep him indoors, but it's like caging him from what he loves. So, we often go out and sit and watch the rain with a throw over our knees."

I think about their simple life together. Happy to just be as long as they have one another. I find it hard to imagine Byron and me at their age, content watching the rain. It's hard to imagine Byron ever slowing down with his endless energy.

"I don't want you worrying about us. We'll be fine," Mom adds.

I want to believe her. I head upstairs to paint until Byron finishes practice.

An hour later, Mom comes into my studio. "It's beautiful, Giana. You really do have a gift."

"Thank you, Mom." I dab color on the canvas. "It's almost complete, though Isabella demanded another five designs."

"You'll be fine, my sweet girl." She places a gentle hand on my shoulder. Why do I get the notion there is more to her words than the pressure of a deadline? She squeezes my shoulder. "Wherever you are in the world, we'll support you."

"And if I decide to stay... for me." Not for Byron or my parents. "What if LA is where I'm supposed to be to expand my business?"

"As long as you make the decision that's in your best interest, for you *and* your career, how can I tell you otherwise? All I've ever wanted is for you to have the chances I never got. I wish I got to spend time in Italy... explore my roots. It's my one last regret."

"It's never too late, Mom."

She pats my shoulder, but her eyes tell me otherwise. "I'll leave you to paint."

Her silence speaks volumes.

Time. Regret. Choices. Is she telling me to go? I lied about staying in LA for me. My heart beats fast when I think about telling Byron I'm returning to Italy for a year or two with only short trips home. Could we manage a long-distance love? My stomach churns, already knowing the answer.

22

BYRON

BEFORE ARRIVING AT MY PARENTS' house, my mother warned me they were going all out this year and making it special. Every year, there is an abundance of food, so I wasn't sure what Mom had planned until now.

Seated at the table beside Brandon, his open mouth tells me he is equally stunned as we read the menu on the table.

Main
Whole turkey with seafood bread stuffing (Alaskan king crab, Maine lobster, Southern Bluefin tuna otoro, and golden caviar from the Caspian Sea),
seasoned with imported saffron and spices and covered in edible gold flakes

Sides
Candied sweet potatoes and butternut squash seasoned with spices from India

Caramelized onions with spices from Egypt

Sauces
Cranberry sauce with Sembikiya Queen strawberries and
dekopon citrus from Japan
Asparagus vinaigrette with Pappy Van Winkle Family Reserve
Bourbon
Gravy infused with Louis XIII Cognac

Dessert
Pumpkin and pecan pies with apple and coconut custard

"Jesus," I mutter under my breath to Brandon. "We'll need to train five times a day to be ready for our next game."

"In three days, we'll still be over the limit to drive," he whispers as Dad stands with Franklin's favorite bottle of Michter's whiskey.

"Byron," Dad says in his deep, authoritarian voice. "Would you like a glass?"

Is this a test? I always feel it is with him being the controlling owner of our basketball team. "No thanks. I'll stick with water."

"Brandon?"

"No thanks, Mr. Hendricks."

"Lola, could you please bring in some iced water?" Mom asks and smiles at me. She stands at the table and reaches for Dad's hand. "We're so happy you can all be here to join our family for a very special Thanksgiving, our first as grandparents." She looks at Penny's parents and smiles. Her parents have been part of our Thanksgiving for the past four years. "We decided to make it a special one to celebrate, even though Summer is sleeping."

"She didn't last night," Franklin says under his breath,

and Penny elbows him. I grin at Penny across the table from me. She keeps Franklin real.

"After talking to Lacey..." she looks at Penny's mom, "... we decided next year we'll have a smaller lunch after we volunteer at a soup kitchen." Mom looks at her, pride shining in her eyes.

Say what? My mother working in a soup kitchen—

"While I enjoy fundraising and the galas, Lacey has shown me the benefits of helping other charities, especially those that support the homeless. I hope you all can join us for a few hours next year before coming home to be truly thankful for our blessings."

"Wow," Jobe murmurs. "I never thought I'd see the day you would fundraise without being in a ballgown and bling. I'm proud of you, Mom." He stands and rounds the table to hug her. One by one, we all stand, too, rounding the table to hug Mom, Dad, and Penny's parents.

"Oh please, you'll make me cry and mess my makeup," Mom says as she hugs us. We return to our seats, and I note the extra seats at the end of the table. She never mentioned any other visitors.

"Let us pray," she whispers. We link hands since Mom has always asked this of us. I regret sitting next to Brandon as I hold his sweaty hand. "Lord, thank you for all the blessings you grant us every day. May you bless this food, and may it nourish and sustain us and strengthen our hearts and minds to do your work. Thank you for surrounding us with family and friends and for guiding us toward gratitude today and every day. Amen."

"Amen."

Lola serves the food. "Lola, we can manage. Please, you and Sergio should join us and enjoy the meal."

Lola looks stunned, though she is not as surprised as me. After working with us for as long as I can remember, even when I was a child, Lola and our chef, Sergio, have never sat with us. Penny's parents' thrifty and charitable lifestyle seems to have influenced my parents. She has no idea how happy this makes me. It offers me hope that next year, Giana's parents could be sitting here at the table with my family.

Jobe left Thanksgiving early, saying he had work.

"I should also go." I stand from my chair in the sitting room. Franklin and Dad have had their fill of whiskey, and the conversation has shifted to the stock market.

I say my goodbyes, and Mom walks me to the front entrance. We stand in the foyer under her chandelier. She hugs me tight before leaning back and staring into my eyes. I know this look. She always gives it right before she lectures us on life.

"I'm proud of you, Byron."

Okay, maybe not a lecture.

"Thanks, Mom."

"I am, and I'm extremely happy you are going to take some time to spend with Giana's family."

"I... didn't say I was."

"It's written all over your face." She looks lovingly at me. "She is good for you."

I grin. "I could be good for her."

She smiles, the creases deepening around her eyes. "I'm sure you are. Don't fight this, son. Roll with whatever challenges are handed out. No relationship is easy, and both of you must give and take equally." *Does she know something I don't?* "We don't get to choose who our heart loves, and I've noticed you are invested in this relationship."

I give my mother a questioning look.

"Dropping everything to rush to her side in Italy? Volunteering to miss a game of basketball is unheard of for you, yet you did it without thinking, for her." Who has she been talking to? "And the idea of purchasing your own jet..." She grins at me. "I love your passion." *Penny.* "It reminds me of your father when we first met. He was quite the romantic." *I can't imagine it.* "Promise me you'll treat this like you do basketball. When it gets tough, don't give up. Be better. Think smarter. It's the best way to navigate a relationship."

I lean in and kiss her. "Thank you." Before I open the door, my mother speaks again.

"I think she's the one, Byron."

My hand freezes on the handle. I turn and give my mother a look, failing to hide the fear of knowing it could be true. Not that I don't want it to be. More that it is true, and there is a chance I could lose her again.

23

GIANA

BYRON PROMISED he would visit after his family's Thanksgiving dinner.

When I heard the knock, my heart thumped in my chest. Why am I nervous? He has met my family and is no stranger to my house. I don't need to pretend with him. This is the first time he has visited on Thanksgiving, and it speaks volumes he would leave his fancy family to visit mine.

I spring from the table to answer the door. Looking through the peephole, I suck in a breath. *He is wearing a freaking suit.* I'm not used to seeing him dressed like this, yet with all his family functions and outings, he would have a collection of designer suits. I yank the door open, then lean against the jamb and stare at him. "You are a very handsome man, Byron Hendricks."

He steps closer to me, his gaze holding mine. "Is that so?"

"Mm-hmm." I eye his fancy navy suit, white shirt, and

pale-pink tie as I imagine what Thanksgiving at his home would be like. "Come here." I undo his tie and slide it off, then loosen the first three buttons on his shirt. "That's more like it."

"And what do you intend to do with my tie?" he says in his best toe-curling sexy voice.

"I'll give you one clue." I wrap the tie around one wrist as I look up into his eyes. He pulls me into his arms and kisses me.

"Giana Monroe. You drive me crazy." He kisses me like there is no tomorrow—only today, this minute, this second.

I wrap my arms around his neck, arch my pelvis to his, and grind against him. He lifts me into his arms and carries me through the door, his lips still on mine. "That's the only way I was getting inside," he murmurs against my lips. "Otherwise, I'd carry you to my car."

I giggle and jump out of his arms, my hands still looped around his neck. "Did I tell you how much I love that you're here?"

He flashes a smile. "Did I hear you say the *L* word?"

I playfully hit his chest. "I love that you're here. Love you in a fancy suit." I waggle my eyebrows.

"And?" He pulls me into his side and nibbles my ear. "What else?"

I haven't told him those three words, although I'm sure he knows how I feel about him. I wanted the first time I say it to him to be special, yet every second I get to spend with Byron feels special. I take his face in my hands and pull his lips to mine. "I like you."

He embraces the humor, wrapping his arms tightly around my waist and pushing his crotch into mine with a single thrust. "You're using me for sex."

I giggle like a horny teenager. Blame Mom's cognac.

"Come and say hi to my parents." I take Byron's hand and lead him into the kitchen, where we are serving dessert.

"Happy Thanksgiving," Mom says to Byron. He goes to her and gives her a hug. "You look very handsome today."

"Just today, ma'am?" he jokes. He moves to my father, now standing by his chair. "Happy Thanksgiving, Mr. Monroe."

"Happy Thanksgiving, son." The way Dad says son makes my stomach flip. I can see in his eyes he likes Byron. He covers his top hand so he has both hands on Byron's, and it almost brings me to tears.

Mom seems more reserved about her feelings for Byron. She wants what's best for me, and mostly wants me to explore my career choices in Italy. She hasn't said it, but I sense she feels Byron will hold me back emotionally. Dad has flipped the situation, showing Byron his support. I move behind Dad and wrap my arms around his middle to lean my head on his shoulder. "I love you, Dad."

Byron leans close to my father. "You know she hasn't told me that yet."

I lift my head and eye Byron. "Do not make me look like the bad person here," I say, half joke, half serious.

"I think someone has had too much to drink," Mom says with a laugh.

"Wait for the right time, son." Dad winks at Byron. *Winks.*

"Okay, let's eat dessert," I suggest, and sit next to Mom. Byron sits beside my father on the other side of the table.

"I hope you all had an enjoyable Thanksgiving," he says on a more serious note.

"We did, thank you, Byron. And we have Giana's new contract to be grateful for. The Lord is blessing her in so many ways."

Fucking hell. I glare at Mom.

"We do. But as I told you, I'm not sure I'm going to accept it."

"New business is always good," Byron suggests. "You have to accept it, Gi."

I twist in my seat to meet his gaze. "It's a contract to remain in Italy for the next season. Maybe two," I say, hearing the quiver in my voice.

"Season? Like spring and summer?"

"No. When Isabella talks seasons, she means years."

Byron stares down at his pumpkin pie and twirls the spoon. "I see." He looks at Mom, then at me. "If it's what you need to do for your career, then you have to do it."

"I told you he would understand," Mom adds. "Byron, you would do the same if it was your career, right?"

I am so angry with Mom right now.

"Without a second thought," he rasps out, his eyes boring into mine.

I scan his beautiful face, his blue eyes framed with long dark lashes. I see hurt there but also understanding. I take his hand and squeeze it. "We were chatting about my travel commitments before you arrived," I say to him. "I need to return this weekend. The movie's release has been moved forward. It'll be for a couple of weeks."

Byron stares at me, his expression unreadable. If I knew what he was thinking—

"Do you remember us talking about the Italian movie and the film stars wearing Leto Designs? That now includes my latest prints. Isabella believes the film stars wearing designs before they are marketed to the public will be the best promotion for our new lines."

He slowly nods as though absorbing what I'm telling him. "I agree. It's a great marketing plan."

Mom serves Byron another piece of pie. "We're all proud of you, Giana."

He glances at me and forces a smile before shoving a spoonful of pie in his mouth.

"Did you have turkey for dinner, Byron?" Mom asks. Why didn't she ask these questions first and allow me to ease into the subject of Italy?

"Yes, ma'am, and a few sides. I declined dessert as I promised Gigi I would eat with your family."

"And we appreciate you being here." She places a spoonful of pie into her mouth. "Our day was good. The weather is still nice enough to sit outside. I'm not looking forward to winter."

"You would hate Italian winters, then," I say to Mom. "It's colder than LA."

"And hotter. Well, more humid in summer," Byron adds.

I hold back a grin, remembering how hot my villa was, especially without power.

The night continues with more and more chitchat, and I regret telling Byron about Italy on a day that's meant to be about gratitude. The mood in the room has dulled, and Mom's small talk makes it worse.

At around eight thirty, Byron stands. "Thank you for a lovely evening. I'm sorry to leave, but I have an early training session tomorrow."

I walk Byron to the front door. "Do you want me to come home with you?"

He takes both my hands in his and stares at our linked fingers. "I am happy for you, Giana." He looks up, and our eyes lock. "I need an early night. Coach has been kicking my ass since I took off to Italy without permission." *What?* "I can't risk further distraction. Enjoy your trip, and we'll catch up when you get back."

We have more time together. I don't leave until Saturday.

"What are you doing tomorrow after training?"

"BJ and I are teaching ball skills to kids in the schools

program. Now that the season has started, we have even more external commitments as players."

"Tomorrow night?"

"Training. Then it's game day on Saturday."

I should know this. I let go of his hand and cup his cheek. "This is not the end of us. It's a work commitment. I hope you understand."

He leans down and kisses my cheek. "Safe travels, Gigi."

24

BYRON

AFTER TRAINING ON SUNDAY MORNING, Simpson ribs Brandon about some chick. His head snaps toward me, his eyes wide like a fucking deer about to be crushed by a truck.

What did I miss?

Brandon and I were no angels when it came to girls. The past six months, though, something seems to have clicked. While I never swore off girls, Giana came into my life at the right time. I wanted security, something safe, and I understand my oldest brother wanting to be in a relationship rather than having one-night stands. It calms your world.

Brandon hasn't mentioned anyone special, but as far as I'm aware, he hasn't been looking. This was always going to be the year we were one hundred percent focused on basketball. This year, we want a damn championship ring.

"What the fuck are you on about, Simpson?" Giana is away, and I'm tense. All I can think about is that dickwad ex being around her. I'm not in the mood for Simpson's bullshit.

Simpson pulls a weird face—one that screams *You don't know shit*. I look at Brandon, and he shakes his head.

"He doesn't know, does he?" Simpson bursts out laughing. "Man, BJ is going down tonight."

I stare at Brandon. "What the fuck is going on?"

I'm pissed Simpson knows something about my best friend before me. Brandon and I tell each other everything. We started college together, and I took him under my wing as a freshman. With his family so far away in Australia, he stays at my house more than he goes back home. He is part of my family, and I'm closer to him than any of my family except for Charlotte. But the last two years, she's wanted to break my balls for any little thing I do to step so much as a toe out of line, so yeah, I'm probably even closer to him than Charlotte.

Simpson coughs, "Charlotte," then practically sprints out of the locker room. The guy has always been a jerk. I'd rather play a full game with a raccoon on crack than be on the court for a minute with him. I turn, expecting my sister to be walking into the room, but it's just Brandon and me.

"What's that dickwad on about?"

Brandon drops his bag to his feet and raises both hands before they fall to his side again. "We wanted to tell you together..."

"Huh? Tell me what?"

He bows his head, unable to look at me.

"What the fuck is wrong with you?"

He lifts his chin and meets my gaze directly. *Christ, who died?*

"Lottie and I are together."

What? "How do you mean?"

"We've been seeing each other a while now."

The fuck? I clench my fists as a ball of anger grows in my chest. Every muscle in my jaw tightens, and I'm unable to speak. I clench my teeth, picturing my *best fucking friend* with my sister in ways I can't erase from my memory because *I know* the sort of thing my friend likes when it comes to sex. He's bragged about it. And now he's with my fucking *sister*? Both have lied to me. Not to mention, he has broken the code that I took seriously. *Family is off-limits.* They took him in, and he took advantage of our friendship.

"You fucker," I grind out.

I push him, and he stumbles back. I shove him harder, and his hands remain by his sides, even as he stumbles. He bows his head again so his blond curls hide his face.

"I know you hate me right now."

"You have no fucking clue," I yell.

I'm trembling with anger. The one thing I can't stand is being lied to. I feel like I just lost my best friend.

Slowly, he lifts his gaze. "I wanted to talk to you alone, but Lottie said we should do it together."

I shake my head. Either way, I still would have been majorly pissed. How had I not known? There were no hints he ever liked her. At times, she was a freaking bitch to him like she is to me. "Fuck!" I spin around, trying to breathe. I turn back and glare at him. "Did this start when you were both in Australia?"

"We became closer then, but the first time was three years ago when we were in college." My eyes want to pop out of my fucking head. "We had a few nights together over the years, but things recently ramped up."

"And you never had the decency to tell me."

"Because I thought you'd react like this." His eyes are full of apology. "I love her."

I see red. I give him one final shove, then collect my bag and storm out of the locker room.

Giana... fuck Italy.

If I ever needed a sounding board for my frustrations, I'd go to Charlotte. The person I'd usually turn to is the one Brandon is banging. I inhale a sharp breath, trying to calm the fuck down. I have never liked surprises, and this one takes the fucking cake.

Inside my car, I hit the accelerator and drive toward the city. There is one person who could calm me down, and it's been a few weeks since I've seen my new little niece.

"Hey, Siri, send a message to Franklin."

"What do you want to say?"

"Please tell me you're home. I'm on my way to yours."

EVEN THOUGH IT'S SUNDAY, FRANKLIN SITS IN HIS FAVORITE armchair in designer trousers and a white shirt. He swirls whiskey around the ice in his glass and crosses his legs, revealing his black leather Gucci loafers. There's no mistaking his billions. Every inch of him is clothed by famous designers, including his Harry's of London over-the-calf socks.

"I'm lost what to do. Frustrated and..." I run my fingers through my hair. I don't mention Brandon and Charlotte. "Why do I feel like I'm at a crossroads?"

"Hmm. Penny mentioned your impromptu trip to Italy."

I lean back on the wide white leather lounge chair. "I'm not suggesting I rush over to see Giana again."

"Absolutely not," Franklin agrees. "The way you assess or see something before deciding on an outcome depends on what you believe. Our subconscious sifts information, and we receive it in a biased way based on our fears and beliefs. It's why I might view and react to a situation differently than you. Sometimes, we need to redefine our process of thinking or overthinking a situation. Change our pattern—"

Penny walks into the room with Summer in her arms. "In other words, you're in love and don't know how to handle it." She offers an understanding smile. Her gentle green eyes make me feel better about being here. "We all go through it. Make decisions we regret, make fools of ourselves. Did I ever tell you about Frank and my previous roommate?"

"This is not the time for storytelling, Penny."

The way Franklin snaps has me wanting to hear it.

She giggles. "Stark naked with a sheet around his head and his package hanging out."

What?

My shocked expression causes Franklin to down his drink. "Now is not the time."

"I think it is," I goad. I look to Penny for more information.

"Perhaps Frank will share his stories, including the one that happened at my parents' house, with you another time. My point is, don't be afraid to be guided by your heart. Not everything we do in life needs to be calculated and with a desired outcome." She rolls her eyes at her husband, as this is how my brother has always lived his life. "And, more the point, you all think Frank is a perfectionist and that is how he won me over. He's not perfect, and his mistakes and admittance of his bad judgment is why I gave him a second chance."

Frank raises his glass to his wife. "You still found me irresistible."

Penny glances down at her daughter and rocks her gently in her arms. "I did. Yet I was wise enough not to let your charm sway my decision in breaking up with you." *Jesus, I wasn't expecting this conversation.* "But your vulnerability at Hugh's wedding made me see how you were willing to change. You showed me that you were willing to be flexible with all the things that were nonnegotiable in your life when it came to me. And now I know nothing in your life is more important than Summer and me." She smiles lovingly at Franklin. He stands, closes the distance, and kisses her, then tentatively kisses Summer on the cheek. He stands behind his wife and looks at me.

"Take everything Penny said and apply it to your life."

"How?" It's why I'm here.

Penny tilts her head at me. "What is nonnegotiable for you, Byron? While I never asked Frank to give up his work or international travel, I asked for him to be flexible with it and to prove that I mean something to him and not to put his work first *all the time*. To be there when I needed him."

"Basically, to stop being a selfish asshole." I grin at Penny.

"Right. But I think all Hendricks have the selfish asshole gene."

Franklin perks up. "Excuse me?"

"Not in a bad way. It's why you're all determined and successful. It takes a special person to succeed, and you need to be a little selfish to achieve the highest of goals."

"What she is saying..." Franklin says casually, "... is we have what it takes, so go get the job done."

25

BYRON

It's the last home game before Christmas. I'm not looking forward to being on the road when Giana returns home.

In the VIP section, Penny's father is on one side of Franklin and Penny is on the other. Her mother is home with Summer. Franklin meets my gaze and gives me the nod. I don't miss the seriousness in his eyes on getting the win. One step closer to making finals. Yet my thoughts shift to his life and his happiness of being with Penny and part of her family. Mom and Dad sit in the row behind him, clapping and chanting with the fans. Charlotte sits beside Jobe. She isn't looking at me. Her focus is on the guy who I haven't spoken to in weeks except for what I need to say at training to keep Coach satisfied.

This season, Giana has been here for our winning home games. When she was away, we lost. I'm not predicting a loss tonight, as I have my eye on the prize of a championship ring, and I'm damn focused on making the top four. But before those winning games, I ran up to her in the stands and kissed her, and she whispered *Good luck*, and it was like she was my lucky charm. Giana is more than luck before a game. Her presence gives me confidence and more drive to win. I stare at the empty seat where she sits beside Charlotte.

Jye calls my name right before the ball hurls toward me. "C'mon, man. Do your thing."

Spinning the ball on the floor until it bounces back into my hands, I drive toward the basket. It takes two bounces to get me into the paint, and I dunk. The fans cheer. It may be the warm-up, but they love to see our skills. And after the extra plyometric training, my leap has improved. They'll see more of that in the game.

Coach calls us in. Brandon and I pull off our warm-up clothes.

I jump up and down. Side to side. High knees for five seconds.

I am ready.

"If Byron is smothered or they double-team him, then BJ, you take the point."

The fuck? Brandon isn't a point guard. He now plays a two or three position. What happened to Dwayne? He's my backup guard. I catch the tic in Dwayne's jaw. I flick my fingers in and out. Clench my fist, unclench. Flick, flick, flick. I roll my neck and stare at the scoreboard, visualizing the win.

"Let's do this," I yell.

"Hands in." Coach is beside me.

"Give 'em hell, Byron."

"Yeah!" I bounce up and down. "We got this. We got this."

Jye wins the tap, and Brandon leaps and grabs it. Before his feet land, he tosses the ball my way as I have sprinted toward the ring. I jump, catch it, two fast bounces, and I slam the ball into the basket.

The crowd roars with excitement.

"Six seconds, baby," I call out. Six seconds to get our first goal. I point to Jye, then to Brandon, and nod, clapping my hands. It's their goal as much as mine.

After that, the game remains tight.

By the end of the quarter, we lead by three.

At halftime, we are up by four.

Coach roasts us in the locker room.

I wipe my face with a towel. Something is off. Fatigue is setting in far too quickly. I shift my mindset and listen to what Coach tells us.

I got this. This is a win.

"Byron, if Jye spins to the basket and takes Kirk out of the paint, then give him the fucking ball. With Kirk out of the picture, no defense will stop Jye."

"Got it."

We head out to the court, jog past the screaming fans, and prepare ourselves for the next half.

"I'll give you a minute's rest soon," Coach tells me. Usually, I only need a minute, but today, I hope for extra time on the bench *if* we are winning.

Brandon makes the first two baskets in the third quarter, giving us a lead of eight points. If I can make a couple of three-pointers, it should mess with the Wolves' thoughts.

I bring the ball down the court, dribbling past competitors as though it's nothing more than a training drill. I yell out Brandon and Simpson. Instead, I pull up and take the three.

Swish.

I hold my hand in the air a little longer, eyeballing Stiner, my opponent. "Where were you, Stiner? Where were you?"

He ignores me, pushes off my shoulder, and leads for the ball. I stay with him, low in a defensive stance, placing extra pressure on him until he makes a crap pass. His teammate fumbles the ball, and it falls out of court.

I clap hard as I walk toward him, grinning and mocking.

Simpson scoops up the ball and stands off the sideline, ready to make the pass. Stiner gets up in my face, trying to deny me the ball. I get a break, and Simpson lands the ball a good distance in front to stop Stiner from intercepting the pass. I keep the momentum going and stride down the court, leaving Stiner in my wake.

Brandon claps his hands, demanding the ball.

I see him in my peripheral vision, although I'm focused on Jye, waiting for him to spin off Kirk and lead toward the key, all while I'm protecting the ball, dribbling and jab-stepping around my opponent, waiting for the ideal moment to pass. I'm not ignoring Brandon. It's the play Coach wants. Yet Brandon is yelling at me for the ball.

Simpson jogs past me and yells, "To BJ."

Realizing Jye can't shake Kirk off, I switch the ball to the other hand to pass to Brandon, but in a split second, Jye breaks free and rolls toward the paint. Caught in the momentum, I twist to give the ball to Jye. My opponent runs at me, leaping into the air to block my pass. I push off my left leg to leap higher—

Pop.

My knees buckle as my leg gives way. He lands on me with a heavy thud before I have aligned my body. I fall awkwardly, but his foot lands on mine, his knee jabbing into the side of my leg, and my ankle inverts.

Snap.

I fall to the hardwood.

"Fuuucckk."

Agonizing pain shoots up my leg. I roll onto my side. *No,*

no, no. I grab my shoe. My hands clamp around my ankle and heel, where it burns. *No, fucking no.* I slam my hand onto the hardwood.

"Jesus."

The umpire blows his whistle to stop the game. I look up at the scoreboard.

Thank fuck Jye made the shot.

Holding my leg out straight, I scramble backward to get off the court. The doctor runs around the court and drops to his knees.

"Where is your pain, Byron?"

"My heel and ankle. I heard a pop, then a snap."

He meets my gaze, his face showing no emotion, and I can't gauge what he is thinking.

"I think it's just a sprain," I gamble. "Strap me up, and I'll be right for the last quarter."

"We'll get you to my room, and I'll assess you there."

The medical staff has gathered around me. They heave me upright, and four of them carry me around the court. Cameras flash in my face. The applause is deafening. Pushing through the pain, I clench my jaw to wave and smile, projecting determination to return to the court.

Charlotte appears, walking briskly alongside the doctor. I bite my tongue before I say something sarcastic. She speaks quietly to the doc, flicks me a look, and drops back behind me. Inside the doctor's room, I'm transferred onto a table, and the courtside staff leaves so it's only Doc, Charlotte, and me.

"We'll win." The positivity inside me is cracking. I glance at Charlotte. She nods and stands against the wall, giving the doctor room to examine me. He tilts my foot a little each way, and I cringe. "Fuuuck." The pain is intense.

"We'll get you an ice bucket and arrange a transfer for imaging."

"An x-ray?" Charlotte asks.

He glances over the rim of his glasses at Charlotte. "And an MRI. We need answers ASAP. Excuse me while I make some calls."

Doc leaves me in the room with Charlotte.

"I didn't see this coming." I shrug. Yet, in hindsight, I was warned. I close my eyes and shake my head. I did everything expected of me. Months ago, at the performance center, Nate highlighted the potential risk of an ankle injury. I have visited the center an extra four times a month to ensure I am on track to strengthening and stabilizing my ankle. *How?* How did this happen?

"Lottie, I have done fucking everything to prevent this from happening."

Charlotte pushes off the wall. "BJ was open. Why didn't you make the pass?"

The fuck?

"You think this is my fault because I didn't make the pass?" I say between clenched teeth.

"I'm saying if you weren't so stubborn, you would have passed it to him and not let our relationship impact your game and decision-making. For years, you two have combined well. This..." she circles her hand between us, "... needs to stop. We all need to move on."

I can't breathe with the anger ripping through my body. Every inch of me wants to scream at her.

"First, thanks for your support. I thought you fucking cared."

"Byron, I do," she says in a softer voice.

"Second..." I say louder, "... Coach instructed me to pass to Jye. He said to wait for him to get open, and I'd better deliver him the fucking ball." Charlotte closes her mouth, her wide eyes fixed on me. "So your *boyfriend* deliberately distracted me from the play. He heard Coach's instructions.

247

Maybe if he hadn't made it look like I wouldn't give him the ball and made a fucking screen or something to help me get it to Jye, then I mightn't be here." I wouldn't be surprised if the entire arena heard me.

Charlotte is beside me, her hand on my shoulder. "You're going to be okay, Byron."

I cover my eyes with a bent arm. "You don't know that."

"Are you in pain?" Charlotte's voice is calming. It's the old Charlotte I used to know.

"Yeah," I mutter without lifting my arms from my eyes. My throat tightens with a mixture of anger, frustration, and fear of the unknown. The way my foot throbs, I'd say it's more than a sprain. "Go back out there and catch the final minutes of the game. We need this win, and you should be there to see it."

She rubs my shoulder. "It's okay. I can stay here with you."

I lift my arm and stare at my sister.

"Thanks for the offer, but you represent the team. You need to be out there." While I love that my sister wants to comfort me, I know what is expected of her, and she has a role to play, just as I do on the court. I know there is a bigger picture where we are both involved, and my family will be waiting for answers. "Tell Mom and Dad I'm fine. Make sure BJ doesn't mess things up."

She offers a half smile. "I'll check back after the game, okay?" I signal with a thumbs-up. "I do love BJ. I always have."

Always? I don't say anything because she has just confirmed they have kept this from me longer than I thought.

While I should be happy she has found a decent guy—I don't know anyone more genuine than Brandon—it's going to take a while for me to accept that my two favorite people lied to me.

I need time.

My cell dings every few minutes with a text message. I missed the last quarter and the win.

I'm in a waiting room, waiting on MRI results. While awaiting the doctor, I watched the highlights of the last quarter on my cell—Brandon playing in my position and scoring ten points for the game.

I am pumped we won. *One step closer, baby.*

While my gut twists with anger at my friend, I can't help the joy of him getting the win for us, but not in my fucking position. Not with the hurt from his lies still stuck in my chest. Not when the doctor tells me it's more than a sprain, and I'm sitting here alone waiting for the results.

> Hey, I wish you were here right now. I miss you x

It's the middle of the night in Italy, but Giana will see the message when she wakes. I need to hear her voice. It's the one thing that will soothe me right now. I swipe on the social media apps, hoping to see her face. The rock-hard lump in my chest slowly melts away. Her smile is all I need. I find an image of her with Isabella, smiling on a stage, and more images of her surrounded by people. I read the caption.

Cibo Creativo has announced a collaboration with artist, Giana Monroe. Their new designer kitchen range is coming soon! Be ready to transform your kitchens.

The collaboration is not news to me, yet seeing her happy and it all coming to life, I'm so freaking proud of her. I flick through more images, and my thumb freezes. *What the actual fuck?*

In a recent photo with Clarissa Carrington, the film star, and Austin Cisterna, the Italian filmmaker, Dante Leto has his arm around Giana. I check the date. Last fucking night. I toss my phone onto the table beside me.

"We have the results," the doctor says as he enters the room.

Perfect fucking timing.

He stands beside my bed and waits for my focus. His expression is serious. *Jesus, just say it.*

"The results confirmed my thoughts. I'm sorry, Byron, but this is the end of the season for you." He's got to be joking. He knows I'll never roll over and die. "You have a ruptured Achilles, along with an inversion ankle sprain. It's a good thing you didn't try to hobble off the court."

A few seconds pass in silence. "But you can fix it, right?"

"You'll need surgery and extensive rehabilitation to prepare you for next season."

"Next season? There has to be a chance I can still play the finals. It's four months away."

He pauses before answering. "While I would like to offer you hope and say yes, I'm afraid if you return prematurely, you could injure it again and worse. If we were dealing with only the ankle sprain, then yes, but a ruptured Achilles is six months. This is not news to you. Your focus should be on rehab and strength training to cope with the workload of an elite athlete and be ready to go next season."

"So there is a chance?"

Doc crosses his arms. "One percent, but—"

"I'll take it. It beats zero chance, and besides, doctors tend to exaggerate."

"Byron, as a professional, I factor in your longevity in the game. If you rush back, it's possible to develop other injuries or rupture it again. Of course, I'll provide what you need to get you back on the court, but my advice is to be patient and do the hard yards so you can have a great season next year."

I shake my head. While I appreciate the doctor's professional advice, he doesn't know my body like I do or how determined I am. An injury is just a hiccup in my grand scheme of winning a championship.

Doc's brow pulls tight as though he knows what I'm thinking. "While I'm here to advise you, I can't stop you from playing."

"Then the next question is, when is the surgery? The sooner it's done, the quicker I can get back on the court."

26

GIANA

THE PLANE BREAKS through dark clouds. The mottled sky ranges from dreary gray to dirty white, reflecting my mood.

With my head tilted back, I watch the ground approach and close my eyes as the plane hits the runway, then bounces. The brakes screech. I stare at the terminal filled with thousands, yet none are here for me. Not a foot on land, and already the emptiness engulfs me. *I should have stayed in Italy.*

Byron hasn't answered my calls, and Mom is angry I declined Isabella's offer, though I know if I change my mind, Isabella will welcome me back with open arms. I open the text from Charlotte.

> Byron is hurting. He is not himself. He is angry at everyone—the world, you, and me. Please understand the pain he is in. I know my brother is a pain in the ass, but he needs you now more than ever. I look forward to seeing you soon. Lottie x

I sent him multiple texts before he responded.

> Please don't be concerned. I am fine. BTW, Austin Cisterna should hire you as his film star. You looked more beautiful than Clarissa Carrington. I'm genuinely happy for you. We can chat more when you get home. For now, I need time to clear my head.

No kisses. Nothing but a subtle hint to give him space. I sent another three texts and crickets. The moment I'm inside the terminal, I call his number—straight to voicemail. I send another text while waiting for my luggage.

> Hi Byron. I'm home. I can't wait to see you. G xx

Part of me wants to drive directly to his house, but I need to see my parents first and check in on Dad. Mom and Dad greet me with excitement, wanting to hear my stories and see all the photos. Dad has a spark about him that I haven't seen in months.

Before heading to my room, Dad chats to me about Byron's garden. I look at Mom, assuming he is mixing his words up, getting them confused.

"Byron took your father to his home last weekend and asked his advice on the garden."

"He did?" I stare at Dad. "You were at his home?"

"He told your father he was the best in his field." Mom looks genuinely pleased. "We mentioned you were returning today, and he said he already knew." *Yet he won't respond to my texts or calls.* "His surgery is today."

A ball of panic grows in my chest. I should have known this.

"Did he drive here?"

"He had a driver with him."

Right.

"If you don't mind, I'm going to go and see him after I unpack."

Mom hugs me. "Of course, honey. We'll see you later. I think he's excited for you to come home."

Could have fooled me.

After closing my bedroom door, I call Charlotte.

"Gigi, you're home."

"I am. How is Byron?"

"I'm here at the hospital. He's groggy. I just stepped out of the room. He ruptured his Achilles and ended up with screws in his ankle."

Holding my hand over my chest, I close my eyes, imagining the pain he is suffering.

"I'll be there soon."

"I'll wait for you. Don't be surprised by his grumpiness. He refuses to accept he can't play the remainder of the season."

"I'll never underestimate his stubbornness and determination."

Charlotte groans. "It's not always a good thing. See you soon."

I shower, change, add a little makeup, and run downstairs to my car. In my head, I consider my words, how to show my support but not pity him. He hates pity.

Imagining him sulking, I take the elevator to the right floor, and a nurse directs me to his room. Through the glass, I see him on the bed, his face whiter than the sheets, and my stomach plummets before rising to my throat. Overcome with nausea, I groan, and Charlotte turns. She walks out to greet me.

"Hey. He's sleeping. Come and get a coffee with me. I have some things to tell you."

We head to the cafeteria and find a table away from most of the people. She asks about my trip, and I tell her all the fun stuff until our coffees are delivered.

Coffee does something to our brain. It's like a trigger to confess, to talk about our troubles. Charlotte dives straight into her and Brandon's secret relationship.

"I already knew," I tell her. Charlotte's eyes pop. "About a month ago, I saw you both in the locker room." I screw up my face. "Sorry. I ran away because... well..."

Charlotte looks bashful and lowers her gaze. "I told him that was a bad idea, but once he started touching me..." She stops talking and looks to me for understanding.

"I never told him."

"I know. When BJ told him, he flew into a rage and has shot daggers at me and BJ ever since."

Oh boy.

"If I got a chance, I was going to leave hints for him but then decided against it because we know how much Byron hates being lied to."

"Yeah." She tilts her head back before meeting my gaze. "How do I fix this?"

"I don't know. He's also angry at me, so I have to tread carefully while he navigates this injury."

"He's devastated." Charlotte gently shakes her head, her eyes watering. "He's out for the season, even though he believes there's a chance he'll play the finals."

"No?"

"Yeah. He'll be replaced by the rookie guard, and if the rookie performs, they won't play Byron, who isn't one hundred percent fit. It's a business. My family understands it has to come before Byron's ambitions."

Shit.

"His world is basketball," I add. "Imagine his mindset if he suffers a career-ending injury."

"And that's what worries me," she says. "The BJ-and-me problem will be old news soon as he loves both of us. It's his future that concerns me. I think about players whose careers have ended because of substance abuse."

"Byron is disciplined and focused. He barely drinks—"

"When he's on top of the world. Remember his freshman year?"

My stomach drops for the second time. "It's a time I wanted to forget."

"Together, we can stop him from falling again."

If he allows us to help.

We return to his room to find Brandon standing beside his bed. We can't see either of their faces, yet we can hear their raised voices.

"It's not about Lottie and you," Byron roars. "You were someone I trusted. Both of you were. So don't give me bullshit excuses."

Charlotte and I stare at one another. She goes to march into the room, but I stop her. "Give them a minute," I whisper.

"I don't give two fucks what you two do now. What I'm pissed about is that I'm lying here because you didn't listen to Coach. You made me out as an asshole on the court. It wasn't about you scoring in my position. You heard the play Coach wanted, and I called it. Then you distracted me, and here I am. Why didn't you set a screen, man? You talk about me, but you're a selfish bastard, and I'm here because of you!" He yells the final blow. Brandon turns and storms out of the room.

"Babe." Charlotte lays a hand on his arm. He doesn't meet her gaze.

"I'm outta here."

"Give him time," she whispers. "He's just got out of surgery."

"I tried," he whispers and shakes his head. "I'll see you later." She touches his shoulder, but he strides away. She watches him walk past the nurses toward the exit.

"You should go and talk to him. I'll stay with Byron."

She wipes a tear from her eye. "He'll come around to us eventually, but this injury has affected him to the point where he thinks everyone is the enemy. I need to be here to support you."

We look into Byron's room. His head is tilted on the pillow, his eyes shut. There are IVs, drains, and cords coming from his limbs. What was Brandon thinking coming today?

I creep into his room, lean in, and kiss his cheek. His eyes flutter open. His watery eyes kill me. My chest constricts. He closes his eyes again. "Not now, Gigi."

I swallow the lump in the back of my throat.

"I'm just going to sit with you a while." I take his hand in mine. He doesn't attempt to hold my hand, but he doesn't pull his away either—a positive. Charlotte stands behind me.

"We're here for you, Byron," she says in a gentle voice.

He opens his eyes, then closes them again. "You should go after your boyfriend."

"I'm staying with my brother." She steps around me and runs a hand over his hair as though fixing his style. "Do you need any pain meds?"

"No," he says without opening his eyes. "I want to rest."

Charlotte refills his water glass and dithers with something on his side table. He rips his hand from mine, twists his upper body away from us toward the window, then heaves. Charlotte rushes around the bed and grabs his puke bag. She stands there holding it for him, sliding her hand over the top of his head to soothe him. He flops back onto the bed, eyes closed, breathing heavily. Charlotte wipes the side of his mouth with a tissue, then puts the bag in the trash.

"I'll notify the nurse," she whispers.

"Lottie," he murmurs, and she pauses in the doorway. "Go to BJ. I said some things I didn't mean."

Her eyes meet mine, and my heart bursts. I can't with all this emotion. I want to stay, but I think these two have much to talk about.

"He'll be okay," she says gently and continues on to speak to the nurse. I take his hand in mine, and this time, I feel a slight squeeze.

"Byron," the nurse says as she enters the room with Charlotte. "I have something to help with the nausea." She has a dish with a syringe and a vial. She adds it to the IV in his other hand. "You'll feel better soon."

For the next half hour, Charlotte and I sit in relative silence while Byron sleeps. We whisper a few things while scrolling on our cells.

"BJ isn't responding to my texts," she whispers. "I asked him if I should go over there, but he's not replying."

Byron's family walks into the room. I stand the moment his parents enter. Jobe follows behind them, along with Franklin.

"I should go," I tell Charlotte. "Tell him to call me if he needs anything." I hug Mrs. Hendricks.

"It's good to see you, Giana." She gives me an extra squeeze.

"I'll come back tomorrow to check in on him," I whisper.

"Thank you."

I turn and look back when I'm outside the room. His

family gathers around his bed, every face etched with concern, especially his father's. I remember his father not supporting his decision to play ball. He wanted him to be part of the Hendricks empire. What will he expect of his son now?

The entire drive home, I'm distracted by worrying thoughts.

As soon as I pull into the garage, I receive a text. I turn off the engine and grab my cell.

> You should have stayed in Italy. You still
> have your dream.

My heart cracks with the final blow. I know what he is doing, and this time, trying to push me away won't work. I'm older, wiser, more experienced than last time and more freaking stubborn when it comes to getting what I want. For once, Byron Hendricks is not going to beat me.

27

BYRON

THE TEAM HAS BEEN on the road for the past three games.

It's been weeks since I attended a training session, and I've barely seen my teammates, who I usually see every day. While the world seems out of sorts, at least I'm home days before Christmas.

I stare out to the pool overlooking LA. It's been a while since I swam, and the memories of Giana in the pool flood back.

She needs to follow her dream while she can because none of us know when it might be ripped out from under us. I'll fight to get back on the court, but I have a long journey ahead of me. I need to be focused.

Giana fussing over me and spending hours at the hospital while ignoring her work are not acceptable. She needs to be painting with a clear mind. How do I tell her we need to give each other space without hurting her? Because when I asked her to leave, I saw the pain in her eyes. She deserves her dream, and I'm taking it away from her.

With a boot on my foot, I hobble on crutches to the kitchen. My chef has left meals for the next two days. I prefer to cook, though I still need to elevate my leg as much as possible. Charlotte has arranged everything. My meals, cleaning, physiotherapists coming to my home, and the team psychologist. We have an appointment this afternoon. I open my cell and find Brandon's number.

> Can we talk?

I need to apologize, and I'm not doing it in a text.

> I won't be a jerk.

I toss my cell on the counter, and before I open the refrigerator, my cell alerts me to someone at the door. I check the camera.

Charlotte.

I hear her rushing up the stairs. She runs into the kitchen, and I'm about to tell her I'm fine, but her distressed expression can't be about me. I saw her yesterday.

Charlotte almost knocks me off balance as she runs into my arms and hugs me, sobbing into my shirt. "He's left."

"What?" I take her shoulder and try to pry her off me, but she tightens her arms around my waist and cries louder.

"He's been traded to Chicago," she says through sobs.

"The fuck?" I'm stunned into silence, my thoughts mashing together in confusion. I pat her back, then hug my sister.

"Is it a done deal? I can talk to him."

She shakes her head. "He's already gone." She leans back and looks me in the eye. Her eyes are red and swollen, like she has been crying for hours. "He didn't even say goodbye. I *hate* him."

I swallow hard. Tears burn my eyes, and I can't fight it. I pull her into my chest for a tight squeeze because I also need to be comforted. I just lost my best friend.

"Who signed the contract?"

"Coach... and Frank."

The fuck?

"Frank said it was in the best interest of both parties. BJ is not a point guard, and Chicago has been interested in him for some time. We signed another guard from Philadelphia," she rasps. "In their meeting, BJ told Frank he thought it was best for everyone if he left." Charlotte's hands scrunch my shirt into a ball as her cries become louder. Her knees buckle, and she leans into me. "I don't know what to do."

"Nothing, Lott. You do nothing. Remember the hurt. Wear the scar like a trophy tattooed on your heart. You'll survive and be stronger for it. In time, he'll understand his mistake. But don't give him the power of seeing you like this." I pat her back. "We'll all make amends when the time is right. You can't force it to happen."

I think about Giana. I need to take a page out of my own book.

EVERY CHRISTMAS EVE, WE MEET AT OUR PARENTS' HOME AND one by one add an ornament to the Christmas tree. Dad opens his favorite bottle of whiskey, and Mum pops champagne and distributes ghastly knitted sweaters that we pretend to like.

This year is different.

She unwraps the sweaters, and after giving everybody their green and red sweater with a reindeer on the front, she shoves the one meant for Brandon back into the packaging. With a fleeting look, she checks to see if Charlotte has noticed—she did. We all saw it. The silence in the room speaks volumes. Everyone is hurt by Brandon's hasty transfer to Chicago. While my father and Franklin signed the contract, Brandon initiated it and without a word to Charlotte.

The fucker.

He has hurt my family.

Crushed Charlotte.

Disappointed me.

Still, I miss him. But I need to show courage and put it all behind me for my sister's sake.

"Quickly, put them on. I have new decorations for the tree and a special one for Summer's first Christmas." Mom beams her radiant smile, and while she loves this time of year, I can tell she feels the weight of sadness that surrounds Charlotte.

And me.

"Give it to me, Mom." Charlotte holds out her hand and moves Summer to her other hip. "When I see him tomorrow at the game, I'll shove it up his ass."

Mom's expression sags. "It won't change anything, darling." She goes to her and takes her hand, pats it softly, then goes to decorate the tree. Dad takes Summer and bounces her on his knee while he sits in his chair, sipping whiskey and talking business with Franklin.

"I can help." I hobble after them on my crutches. I'd rather be decorating than listening to my father and Franklin discuss numbers and the stock market. Jobe is in the corner chatting to Penny. Odd, because I also noticed he was sitting with her at our last family dinner when I thought he didn't want to hear about happy families and the benefits of commitment.

When Mom leaves the room, Charlotte stands beside me to admire the lights on the tree.

"Have you heard from him?" I whisper.

She shakes her head.

"Same, and he's blocked me on social media."

"What?" she snaps. "I thought it was only me?" She quickly wipes her eyes. I hate how fast the tears well in her eyes, revealing her shattered heart.

Fucking coward.

I'm furious. "He knows he's fucked up."

"Don't make excuses for him," she says in a hoarse voice. She wraps an arm around my waist and leans her head on my chest. "Besides, I know you're hurting as much as me."

Mom enters the room with the rest of the family following her. "Franklin, please hold Summer while you add the final decoration. And this year, I have decided we all get to open one present tonight."

Charlotte forces a smile in an attempt to brighten our mood. She turns to me and lightly punches my shoulder. "We're going to have a fun night. Because if we're sad, it means he's won. And we can't let that happen. Ever."

"Especially not tomorrow," I murmur.

It's one Christmas I'm not looking forward to. For the first time, I'm contemplating avoiding the game and watching it on the television.

"You're not staying home and moping," she says, wide-eyed.

"Christ, can you read my thoughts?"

"I know you." Her brow pinches. "And you're not leaving me to face him alone."

I pull her in for a hug. "I'll be there for you, Lottie."

It's our home game, and we are playing Chicago. No—we are playing Brandon Johns. We never thought this is what our Christmas would be like.

He hasn't returned my calls or texts. He is treating Charlotte the same way, and I'm livid. Years of friendship gone. Burned. Evaporated in a puff of smoke. Despite how much it will hurt to watch him play for another team, I'll sit on the bench and scrutinize his game.

My gut is still tight after last night.

We didn't joke around like we usually do. It was more about presents for Summer, even though she is too young to understand. Mom needed a distraction from all the drama, and there was barely a moment when Charlotte didn't have Summer in her arms.

The music ramps up, and I focus on what is happening around me in the locker room. Our team is motivated. Coach has barely mentioned Brandon, and it's probably a good thing. My attention is on Drew, our new point guard from Philadelphia. I watch his every move, how he warms up, even the way he prays. The players gather and proceed to the tunnel, all shouting a chant.

"We've got this."

"The game is ours."

Charlotte is beside me. I hobble on the crutches, following the guys in the tunnel past cameramen and journalists.

"How are you, Byron?" A camera is shoved in my face.

I fake a smile at the lens. "Recovering well. Ready to watch my team get the win."

"Can you give any insight as to why Brandon Johns made a hasty exit?"

Charlotte pushes between me and the camera. "Sorry, we need to get to our seats." We head straight to the courtside seats behind the players. She keeps her chin high, refusing to look at the opposition. My parents are not sitting in the VIP seats, instead choosing to remain in the glassed corporate box, where they have sat ever since my injury.

Charlotte and I find our seats, and I lean close. "Remember, the cameras will turn to us without warning, so I need your best poker face, no matter what happens or how you feel."

"I know," she murmurs, taking a moment to adjust her long, blonde ponytail over her shoulder. I give her another look and notice the heavier makeup, the longer lashes on her eyes, and her bright red lipstick. She is dressed to impress or to ignite regret in a certain player.

In the final minutes of the warm-up, I unbutton the top two buttons of my shirt. In my mind, I was prepared for the onslaught of emotion at not being on the court, but not how much it would hurt seeing my best friend on the opposing team.

What do you call a friend you've barely uttered a word to in weeks?

He still gets to do what he loves, and I'm on the sidelines, dressed in a fucking suit and in a post-op boot.

When the players line up on the court, Brandon refuses to look our way. Not once does he look at Charlotte until the final quarter, when Charlotte calls out to the team. I look up to the circular scoreboard overhead to see Charlotte's and my faces on one of the screens. I assume the commentator is talking about our family. I give a little wave, but Charlotte is watching Brandon. The camera enlarges her pretty face. One of the opposing players looks up at the screen and nudges Brandon. He looks at the screen, then his gaze darts to our players and Charlotte. His expression sags, and his gaze flits to mine. He gives a subtle nod before focusing on the ball. Most people would have missed it, but I didn't, and

I recognized the look in his eyes. There's a slight chance we'll come out of this as friends on the other side.

We get the win. It wasn't in contention, and Brandon played less than his best. It's not surprising, but I know him and his skill level. He was more than capable of coming away with twenty points, not a mere six. He'll bounce back. I wouldn't underestimate his drive to win. He passes us as he heads to the tunnel with his team. Charlotte calls out to him. I walk ahead slowly, hobbling along, following my team into the tunnel.

"How are you?" she asks in a quiet voice.

"Fine."

I slow up. He'd better not break her fucking heart.

"Why didn't you call me? We could have worked something out."

Silence.

"Why haven't you returned Byron's calls or mine?"

"I have a new phone and a new number."

What?

"Why?"

Come on, Charlotte. No desperation in your voice.

"Because I threw the old one in the lake?"

"You're a coward."

"It's fate, Lottie. We're not meant to be."

I turn to see him walk away from my sister. A message loud and clear—he's starting anew. "Lottie," I call out. She looks from Brandon to me. Even from here, I see her red eyes. I shake my head and gesture toward the tunnel. She strides over to me with a straight face.

I turn back to Brandon, and his gaze meets mine. "I'll see you on the court next year," I warn him. He looks away and, with his head down, follows his new team into the tunnel.

Charlotte and I walk past the cameras. She manages to hold it together. Closer to the locker room, we dart into one of the storerooms. She takes one deep breath, then lets it all go. I hold her tight while she cries muffled sobs into my shirt. It's going to take more than a nod to forgive him for breaking my sister's heart.

"This is why you were always off-limits to my friends," I whisper. I hold her tight and allow her to cry for the next fifteen minutes.

When she finally comes up for air, she thumps my chest. "Fate, my ass."

28

GIANA

Dawn.

The sun has barely touched the horizon.

Like the certainty of the sun rising and setting each day, I refuse to wait another minute to confront Byron. I can't avoid the inevitable. We have slipped effortlessly into a relationship, sliding the problems of the past and how we have dealt with them under a very thick rug. We've danced over and around it so we don't trip and spoil the fun of the last few months by arguing. But all real couples argue, or at least debate, at some point. Sometimes, you have to in order to move forward. And if we want to move forward, we need to discuss how we deal with complications like adults.

He's pushing me away rather than discussing our emotions. Sure, he is angry, hurt, and frustrated. While yelling doesn't resolve anything, I'd rather that than the silence. My plan is to talk to him in a calm way so he'll hopefully open up about his feelings.

Imagining how the 'debate' will pan out, I practice positive reactions while driving to his place. I check my facial expressions in the mirror, practicing my best poker face if he says something negative. I'm not about to smother him with positivity because I know he is hurting, and too much sunshine will burn him when he's feeling down. Instead, I want to offer a gentle warmth and let him know I'm here for him.

After parking my car out front, I use the passcode to his gate, then stand at his door, knowing the cameras will alert him to my presence. I tap in the code to his front door and let myself in.

He's not in the kitchen or out on his beautiful balcony watching the sunrise reflect off the water of his pool. Without knocking, I march straight into his bedroom and swing open his door. He is sitting upright with pillows behind his back.

"Clearly, I need to change the code," he says without looking at me.

For a moment, I'm distracted by his tanned bare chest, his muscled abs, and the beginning of the V on his hips, where the sheet falls loosely over his skin.

"So he talks," I remark sarcastically. I walk over to his bed, take the cell out of his hand, and tap on my number. My cell buzzes in my handbag strapped over my shoulder. "And this works." I toss his cell onto the white sheets, then fold my arms and glare at him. "What's your excuse?" He turns his head to the window and stares out to his beautiful garden. I move to block his view. "Oh no. You don't get to ignore me today."

This is not what I foresaw happening. What happened to calm Giana?

He tilts his head back, leaning it against the headboard. "Why are you here?"

Still, he refuses to look at me. I take a deep breath to slow my racing heart. "To talk. Resolve our problems. Talk about the future."

He shakes his head. "No, Giana."

I flinch at his tone, and the fact he called me Giana and not Gigi. In the seconds of silence, I momentarily avert my gaze to the wall. My painting of *our beach* hangs on the wall. It's not my best work, yet it means a lot to Byron, and for him to have it in his room reminds me all is not lost.

"Why are you here in LA? You left. You can't just—"

"Do not tell me what I can and cannot do," I yell, louder than I intended. "I am here for us, and I'm not about to let you ruin our chance." I inhale a sharp, angry breath. "Deny it all you want, but we have something special, and you're running from it."

Byron throws back the covers, stands, and balances on one leg while his foot in the black boot hovers above the floor. He stares down at me, his blue eyes a darker shade than I remember. He narrows his eyes at me, almost glaring. "I'm not running away from shit. I'm giving you a chance to leave."

"I don't want to leave," I yell, then point a finger at him. "If you want out, then say so. Be the coward. Or is this all too close to how you were in your freshman year? Poor Byron didn't get on the court, the coach wouldn't give him a chance. Now you're feeling sorry for yourself all over again. Lick your wounds, do what you need to do, then grow the fuck up."

His face turns red. "I want out," he says slowly, between clenched teeth. "I want you to leave. Now."

I hate that we have come to this. We're acting like petulant teenagers. I push him. He stumbles back. I push him again so he falls onto the bed. "Make me, asshole." I grab his chin and raise it so he is looking at me. "Six years ago, you made one wrong move that ruined everything we had. Don't—"

He grabs my wrist and holds it away from his face with a grip tight enough to cut off my blood supply. His eyes bore into mine. "You don't get it, Gigi," he whispers angrily.

Gigi. I have an edge.

"Yes, I do. You're trying to push me away, thinking you're saving me from making a big mistake." I lean closer so our faces are inches apart. "I beat you to it. I'm here to save you from making one of your own."

He gently shakes his head as tears well in his eyes. "I can't let you do that."

The world stills. I pant as though the air in the room has thinned, making it harder to breathe. He's not being an asshole. He's not acting selfish, thinking about himself or his career. It's not about him falling from grace and turning to alcohol or substance abuse again. He is thinking about me. He believes he is saving me from him, the one person I don't want saving from.

I lean down and kiss his lips once, softly, then again. "Too late. I already have."

He flops back onto the bed, pulling me onto him. We kiss each other with desperate passion, lost in the moment, his hands hold my face so I can't break free. This is our first real argument. The last time, he ran away from our problems, and I sprinted in the other direction all the way to Italy.

"If this happens again... the only place we run to is each other's arms," I tell him.

Byron leans his forehead against mine and squeezes his arms around my back as though he's afraid to let go. "I can't think of any other place I would rather be than wrapped in your arms. Promise me you'll never let me go."

I never will. Never again.

EPILOGUE

BYRON

February…

Light stretching and strengthening exercises are now part of my daily routine. While I'm focused on rehab, the time away from the court has given me time to think—to ponder my life and our life together.

Franklin and Penny gave me advice and asked me what was nonnegotiable. Without me giving them an answer, they implied I needed to find flexibility in my other commitments if I wanted a successful relationship. Basketball controlled me. The more I stay away from the court, the more I realize it was an unhealthy obsession. I love the game, but I want the control to be mine—to keep the ball in my court and the freedom to decide how I want to play the game. Months ago, Jobe spoke about me being a pawn when I thought I had control. Now, it all makes sense.

It's something I'll discuss with my agent.

I squeeze Giana's hand as we enter my parents' home

and slowly make our way to the formal sitting room. My limp is less noticeable now. My family stands, and hugs are shared. "Sorry we're late."

"You're not late, darling," Mom says, holding both my shoulders after we hug. She looks over me. The same eyes as mine shine with concern. "How are you? Are you on track with your rehab?"

"I am. Oddly, I'm enjoying it."

"Wonderful." She turns to Giana. "And how is your painting coming along?"

"I'm almost finished." Giana looks bashfully at me.

"What painting?"

Mom looks coy. "Giana is painting something special for our bedroom."

I smile at my beautiful girl.

"And..." Mom spins, making the light fabric of her floral gown swish and sway. "What do you think?"

"It suits you perfectly. You look stunning." Hearing the excitement in Giana's voice, I look at Mom more closely.

"Is it one of yours?" I ask Giana.

"Byron," Charlotte chastises. "You should know this."

I shrug and walk over to stand beside Jobe chatting with Penny.

Penny rests a hand on his forearm. "Thank you. I appreciate it." She then moves to stand beside her husband.

"You're popular tonight. Handing out favors to everyone."

"She's upset. I couldn't say no."

"About what?" I push.

"Her friend, Zara, moved to London, and she only told Penny a week before she left. Some things were said in the heat of the moment, and now Penny is worried about her. She asked me to check in on her while I'm there."

"Will you?"

Jobe groans. "Have you ever said no to Penny?"

I huff out a laugh. "About favors... do you have an update?"

"It's a done deal." He hands me a key.

I pat his shoulder. "I appreciate it." I slip the key into my pocket. "So, any clue why we're all here?"

He shakes his head. "I thought you'd have some insight."

"Nope."

"I can't stay anyway. I have a business arrangement."

"On a Sunday?" I study my brother's face, and the mask cracks. "You seem to have a lot of business appointments on weekends. Maybe it's an excuse to leave."

His brow furrows.

"No judgment here. Eventually, your secret will get out, and we'll find out who she is."

"There's never just one," he says dryly. He looks over to Franklin and Penny as though he is hiding something.

Something tugs on the leg of my trousers. "What the..." I look down to Summer crawling over my feet. "Hey, princess." I scoop her up, holding her in the air before lowering her to my face and planting a kiss on her cheek. Giana holds out her hands, and Summer goes to her without hesitation. I turn back to Jobe, but he has moved toward Dad, who is pouring four glasses of whiskey. Mom pops a bottle of champagne.

I take the whiskey from Dad as Lola walks through the room with a silver tray of appetizers. "Thank you, Lola." I pop a mini lobster roll in my mouth. We must be celebrating something special.

Penny comes to take Summer from Giana. "She moves so fast I can barely keep up."

"She is so cute," Giana coos. They talk briefly, then Mom signals that she wants to say something, so Penny moves to stand beside her husband.

"We have exciting news," Mom announces as she moves to stand beside Charlotte. "You all know Carson and I intend to travel more, this time for leisure," she emphasizes. My father spent half his life flying around the globe for work. "And Frank is stepping away from the team to spend more time with his family and to focus on Hendricks Capital Management. He's had too many fingers in the pie and, unlike his father, knows the right time to let things go."

I'm not surprised. But wait, who will be heading up the LA Sharks?

"While we have loved our journey owning a basketball team, we are promoting Charlotte to CEO before taking over the ownership." Mom looks fondly at Charlotte.

"Please raise your glass to your sister..." my father adds, "... and her ideas on how to propel the team forward and maximize our success."

"Congratulations" sounds around the room as everyone toasts. I throw my whiskey back, then move toward Charlotte. She flashes a big smile, the pride oozing out of her. "Well done, Lottie." I lean in and hug her. "I hope you enjoy babysitting grown men."

She laughs and clinks her glass with mine. "I'm used to it. Older brothers who behaved like idiots helped the transition."

I pat her back. "What's the first change you intend to enforce?" Every new CEO has ideas of how they want to revolutionize procedures, even if it's not broken.

"I'm going to have more say with player selection and oversee the coach's decisions."

I nod, thinking it's a ballsy move. "Good luck with that."

"I was going to ask you to pop into my office. I have a proposition for you."

"Yeah, what is it?"

"I won't go into detail here, but I'm hoping you might be part of the offensive coaching team, at least until you're fit enough to play. It's also about the future and our family's future with you remaining with the team when your playing days are over."

Giana comes to stand beside me. "Sorry, I couldn't help overhearing."

Wrapping an arm around her shoulder, I kiss her forehead and pull her into my side. "What do you think?"

"Something to consider. Coaching is strategic, right?" I nod. "And you're a math genius. It makes sense to coach and use your strategy intelligence off the court."

"Maybe." I love the idea, though getting back on the court is still a priority. For the future, it could be a viable option to coach and remain in the game.

"Give it a shot. Even for a month," Charlotte suggests.

"He will..." Giana says for me, "... and he'll excel like he does at everything."

I shake my head and smile at Charlotte. "She makes me the happiest man on the planet. How am I so lucky?"

Charlotte touches both of our arms. Her eyes flick from mine to Giana's. "You're both lucky to have each other. Never forget that."

A piece of my heart cracks for my sister, knowing she still hurts.

"Everything happens for a reason," Giana says gently. "I know the pain, but you'll be stronger for it. For now, I think you're meant to be right where you are... the CEO and the face of the LA Sharks. You're good at what you do. Keep your eyes open, and when you least expect it, love will hit you smack in the face."

Charlotte gives Giana a quick hug. "I hope so. It will be the only time I'd welcome a broken nose."

"Is that what happened to us?"

She places a hand on my shoulder. "You came at me so fast—"

"Like a wrecking ball," Charlotte finishes, and they laugh.

I'll take it as a compliment, especially if it makes my sister smile. Charlotte gives a gentle punch to my shoulder and works her way over to Jobe.

Giana curls into me, then leans back and holds my gaze.

I reach for her body, bracketing her waist and rubbing her hip bones with my thumbs. "I know that look."

"What look?" Her voice is sweet and smooth like honey.

"The one where you want to take me out back and fuck me," I murmur against her lips.

"Clearly, you don't know me," she says in carefully spaced words. *What?* "Because I was about to tell you I love you."

A rush of adrenaline tingles through my body. It takes my breath away, and I'm stuck for words. "Finally," I murmur, unable to hide the huge grin growing on my lips. We got our special moment, and I wasn't expecting it at all.

THREE MONTHS LATER...

INSTEAD OF DINING AT BLOOMS FOR A DATE AS PROMISED, I surprise Giana by taking her in the helicopter along with my instructor to Downtown LA. My instructor speaks to me as we fly toward the helipad of Hendricks Capital Management building. Since Frank is owner and CEO of HCM, he leases the lower floors to other businesses. When the first-floor business vacated, he spoke to Jobe about leasing it. Instead, I bought the entire floor from my brother as an investment.

"It's going to take a while for me to get used to this," Giana shouts. "But I love it. The view is sensational."

"It is." Her excitement has me grinning all while maintaining my focus and listening to the instructor. A set down surrounded by skyscrapers has adrenaline pumping through my veins.

"Where are we landing?"

"On the HCM building."

"Are we visiting Franklin?"

The instructor's voice cuts in for the vertical landing set down.

We balance out, descend slowly, slower until we have set down. "I'll see you next week," I say to my instructor, spring out of the side door, take Giana's hand, and help her down. Bent over, we run, her hand blowing over her face with the force of wind from the blades whipping around our bodies. Inside the doors, she flings her arms around me. "That was exhilarating." She leans into me and kisses me. "Thank you."

"No, thank you," I murmur against her lips.

"For what?"

"Trusting me." My voice cracks as my words are not only for today. "For giving me another chance." Her gaze flicks over my face, and before she can say anything, I take her hand and lead her to the elevator.

"Why are we here?" she whispers.

I grin, thinking about her reaction. "It's a surprise."

"For Franklin or me?"

"You." We are not visiting Franklin. The elevator door opens. The three-month renovation has proved to be the best impulsive decision I ever made. Stepping forward, I squeeze her hand as we walk into a foyer where a chandelier hangs above us.

"What is this?" she asks, her head turning back and forth, taking in the room.

The bare walls are all white, the high ceiling is white, and the hardwood floors were laid only a few weeks ago, the scent of paint still lingering in the air.

"It's for you," I whisper. "All you need to do is think of a name for the signage."

Her eyes widen as she studies my face. Her delicate hand goes to her throat as though she is incapable of speaking.

"Giana Monroe's art gallery. A place to house your famous work for display or to sell." I lead her to a room at the back that has floor-to-ceiling glass windows looking out to the bustling streets. It's a corner room and has the best view. "This is your studio for you to work when you please."

Giana throws her arms around my neck. She hugs me, then slowly, I realize she's not laughing. Muffled sobs sound against my chest.

"Hey, hey, hey, I thought you'd be happy." I take both her shoulders and pry her off me. Tears stream down her flushed cheeks. Fuck, have I messed up?

She shakes her head. A sharp pain grows in my gut. Jesus, she has a different vision for her future. *Fuck,* she's returning to Italy? Giana continues to choke out sobs.

"Talk to me, Gi."

She lifts a finger and flicks tears off both cheeks. "My makeup is ruined."

"Here." With my thumbs, I wipe the black lines from beneath her pretty eyes. "Perfect."

She coughs out a single laugh. Her lashes flutter, and she gives me her standard bashful look. "How am I so lucky to have you?"

My shoulders loosen, and I blow out the tension in a breath. "Fuck, Gi. I almost called Jobe and said we need to sell."

Her soft hands cup my face. Her gaze fixes on mine, staring deep, full of love. "You are the most thoughtful, loving, caring man on this planet."

I grin at her. "I enjoy being upgraded from selfish." Moving her hands to my mouth, I kiss her knuckles while holding her gaze. "If I knew how good it felt, I would've stopped being an asshole years ago."

She pulls her hands from my lips and loops them around my neck. "Truth is you were never an asshole, merely focused on your dream. And now, I feel like the asshole, with you doing this for me, for my dream." Her chin dips, and I rest my chin on the crown of her head.

"It's for us, Gi. Our future. Not just for you."

"Our future," she whispers and snuggles into my chest. "To repay the favor, do I need to buy you a team to coach?"

I laugh, then wrap my arms around her and hold her tight. "I already have that," I say, contentment settling in my chest. "I only need you."

THANK YOU FOR READING GIANA AND BYRON'S STORY

I hope you enjoyed reading THE WRONG MOVE as much as I did writing it.

If you want to read more you can download the bonus epilogue at: https://dl.bookfunnel.com/83yh3g4jhu

THE WRONG PROMISE Book #3 in the series is Jobe Hendricks story. You can order it on Amazon now.

Want more of the characters in this book?
Penny & Franklin's story is THE WRONG PROPOSAL Book #1
in The Hendricks Billionaire Series
Brandon Johns (BJ) is originally from my Australian sports series.
You can read about Brandon in Winning the Player.

If you want more of my books please follow me on Amazon, and be notified about my next book release.

If you are on Facebook please join my Reader group. We have a lot of fun talking about books.

Please join my <u>mailing list</u> to be notified of my next release.

You can learn more about me on my <u>website.</u>

ALSO BY LEESA BOW

Beautifully Broken Prequel (Beautifully Wild Series): https://dl.
bookfunnel.com/b5myspjim6

The Wrong Proposal Epilogue (The Hendricks Billionaires) : https://dl.
bookfunnel.com/dxpg42qko3

The Wrong Move Epilogue (The Hendricks Billionaires): https://dl.
bookfunnel.com/83yh3g4jhu

www.leesabow.com

ACKNOWLEDGMENTS

First and foremost, to my husband, and my family. Thank you for your encouragement, love, and support of my writing journey.

My gratitude extends to my amazing editors. To Kaylene Osborn at Swish Design and Editing. Thank you for all your expertise, for answering endless questions, and for making my book shine. You are my rock! And a big thank you to Nicki and Rachelle!

To Virginia Tesi Carey for proofreading, and helping to eliminate all the Aussie terms in my writing.

To Letitia Hasser at RBA Designs, thank you for my beautiful cover.

My appreciation extends to my Facebook reader group, and all the blogging community for helping to get my book out to the world. You all make the book world a much better place.

To my author friends, I can't express enough gratitude for all your advice and inspiration.

To my beta readers Carol and Robyn. Thank you for reading on short notice and finding the little things to help my story be the best it can be. A special thanks to my beta Cheryl.

To my readers. Thank you for your endless support, and most of all, for loving my stories. Some of you have been with me from the start of my author journey, and to others, I'm a new author. What I love most is you all embrace my characters and stories and love them as much as I do. Thank you for reading, reviewing, and talking about my books to your families and friends in book clubs and blogs.

I appreciate everything you do for me.

To my friends from my home town Broken Hill who have gone on to do fantastic things around the world, you are my inspiration.

To my daughters who played basketball and trained hard every day. You made me so proud of your work ethic. Basketball was ingrained into our lives and I'll always be proud of your achievements. The Australian basketball community kept you focused as teenagers to be the best you can. I was destined to write a basketball story, and can't wait to write more.

ABOUT THE AUTHOR

Best selling Australian author, Leesa Bow lives in sunny Queensland, Australia. She spends her spare time with her family, and catching up with girlfriends for coffee or a wine.

Leesa loves to keep fit at the gym, in the pool, and walking surrounded by nature. Importantly, Leesa keeps it fun with laughter in her life.

She loves nothing more than to curl up with a good book, and a glass of South Australian wine. Or if its by a pool then a cocktail is preferable.

Leesa's love of travel inspires the next story. She hopes her books transport the reader around the world by the words on the page.

www.leesabow.com